IN THE SHADOW OF DEATH
A Margaret Spencer mystery

STUDIO

In the same series:

Death in a Family Way

Cataloguing in Publication Data

Southin, Gwendolyn, 1930-

    In the Shadow of Death

    (A Margaret Spencer mystery ; 2)

    ISBN 1-55207-033-6 (Cloth), 1-55207-037-9 (Trade paper)

    I. Title. II. Series: Southin, Gwendolyn. Margaret Spencer mystery ; 2

PS8587.O978I5 2002	C813'.6	C2001-941471-4
PS9587.O978I5 2002		
PR9199.3.S68I5 2002		

For our complete catalogue of books
in English and French, please consult our web site at
http://www.rdppub.com

In the Shadow of Death

A *Margaret Spencer mystery novel*
by Gwendolyn Southin

ROBERT DAVIES/STUDIO 9 BOOKS

ISBN 1-55207-033-6 (Cloth), 1-55207-037-9 (Trade paper)

Ordering information
United States:
Studio 9 Books, 162 Margaret Street, Plattsburgh, NY 12901
☎ 518-298-8595
Also available from Koen, Ingram and Baker & Taylor

Canada:
Starbooks Distribution
100 Armstrong Ave., Georgetown, Ontario L7G 5S4
☎ (905) 877-2828 🖷 (905) 877-4410 SAN: 118-8801
E-mail: sales@starbooks.ca

or from the publisher (special & group orders):
Studio 9 Books
Montreal, QC H3H 1A7, Canada
☎ 514-934-5433 🖷 514-937-8765
e-mail: mail2@rdppub.com

UK, Ireland, Europe (France excepted):
Worldwide Book Distribution,
Unit 9, Oakwood Industrial Park,
Gatwick Road, Crawley, West Sussex RH10 9AZ
☎ 44-1293-456300 🖷 44-1293-536644

France:
Éditions Casteilla,
10 rue Léon Foucault, 78184 St-Quentin-en Yvelines Cedex
☎ 01-3014-1930 🖷 01-3460-3132

We wish to thank the Sodec (Québec) and the Department of Canadian
Heritage for their generous support
of our publishing program in both French and English.

This book is dedicated to my husband Victor Southin,
my publisher, Robert Davies and my writer's group,
The Quintesessential Writers —
Your encouragement has been invaluable.

Prologue

"There are problems, Mr. Smith."

"What do you think I pay you for?" Over his steel rimmed glasses, Lenny Smith glared at the well-dressed, slightly built lawyer. "You're supposed to look after all the problems."

Harry Spencer inched closer to the edge of his chair. "But do you really want to acquire a fraudulent business? Friendly Freddie's Used Cars has been operating very close to the line, certainly. Over it, probably. Some of their dealings are . . . " he paused . . . "highly questionable."

"How do you think I made my money?" Lenny answered. "Being weak at the knees?"

"But . . . " Spencer stammered, "what about your good name . . . ?"

"I'll worry about my name, Spencer. You just get them to take my offer. Let's see the papers."

Spencer was thorough and methodical in nature despite his nervous anxiety, and went over the contract clause by clause, pointing out the legal potholes and ethical dangers as he saw them.

"That's enough!" His client jumped to his feet and glared down on the hapless lawyer.

"But Mr. Smith, I—" Spencer stuttered.

"Go on home, for God's sake, Spencer. Go home. You're out of your depth here. Leave it with me, I know what I want."

Dismissed, humiliated, and exhausted by the abuse, Spencer left the office without another word.

Lenny leaned back in his soft leather chair and reflected on the events of his rotten day. It had started with a visit to his doctor. The old quack had tried to scare him — imagine! — by saying that if he didn't take life easier, his heart would surely give out. The man had even had the unmitigated gall to suggest that Lenny let his two sons take over the business and earn their keep. What a laugh! In fact, it was just the opposite. The very thought of his two inept offspring trying to run Leonard Smith and Sons Ltd. — his business — was enough to give him a heart attack. Then came that godawful lunch with his nagging wife, who was incapable of passing a single hour without finding fault. Always made him feel like ordering the Alka-seltzer blue plate special! And now Spencer, his idiot lawyer, was trying to scuttle his latest car dealership acquisition because of "ethical problems." Thinking about that insipid shyster nit-picking over every little detail of another run-of-the-mill deal gave him gas. Didn't these guys have any understanding of the meaning of the word "business?" He pulled the telephone on the desk toward him and lifted the receiver before dialling the only number in town where he could be sure to find some relief. "I'm leaving the office now, hon," he told her. "Make me something nice to eat. I told my wife I have a late meeting."

As always, Smith made sure he was the last to leave the office, and being a man of habit, pulled his pocket watch out to make sure that it was precisely six o'clock before gathering up the contract papers that Spencer had left him and stashing them in his briefcase.

Then closing and locking the door carefully behind him, he rode the elevator down to the underground garage and walked toward his black Cadillac De Ville waiting in its reserved parking spot.

As he bent to insert the key into the door, a sudden movement reflected in the car window made him whirl around, but in one astoundingly swift action a chloroformed rag was thrust into his face. As he collapsed gagging onto the concrete, a woolen blanket was thrown over his head, muffling his already weakening cries. He was unconscious in less than fifteen seconds. Silently, one of his shadowy aggressors opened the trunk of the nondescript Ford that had been parked next to the Caddy; the other two effortlessly picked the financier up and threw him inside.

CHAPTER ONE

Harry Spencer carefully parked his conservative blue, impeccably clean Chrysler sedan the requisite distance from the sidewalk, put the push-button transmission into "park," pressed his foot firmly down on the emergency brake despite the fact that the street was perfectly flat, then eased out of the comfortable leather bench seat, gazed back and forth disapprovingly, and carefully locked the car door. Checking a slip of paper more than once to make sure he had the street number right, he marched up the wooden stairs of the house and pushed the electric door button with a determined thrust of his index finger.

"Yes? Can I help you?" an unfamiliar woman asked through the partially opened, chained door, her suspicious stare combining with a high-pitched voice to pierce right through Spencer's thin veneer of confidence.

"This is 4750 West 2nd Avenue, isn't it?" His self-assurance faltering now, he looked anxiously at the brass numbers nailed beside the door. "I . . . uh . . . I thought my wife Margaret lived here."

"Your wife? Sorry, no. Just me, and I'm sure we're not married." She was about to close the door when a new thought came to her. "You don't mean Maggie, do you, by any chance? Maggie Spencer? She lives downstairs in the basement flat."

"Downstairs?"

"Yes. Blue door. Powder blue. Around the side of the house."

"Thank you," he said stiffly, then turned, walked down the steps and around to the side of the house, took a deep breath and rapped loudly on the door.

"Harry!" Margaret Spencer greeted her estranged husband with a mixture of surprise and suspicion. "What are you doing here? What's the matter?"

"Are you aware, Margaret, that multi-family dwellings are strictly illegal in this part of Vancouver?" Harry demanded in an aggressive voice. "You could be in serious trouble with the city by-law department, you know."

"Oh, come on, Harry," she replied, "I seriously doubt that." She stepped aside for him to enter but ignored the hat he had removed from his head and was holding out in an expression of well-worn intimacy, expecting her to take it from him as she had always done when they were living as man and wife. "With the scarcity of housing in this city, the by-law officers have been turning a blind eye since the war." Then, watching him look with some unease for a piece of furniture to put his hat down on, she added, "And you know it."

Harry flushed then responded lamely, "No one is above the law, Margaret."

Once a lawyer, always a lawyer. In desperation, he balanced the hat on a tiny end table and turned his head to her again.

"So what brings you here, Harry?"

"Do I have to have a reason? I'm still your husband, you know! Or have you forgotten?" When she blushed but didn't answer, he decided to try a different tack. "You look very well, I must say, Margaret."

Maggie felt a sudden stab of remorse that she couldn't say the same for him. "You look a bit tired, Harry."

"So would you be if you were in my position," he answered tersely.

Maggie refrained from asking what that position would be. "Would you like a cup of tea, then?"

He lowered himself into one of the two basket chairs. "I hate to put you to so much trouble." He looked around the small room and sighed. "Barbara told me how cramped this place was."

"It suits me fine."

"Margaret," he said, getting up again and following her into the tiny kitchenette. "Look here. I've come to ask you once more to forget all this nonsense and come back home where you belong. With me."

"It's too late for that, Harry. I'm used to living on my own now."

"But we can work something out," he pleaded. "I'm sure we can. We'll go out more. You'd like that, wouldn't you? And you love the house, you know you do."

"Yes," she mused, looking around her modest quarters. "I always did." She poured the boiling water over the tea, then reached up to a shelf for the cookie tin. "You still like your tea black?" she asked.

"You see," he said triumphantly, taking the cup from her. "You remember how I like my tea."

I'm hardly likely to forget that in less than a year, for Heaven's sake.

As she followed him back to the living room, Emily, Maggie's cat, who always had a soft spot for Harry, waited until he sat down, then jumped into his lap and started to knead and purr ecstatically. He automatically rubbed behind her ears as he sipped the tea.

"And I also remember how you were so against my working," Maggie said, watching the traitorous cat sucking up to her husband. She had adopted the animal after Emily's owner, a miserable old client of hers from the Southby Detective Agency, had come to a very sticky end. To her astonishment, the cat had preferred Harry's touch to hers right from the beginning.

"But, Margaret," Harry went on, taking an enthusiastic cue from his success with the cat, "we can change all that. Just give up this stupid idea of working for that . . . that detective. I've nothing against you having a more . . . er . . . refined kind of employment. Nothing at all. Perhaps we could even find a small place for you in the firm."

The thought of working at Snodgrass, Crumbie and Spencer, Barristers and Solicitors, gave Maggie the shivers. She took a sip of her tea while she let that thought ebb away. "You see, Harry, it's just that I'm happy where I am."

Angrily he slammed his cup down on the coffee table with a furious crash. "Well, she knew, didn't she? Mother told me you wouldn't listen, and she was right!"

He pushed Emily off his lap in agitation and stood up.

"How is the old battle-axe, anyway?" Maggie asked in a voice sweet with sarcasm.

Harry's face turned a mottled red. "What has happened to you, Margaret?" he asked as the cat, having licked her ruffled fur into place again, rubbed up against his leg. "My mother deserves better than that."

"Well, Harry, this is my house, you know," Maggie replied, calm now. "I can say and do just what I like."

Carefully ignoring the cat at his shins, he made a show of brushing the hairs from his trousers and with all the dignity he could muster, walked to the front door of the apartment, Emily padding sadly behind in his wake. "You'll come to your senses one of these days, Margaret, I can tell you that. I just hope it's not too late."

Maggie watched as he threw open the door. "Harry," she said suddenly, picking up his hat and tendering it in a kind of peace offering, "have you heard from Midge?"

"Midge? No. Why?"

"She's not mentioned Jason lately. I Just wondered if everything is fine between them."

"Perhaps she's come to her senses and found someone from her own class," Harry said pompously. He had never taken to their younger daughter's non-conformist boyfriend.

"Jason suits Midge very well, Harry. He's fun. He makes her laugh" Maggie answered as politely as she could, steaming underneath.

"There's more to life than fun, Margaret. Which I'm sure both of you will find out soon enough."

"So you keep telling me, Harry." She saw him out and watched him stride down the path to the street. As he bent to insert the key into the lock of his pristine Chrysler, a battered old Chevy drew up behind him. Maggie's boss, Nat Southby, emerged from the wreck and the two men glared at each other wordlessly before Harry slipped behind the wheel of his car and drove away, tires screeching as he accelerated around the corner.

"What's up?" Southby asked Maggie as he closed the door behind him and took her in his arms. Then he bent down to pick up Emily, but the cat, fur ruffled, struggled to get out of his grip. "What's wrong with her?"

"I hate to say this, Nat, but she still dotes on Harry," she answered, blushing.

Maggie Spencer — Margaret to her erstwhile husband — looked at the plump, kind face of her boss, lover and owner of the Southby Detective Agency and thought what a difference he'd made to her life. She had gone to work for him in March 1958, just over a year ago, and hadn't regretted one day of it, even though she'd had a close scrape on her first job. He was somewhat overweight, true enough, sloppily casual in his clothes, and still fighting an uphill battle to give up smoking cigars, but he treated her as his equal and made her happy. She wouldn't change one single thing about him.

"So. What did he want?" Nat mumbled as he followed her into

the kitchen.

"Oh, just the usual. You know. Give up my job and be a dutiful wife and mother again."

"Maggie," he said softly, putting his hands on her shoulders. "It's been over a year since you left Harry. Your family must realize there's more between us than just work."

She nodded. "I suppose they can't help but suspect, Nat. I just haven't had the guts to bring it out in the open." She handed him a bottle of wine and a corkscrew. "Ah, let's forget that for a while. Here, make yourself useful while I prepare dinner."

They had reached the dessert and coffee stage when the phone rang, breaking into their intimacy. "Let it ring," Nat said. But Maggie couldn't. Old reflexes die hard.

It was Barbara on the line, the elder of her two daughters. She had never forgiven her mother for leaving Harry and the family's spacious Kerrisdale home. The fact that Maggie was perfectly happy living in Kitsilano hadn't sunk in: the rent here was affordable, the neighbours were interesting and the flat had the added bonus of being near the sea.

"I've got to talk to you, Mother."

"Can I call you back, dear? I've company for dinner."

"You've got that awful man Southby there, haven't you?"

"Who I invite to my house is my business, Barbara. Now, what's the matter? Baby's not sick, is he?" she asked.

"No, apart from his teething and me not getting enough sleep. But the pediatrician says that Oliver is very advanced for his age." Maggie noticed that Barbara's usually petulant voice took on an almost happy tone when she spoke about her infant son. "But that's not what I called about. I've just spoken to Father. He's terriblyy upset over your conversation with him. Don't you realize how helpless he is on his own?"

"What's wrong with his housekeeper?"

"He fired her."

Maggie looked down at her bare left hand, the impression of

the wedding band she had worn for twenty-eight years still show-ing. "Well, Barbara, he'll just have to find another one, I suppose. In any case, it really is no concern of mine."

"For goodness sake, Mother, people like you and Father don't break up after being married all those years. Don't you care what you're doing to the family? Charles and I find it very embarrassing. None of our friends' parents are separated. Your place is with Daddy."

"You mean I'm ruining your image? Barbara dear, I really have to go. I'll call you back later." Maggie replaced the phone on its cra-dle with a world-weary sigh.

Nat fiddled with his coffee cup, making a determined effort not to be the first to speak.

"Why don't they all just leave me alone, the lot of them?" Maggie demanded. Her happy mood gone now, she started to stack the plates, crashing them one by one into the sink with a little more vigor than necessary. Despite her protests, Nat came over to help her by drying the dishes but, sensing that she needed to be alone, hardly said a word and left soon after.

Before getting ready for bed, Maggie let Emily out into the gar-den and stood for a while at the kitchen window watching the cat chase imaginary beasts under the bushes. Then, feeling complete-ly exhausted and morose, she sank down into her armchair, closed her eyes and thought back to how stultifying her life had been before she went to work for Nat Southby. But here was Harry still doing his best to bully her back to that life, and Barbara loading her with guilt. Then there was Nat, not unexpectedly wanting their relationship to be even closer. *I have to get away. I'm being pulled in so many different directions, it's like a tug-of-war and I'm the one in the middle.*

The next morning, Maggie rose with new determination, ate a small breakfast and arrived at the office promptly at nine, pushing the key into the lock, and stepping briskly into the small, stuffy rooms of the Southby Agency. She dumped her bag on her desk, flung open the window that overlooked Broadway, and leaned out to breathe the warm June air and watch the bustling crowds below. She turned as Nat walked whistling into the office and watched him throw his hat at the wicker stand as he did every morning. As usual, he missed. He waited for the usual reprimand from Maggie, but this morning she gave him only a fleeting smile. "Still out of tune with the world, dear?" he asked, bending to retrieve the hat.

Maggie sat on the edge of her desk. "I've got to get away, Nat. Somewhere. Anywhere."

There was silence as he straightened up and placed the hat on the stand. "You want to leave me?" he ventured at last, with a worried look.

"Just for a while, a couple of weeks at most. I really have to clear the cobwebs from my mind."

He breathed a sigh of relief. "Is this to do with Harry turning up yesterday at your flat?"

She nodded. "That and the call from Barbara."

"Could you wait until we're not so busy so we could go away together?"

Maggie shook her head. "No, Nat, it isn't that. I just need to get away on my own, and right now."

"I see. Well all right, where would you go?"

"Jodie, my landlady, has a sister living in the Cariboo district. She and her husband run a dude ranch up there."

"Sounds suitable, I suppose. But while you're away, who'll run the office?"

"Nat Southby," she declared firmly, "sooner or later you're going to have to face the fact that we're going to need some extra office help anyway. The business has expanded and we can't do everything just the two of us any more."

"I suppose you're right," Nat replied gloomily. "I just hate the thought of having to go that route again." He pretended to duck as

18

he added, "With my luck I'll end up hiring another bossy Maggie Spencer."

Later that morning he looked up to see her standing in his office doorway. "I've just put an ad in the Sun for part-time help. Set things in motion."

"You've what?" he exploded. "We've not talked this out, Maggie!"

"Oh, I knew you'd just keep putting it off, Nat. And I'm serious about having a couple of weeks vacation."

"But where would we put the girl?"

"All we have to do is move a couple of the filing cabinets in here, then buy a second-hand desk for me. . . ."

"But—" Nat took a stab at cutting Maggie off.

" . . . and a bit of shifting of the furniture in the outer office," Maggie continued gaily. She stopped to think for a moment. "Yes, that should do the trick very smartly. Put my new desk across that corner near the window, move the small table to the other wall . . . then there would be plenty of room." She walked out of his office, then came back. "I'll leave you to find me a new desk. Okay, Mr. Private Eye?"

And with a neat swirl of her hips she exited, leaving Nat staring glumly at the closed door.

Later that afternoon, after a spell during which neither of the two had so much as spoken a word out loud, Maggie finally decided to break the tension and called through the open doorway, "Nat, give me your schedule for the rest of the week, would you, so that I can confirm your appointments?"

He walked out to stand beside her desk and gave an ostentatious sigh. "I suppose it's about time that I started doing my own phoning." Then an impish grin broke out on his rumpled face. "No, wait a minute, on second thought you carry on as usual until we get ourselves this new Girl Friday you're hiring. And by the way," he added, looking at Maggie's astonished face, "Murphy's Stationery over on West 5th has a good selection of used desks. You just go over there later on and pick one out. They'll deliver." The grin on his face turned into a broad smile as he tasted Maggie's scarlet lipstick that was now on his lips too. "Wow! Maggie," he said expansively, "as long as we're at it, what else would you like?"

~

A few days later Maggie, flipping up her day diary to Wednesday, June 10th, saw that secretarial applicant number four was due in the office at 10 o'clock. Applicants one and two had been fresh out of high school and were obviously looking for jobs to tide them over until something better turned up, and number three's typing skills were somewhere south of nil. *Well, number four can't be much worse, I suppose.*

Promptly at ten she heard heavy footsteps clumping their way up the stairs. The door banged open against the bamboo hat stand, making it wobble precariously. A woman in her forties stomped in and Maggie's gaze travelled automatically upward to the top of the visitor's head. She was at least five eleven, dressed completely in brown from her felt hat, sporting a small pheasant feather tucked in the grosgrain ribbon, to the serge, double-breasted suit, lisle stockings and brown oxfords. The only concession to contrast was a no-nonsense white shirt. Maggie tried not to gasp as her small hand was crushed in the candidate's oversized paw.

"Henny Vandermeer," the woman said. "Here for job." She dumped a huge, bulging tapestry bag beside the visitor's chair and sat down heavily.

Maggie eyed this new applicant with trepidation. "You do understand that we are only offering part-time employment?" Maggie said tentatively.

The woman nodded. "*Ja.* I understand," she said in a thick accent. "Suit me fine. I haff two kids at home."

Maggie hesitated before asking the next question. "Are you a single mother, Mrs. Vandermeer?"

20

Henny Vandermeer drew herself up. "Single? I haff you know, I am respectable married woman, Mrs. . . . ?"

"Spencer," Maggie answered, then quickly moved on to her next question. "You've worked in an office before?"

"I haff my references right here," the woman replied. She dug into the bag and hauled out a ball of thick natural wool and a length of knitting speared with two wooden knitting needles which she placed on Maggie's desk. A packet of wrapped sandwiches, a thermos and several sheets of wrinkled paper followed in short order. "See?"

Maggie took the proffered papers and quickly glancing through them, saw that indeed each one sang the praises of Henny Vandermeer. And all said how sorry they were to lose her. "You have worked in a number of places, I see."

"Ja. Never fails. No sooner I get an office going right, then that office close down or they haff to cut back on staff." She sat back in the chair and surveyed the room. "I see you haff good typewriter?"

"Yes. You can type?" Maggie said, hoping the answer would be "no."

"Oh, ja. Got top A in typing school."

Maggie's heart sank. "But English is not your mother tongue."

"But I speak English just fine. Ja?" She looked towards Nat's door. "The boss he is in there?"

"Mr. Southby's out at the moment, Mrs. Vandermeer, and in any case you would be working principally for me." *That should be enough to scare her off.*

"You call me Henny. But I should see boss anyway."

Maggie stood up. "I'm sure he'll be sorry he's missed you. Well, we'll get in touch with y—"

"So, when do I start?" Henny cut in, reaching down to pick up her bag and hardly even glancing at Maggie.

"Start?"

"Tomorrow is Thursday," Henny went on. "You show me round now, and I come to start in morning."

"But you said you needed to see the . . . the boss."

"Change my mind. You'll do fine."

Oh-my-God! What will Nat say? "Mrs . . . I mean Henny, are you sure you want to work here?" Maggie handed the woman's papers back to her. "It can be quite hectic. You see, Mr. Southby and I have some very unusual clients. We are an investigating firm. Detectives, you know . . . "

"You keep those to show boss," Henny answered, thrusting the papers back into Maggie's hands. "I know you detective agency. I look you up. I be good at investigating."

"But you wouldn't be doing any investigating," Maggie explained, keeping her voice calm, with no little difficulty. "What we are looking for is someone to do all the office work — typing, filing, answering the phone, that kind of thing. So you see. . . ." Her voice trailed off.

"*Ja.* That's why I'm here. Now show me what I haff to do."

Maggie stood up. *Oh, what the hell! There's no more applicants so he'll just have to put up with her until I get back from Williams Lake. Anyway, all those recommendations must mean something, I suppose.*

"I've hired our new Girl Friday," Maggie told Nat when he arrived later that afternoon. "Her name is Henny Vandermeer and she starts tomorrow," she finished with a breathless rush.

"Tomorrow! That's a bit soon, isn't it?" He looked closely as Maggie. "What's up? You seem nervous. You didn't hire one of those kids you interviewed, did you?"

"No, no. She's forty-ish, married, and has two kids at home." Maggie took a deep breath.

"Vandermeer? Sounds Dutch."

"I don't really know. She has a thick accent though." Among other things.

"Well, if you're satisfied with her, my dear, she must be okay."

"Of course, I'll give her a week's training before I go," Maggie added.

22

"Gosh, you just can't wait to get away from me, can you?" Nat asked glumly.

"It's not you and you know it, Nat," she replied warmly as she slipped an arm around his waist. "I don't want to leave you. Just my blasted family." But Maggie wasn't being totally honest; Nat's love for her was part of the problem.

That evening, Maggie phoned Harry.

"What do you want, Margaret?" he asked stiffly.

"I wondered if you would do something for me, Harry?" Then before he could answer she quickly added, "Could you look after Emily while I go away for a couple of weeks."

"The cat! Is that all you want me for? A cat sitter?"

"I need to get a way for a while," she explained.

"Well. At long last you see my point."

Maggie could picture him gloating. "It's not that, Harry, not that at all. . . ."

"You've made your bed, Margaret Spencer, and as my grand-mother would say, now you can lie in it. Goodnight."

Fuming, Maggie replaced the receiver. *Why did I ever make that call? And what the devil am I going to do with Emily?*

The next morning when Maggie looked out of her bedroom window, she saw blue sky and the sun shining brightly. *A beautiful day! A new day!* But there was something nagging at the back of her mind. *What is it?* The feeling persisted right through her breakfast. *What's wrong?* As she showered, she couldn't shrug off the sense of impending doom. It wasn't until she was towelling that it came to her. *Oh my God. Henny!* She raced back into the bedroom, slipped into the skirt and blouse she had worn the day before, and after making sure Emily had food and water, ran to her car.

The traffic seemed slower than ever. *I must get to the office before Nat meets Henny.* But she was too late! Even before she entered the outer office she could hear the thick guttural voice.

"Mr. Nat. You in there?" The woman was banging on Nat's door and then putting her ear against it to listen. When a muffled answer came through the connecting door, she turned to Maggie. "What he say?"

"I think he said yes," she answered, trying not to smile. "You've met Mr. Southby, then?"

"Ja. He said fast hello and then went in office quick." She waved a mug in the air. "He likes coffee, ja?"

"Ja . . . I mean yes," Maggie answered, flustered. "That's very kind of you to make it".

"That my job, ja?" She turned back to Nat's door.

"Never mind, Henny, I'll take it." Grabbing the mug from her assistant's hand, Maggie tapped lightly on the door. "It's me, Nat. Open up." The door moved inward, just enough for her to slip through before Nat quickly shut it again.

"Who is that woman?" he hissed.

"Henny." She smiled sweetly. "Our new Girl Friday."

"Well, get rid of her."

"Now, Nat. You've got to give her a chance." She reached for his in-tray and extracted the papers she had left for him. "Look, these are her references. Everyone praises her."

"But she speaks some strange patois. Doesn't she understand English?"

"Yes, of course she does. It's just her Dutch showing through, and you don't want to seem prejudiced, I'm sure, do you? Don't worry, she'll be able to cope. After all," Maggie added with a coy smirk, "she only has to copy what you write. You'll just have to watch your spelling a little. And besides," she finished, turning to go out, "she was the best of the bunch."

The next week was a nightmare for Nat. Henny decided that she was going to mother her new boss, to his chagrin. "Maggie, look what she's brought me," he said, pointing to a plate of large, lumpy oatmeal cookies. "You know how I hate oatmeal cookies!" He pushed the plate toward Maggie. "Here, you have them."

"Oh, I couldn't possibly deprive you, Nat, I wasn't raised that way!" She made a jaunty exit, humming a catchy tune.

But despite her peculiar accent and odd (to Southby) habits, Henny worked hard at mastering the office procedures Maggie had set up. The filing was up to date, so it was just a matter of keeping on top of it. She even got the hang of typing up Nat and Maggie's case notes. Answering the phone was something of a problem though, as she tried to have an intimate conversation with every caller. However, things did progress, and two days before Maggie planned to leave for her trip, she was confident that their new office help was as good as she would ever be. Simple rules had been established: the phone was to be answered professionally and Henny wasn't to ask the caller personal questions. She would only type what Nat or Maggie had actually written and not what she thought they might have meant, and she would stay out of the boss's office — he didn't want it dusted or even the ashtray emptied, she was the office help and not Maggie's replacement — and finally, she would refrain from giving gratuitous advice to the clients while they waited. They had already lost one prospective client who decided to follow Henny's advice and solve his problem on his own rather than pay "good money" to see Mr. Southby.

"I'm going upstairs to Jodie's tonight," Maggie called out to Nat as she tidied up her desk before leaving the office. "She's got a map of the Cariboo district that will help me get my bearings."

"Mind if I come along?"

"Be my guest," she answered smiling. "I'll see you around seven."

It was shortly after six-thirty that evening when the phone rang.

"Oh damn! That will surely be Nat to say he's going to be late getting here."

But it was a different voice she heard, and she almost dropped the receiver in surprise.

"Harry here, Margaret. Tell me, when do you plan on leaving for your vacation?"

25

"Er . . . Friday, Harry. Why?" she asked nervously.

"What arrangements have you made about Emily, then?"

"Emily? Well, at this point I'm hoping my neighbour will. . . ."

"I'll take her," he interrupted.

"But . . . " Maggie was speechless. "Are you sure, Harry? I mean, you seemed so against the idea when I spoke to you on the phone, and I'm . . . er . . . I'm sure my neighbour would—"

"No, that's all right. I've changed my mind. Can you bring her over tomorrow evening?"

"That's very kind of you, Harry, but . . . " Maggie was wary, waiting for the other shoe to drop.

"I think a vacation from that place is just what you need, Margaret. I'll be happy to chip in and help. Where do you plan on going, anyway?"

"A dude ranch. It's just outside Williams Lake."

"Dude ranch! What's it called?"

"I'm not sure, but it's on Wild Rose Lake."

"Why the devil a dude ranch?" He went on without waiting for her reply. "But I suppose that's better than working for that detective. I'll see you around seven o'clock then."

Spencer hung up before she could respond.

Now what's he up to?

A short time later, Jodie, Nat and Maggie were poring over a map of central British Columbia. "See," Jodie explained, pointing to a small dot next to a large lake. "That's Williams Lake. And this," she added, indicating a road that branched off to the right, "is the road to Horsefly." She circled the road with a pen.

"What a crazy name."

"It is, isn't it?" Jodie agreed, and then continued. "But you'll only take that road as far as Wild Rose Lake." She drew another circle. "It's about twelve miles along."

Maggie put her finger on Vancouver then moved it up the map to the lake. "Whew!" she exclaimed. "I didn't realize it would be so far."

26

"Well over 300 miles if its an inch!" Nat commented, looking over her shoulder.

"You're going up by train?" Jodie asked. Maggie nodded. "Well," Jodie continued, "you know of course that it travels north from Vancouver to Prince George on Mondays, Wednesdays, and Fridays and south on Tuesdays, Thursdays and Saturdays."

"I'm leaving at seven this Friday," she answered, and then turned to Nat. "Yesterday when I slipped over to buy my ticket, the station master told me that line between Vancouver and Squamish was only completed three years ago."

"And did he tell you that there are still occasional rock slides on that line?" Jodie asked.

Maggie shook her head and laughed. "No, he didn't. He kept that bit to himself."

"Well, don't worry. It's been fairly dry lately, so there shouldn't be any problem. The train gets into Williams Lake around seven in the evening. It takes about twelve hours." She started to re-fold the map. "But Kate will be there to meet you."

"You've been up to your sister's, then?" Nat asked.

Jodie nodded. "Last fall. I must admit it's beautiful if you're into space, cows and horses. I prefer the city myself."

"What about your sister?" Nat asked. "How's she coping with the great outdoors?"

Jodie laughed. "Quite well, considering."

"Considering what?"

"Considering she's twenty-eight and still a bit of a kid."

"Why do you say that?"

"Being the youngest in our family, she was spoilt rotten. Then when she was barely out of high school, she ran off to Montreal and married some low-life. Thank God, my father managed to step in and have the marriage annulled."

"How did Kate feel about that?"

"Relieved, actually. He'd begun to knock her around. Put her right off marriage, for a while, that is." She picked up a silver-framed photograph and handed it to Maggie. "This is a recent one of her. As you can see, she's very pretty."

The photograph showed a young woman, blonde hair tied back in a pony tail, wearing blue jeans, a red plaid shirt, and western boots. She was holding the reins of a chestnut mare, but standing several feet away from it. "My. She doesn't look twenty-eight," Maggie commented, handing it back.

"No. And Doug, her new husband, is a good eighteen years older," Jodie said ruefully. "She's gone from one extreme to another."

"You don't like this one either?"

"Mm-m-m. There's something about him. . . ." She shrugged. "But I will say this, if you're looking for a peaceful vacation, they can provide it."

"That's just what I want," Maggie replied picking up the map.

Later that evening in the downstairs suite, Nat drew Maggie toward him. "I'm really going to miss you. I just wish I was going with you."

"I'm going to miss you, too," she answered with a coquettish smile, kissing him. "But at least you've got Henny!"

It was early Thursday evening. Maggie stood beside her bed and surveyed the pile of clothes that still had to be crammed into her suitcase. She reached down to pick up her slippers and saw one of Emily's toys lying next to them. It squeaked as she picked it up and she realized with a sudden pang how much she was going to miss the independent, unpredictable creature. She glanced at her watch. Almost six thirty. She'd have to scoot if she was to make it over to Harry's by seven, as per his summons. She had already prepared the cat carrier for the journey so all she had to do was locate the elusive feline, who naturally had disappeared as soon as she saw the cage emerge from the closet. By the time the chase was over, both Maggie and Emily were worn ragged, and the cat continued her protest as they went out the door, into the car and all the way across town to Maggie's old home on Kerrisdale's staid Elm Street. If the cat's protests were unnerving, so were the unwanted memories that came flooding back to Maggie as she drove into the driveway, parked, rang the doorbell and waited for Harry to answer.

She followed her husband along the all-too-familiar hallway and into the dining room where she set the carrier down and released Emily, who was by now frantic. The cat immediately ran into the kitchen and sat staring at the cupboard where her food used to be kept.

"You see, Margaret," Harry said with a self-satisfied smile, pulling out a chair at the dining room table for his still-frazzled wife to sit down, "Emily is pleased to be home. Would you like some coffee?"

She was about to refuse when she saw the effort he'd made to welcome her. Her favourite coffee mugs were waiting on a tray. "Thanks, Harry. That would be nice."

"I still don't quite understand about this dude ranch," Harry said, once the coffee pot and cream were in front of her. "Couldn't you have found a nice hotel in Victoria, perhaps?"

"I need to get right away, somewhere new, Harry."

He watched her as she looked around the room. "You know, Margaret you could have all this back. Your home, your garden — all the things you loved. They are all waiting for you."

As she gazed around she realized how much of her was in the room. It was still the same, the Wedgewood china she had purchased when they had first been married still in its walnut cabinet, the pictures they had chosen together, the drapes, even the carpet on the dining room floor had not moved an inch. Then she looked at Harry and realized that he hadn't changed either. He would still be as demanding, and suspicious of her new-found freedom. He would never stop nagging at her to give up the job she loved. And then, of course, there was her relationship with Nat, which Harry probably suspected but couldn't bring himself to ask about. Sooner or later she'd have to face that.

"Mother knows how much I want you back," he continued

29

blithely. "She's such a generous soul, you know. She said she would be quite willing to forgive and forget."

"Forgive . . . ?" Her mind went back to the last time she had entertained her mother-in-law, Honoria Spencer, in this very dining room. It had not exactly been a crashing success. Honoria had demanded she get rid of Emily or she would not darken their door again. Margaret had taken the opportunity and chosen Emily, scandalizing her husband. That thought brought her mind back to the present. "I'm sorry, Harry, what did you say?"

"I said," he replied. "She is willing to forgive your . . . er . . . unkind words to her."

"That's awfully nice of her. But she needn't worry, because I'm not coming back." She put her mug of coffee down purposefully on the table. "This was not a good idea, Harry." She picked up her purse and controlled her impulse to run to the front door. "You still can't understand, can you?"

"No. I don't understand," he replied, raising his voice. "I gave you everything you could possibly want—"

"Yes, everything except the freedom to be myself."

She was still shaking when she reached the relative safety of her own front door. She marched into her bedroom and stuffed the final things into her case. *How could I have been so stupid? I should have known what would happen. And how the hell do I get Emily back now?* "Damn! damn! damn!"

She snapped the suitcase shut. *Well, there's no point in worrying about it for the time being. It's just another problem that I'll have to face when I return.*

The next morning when Nat came to drive Maggie to the train there was a distinct feeling of shortness between them. "I forgot to ask," Nat eventually said, trying a new tack as he stowed her suitcase into the trunk of his car. "Who's finally looking after that cat of yours?"

"An old acquaintance," she answered curtly. "Don't bother yourself about Emily. Anyway, we'd better get a move on if I'm to catch that train."

30

CHAPTER TWO

By the time the train had reached the coastal mountains after short stops at the small towns of Squamish, Whistler and Pemberton, Maggie was in a very different mood. The scenery, which could hardly get any better, had pushed her Vancouver worries and thoughts of husband past and boyfriend present to the back of her mind. She peered out of the dusty window of the three-coach train, awestruck by the rugged beauty of the mountains, their snow and glacier peaks glinting in the clear morning sunshine. Then the scene changed in a flash, or so it seemed, to sheer tranquillity as the track ran beside Duffy Lake, where broad forests of dark green fir trees and slate-colored peaks were reflected perfectly in the still water. Before reaching Lillooet, the train made a couple of stops to let passengers off. Most of them were met, and she watched as they threw their bags into battered pick-up trucks or old cars. It all seemed so homey. Once the train even stopped to let a passenger off in front of his house. She watched the man throw his bag over the fence before hopping over it himself, then turn and give a cheery wave to the train engineer who gave an answering toot of the whistle before continuing down the track. But the area was so remote, the roads that ran beside the train tracks so narrow and dusty, that she had to wonder how people could possibly live happily in such isolation.

In the small town of Lillooet there was a half-hour lay-over, giving her time to stretch her legs and buy a take-out lunch. Feeling refreshed, she settled into her seat once again to watch the landscape change; now there were sand dunes and hills that the winds had carved into miniature castles and fortresses. Stunted fir trees and an abundance of wild sage were the only greenery in this sparse, desert-like area. Then the train emerged from the dunes, and the track ran through forests, open ranch land and around lakes before a brief stop at Lac-la-Hache. Maggie, very tired and stiff after the long hours of riding the rails was glad that she would soon be in Williams Lake.

Kate Guthrie, as good as her word, was at the station to meet her and soon had Maggie's luggage in a Land Rover. Maggie, used to Jodie's exuberance, found Kate extremely quiet and remote, and several attempts at starting up a conversation fell flat. By the time they reached the turn-off to the ranch, she was beginning to wonder if coming all this way was such a good idea after all. It was dusk when they arrived at the end of the private dirt road that led to the Guthrie's ranch. Kate turned off the engine in front of a large log house, and Maggie's mood now changed again: she felt the peace of nature reaching out to her as she got out of the car and looked around. In the near distance she could see barns and out-buildings settled on a gentle, sloping acreage now enshrouded in a swirling mist. The strangeness of the scene was accentuated by an odd snuffling sound. She turned to find a number of brown and white cows, their heads hanging over a Russell fence, surveying her with interest. "Nice cows," Maggie said nervously, backing away in haste from this unexpected, real contact with nature.

"Steers," Kate corrected her. "Not cows." She unloaded Maggie's suitcases and carried them to the front door which she opened with one hand, and was immediately greeted by two huge Golden Labrador retrievers. After slobbering all over Kate, they turned their attention to Maggie who found to her dismay that she was being pushed back towards the fenced-in steers. "Down! Down!" Kate ordered. Giving Maggie a final lick, the dogs backed off and followed Kate inside.

"I'll show you to your room. Supper will be ready in twenty minutes," Kate said. And still carrying Maggie's luggage, she started to lead the way up the wide staircase.

"I can manage those," Maggie said, reaching for the smaller case. "Perhaps your husband could—"

"My husband is out of town."

"Then let's take one each," Maggie proposed, firmly taking the largest out of Kate's hands.

After a long hot shower, Maggie changed into fresh clothes and found her way downstairs to join her hostess in a comfortable kitchen-cum-dining room. The honey maple oval table, set for two, was positioned in a bay window overlooking the lake. Kate, with the two labs sitting at her feet on the linoleum tiled floor, was perched on a stool drawn up to a workmanlike island, preparing a salad.

"What can I do?" Maggie asked.

"Nothing. It's all done." She poured Maggie a glass of wine but continued to chop.

"Are there other guests at the ranch?" Maggie asked, looking for a chance to break the ice.

"You're the only one at the moment. But we're fully booked for the summer." There was another uncomfortable silence, then Kate said suddenly, "Jodie told me you work in a detective agency."

Maggie, surprised at the comment, laughed. "Yes, though if someone had told me a couple of years ago that's what I would be doing, I'd never have believed them."

"Do you investigate missing people?" Kate asked as she placed the food on the table.

Maggie nodded and then sat down. "A great percentage of our services involve looking for people. Why? Did you lose someone?" She began to smile but the look on the girl's face stopped her cold.

"It's Doug, my husband. He left on Sunday, June 7th to buy some horses, and . . . and I haven't heard from him since."

"But that's nearly two weeks ago. Where was he headed?"

"Over to the Alberta border, the McDougalls' ranch. He should've been back by last weekend."

"Did you call them?"

"Yes. Last Saturday. But they told me that he'd never arrived at all."

"Why hadn't they called you?"

"They said as it had been a tentative arrangement, they simply thought he'd changed his mind."

"Have you called the police?"

"Yes. Right after I spoke to the McDougalls, but Brossard said to wait a few more days and if I still haven't heard from him, then they'd look into it."

"Who's Brossard?"

"RCMP." Her eyes brimmed with tears. "I just don't know what to do."

Maggie placed her hand on Kate's. "What about your hired help? Do you think they would have any idea where else he could have gone?"

"I asked Hendrix — he looks after the horses and helps Doug run the ranch — but he said that Doug's probably just gone off on a toot." She wiped her eyes, then added, "Hendrix doesn't like women very much in general and me in particular."

"Has he been here long?"

"He came with the ranch when Doug took it over from his father."

"How long ago was that?"

"About twenty years, I think."

"That is quite a while," Maggie agreed.

34

Kate composed herself, arose from the table, and carrying their coffee led the way into the den. "It's cosier in here."

Maggie's first impression of the den which opened off the kitchen was that it was anything but cosy. It was at least double the size of her whole basement suite, and its atmosphere wasn't improved by the leering wolf's head hanging on the facing wall, baring its fangs and fixing its malevolent eyes on her as she sidled over to a huge leather armchair. Fortunately, the antlered head over the massive fireplace was eyeless, and the grizzly bear rug — complete with head — which lay in front of it seemed to be asleep. She looked for guns and soon found them, at least a dozen, locked in a glass-fronted cabinet.

Kate put the cups down on a coffee table made of a large slab of varnished maple burl. "It's quite a room, isn't it?"

"How long did it take you to get used to all the wild life?" Maggie asked indicating the wolf's head.

"I never liked it much. Still don't. But it's Doug's room."

"Yes. I can see that. He must do all his business in here," she added, nodding at the leather-topped desk and matching chair. The only feminine touches in the whole room were a number of water color landscapes. "Jodie says you worked in Vancouver before you were married?"

Kate nodded. "I did. For Teasdale Advertising."

"Sounds like it was an interesting job."

"It was, you know. I started there as a copy writer, but Ray Teasdale discovered I could draw and he started training me to be an illustrator. Then I met Doug."

"End of career?"

Kate nodded again. "Shame, really, in a way. I liked my job."

Maggie took a sip of her coffee and tried to stifle a yawn. "That train ride really took it out of me." She struggled out of her chair. "Who painted the water-colors?"

"I did. They're not very good, though."

"Better than I could do. Is this a view of the lake?"

"Yes. From the deck out back."

"And this one?" Maggie asked, pausing in front of a scene of pasture land with a background of steep craggy hills.

"That's way up on the border of our property — Black Adder Ravine. Doug took me up there by jeep when I first arrived."

"So you went back and painted this?"

"No. I did it from the photographs I took," Kate answered. "My camera went everywhere with me in those first few weeks."

"You haven't been back?"

"He said once I'd got used to riding Ginny we'd go back." She stood silent for a moment. "Al — he's Hendrix's eighteen-year-old son — has been teaching me to ride, and he says I'm ready now. I was going to surprise Doug. . . ." Her voice quivered. "Do you ride?" she asked, with an effort to be the proper hostess.

"Used to," Maggie answered. "And I'm looking forward to trying it again. Perhaps Hendrix can find a gentle horse for me too."

"We'll look into it first thing in the morning."

"Another thing we could look into in the morning is your husband's whereabouts, Kate. Let me sleep on it."

Maggie fell asleep immediately, and apart from a disturbing dream in which Henny was banging on the door yelling that Nat was on fire, slept fairly well. When she awoke, her guilty feelings of having left her boss to the "tender" mercies of their new Girl Friday were firmly behind her. She slowly focused, then rolled over to look at her travel clock. *My God! It's nine o'clock.* Throwing back the covers, she quickly washed and dressed for the day.

The table in the kitchen was set for one, and propped up against a bowl of fruit was a note addressed to Maggie.

Help yourself. Eggs and milk in the fridge, cereal on the counter, bread by the toaster. Gone to feed the chickens.

Kate

Maggie was just finishing her breakfast when the back door opened and Kate walked in with a wire basket of eggs. "I've spoken to Hendrix and he's getting Angel ready for you. You'll love her, she's such a pet."

"I didn't bring riding gear, Kate, do you think—"

"Jeans will do. That's what everyone wears around here."

"Oh, super. I'll go and change. Then you can have the pleasure of introducing me to Angel." She paused in the doorway. "By the way," she added, "did you call the police again?"

Kate nodded. "Corporal Brossard said that since it's nearly two weeks since Doug left, he will definitely start looking into it."

"There. That's something, anyway. But I think it will still be a good idea to sit down together and review some of the details of his disappearance. After my ride?"

Maggie and the horse eyed each other warily. "Ever ridden before?" a raspy voice said behind her. She turned to find a heavy-set man in his mid-fifties. He was dressed in jeans, western boots, red-checked shirt and wore the biggest Stetson hat she had ever seen. This must be Hendrix, she thought.

Kate made a somewhat perfunctory introduction and then hurried off to attend to her own mount.

"Not for quite a while," Maggie answered, picking up on his comment and trying not to stare at his hat. "My sister has a riding stable in Norfolk, but I haven't been back there in a while." She put out a tentative hand to stroke Angel's nose.

"Then you never used a Western saddle?" He pointed to a mounting block. "Here, climb up."

Maggie was terrified that she would make a complete fool of herself and go flying right over the horse and land on the ground. But to her surprise she found herself astride the animal. Hendrix adjusted the stirrups. "Okay," he said, "Let's see what you can do." Swinging himself onto a huge chestnut mare, he leaned toward Angel and took the leading reins in his hand as they headed out of the enclosure and onto a well-marked trail. After some initial nervousness Maggie found herself adjusting to the horse's gait, and she soon even managed to take the occasional glance at the open range as they plodded up towards the distant hills.

Hendrix broke the silence. "You a friend of Kate's?"

"No. I rent a basement suite from her sister in Vancouver." Her gaze wandered up ahead to where Kate, looking very much at home on her horse, was chatting with the young ranch hand keeping pace beside her on his grey mare. "Kate looks as if she's doing okay."

"Yep."

"She's worried about her husband."

"Huh!" he snorted.

"You don't think she has cause to worry? He's been away for nearly two weeks now."

"Used to go away all the time before she came along." He leaned over and handed the reins to her. "Try riding on your own."

"If you're sure she won't charge off with me clinging to her neck."

"Just do what I showed you," he added. "Head for those hills up there."

"That seems an awfully long way."

"You'll make it," he answered in his terse manner. "You seem like a natural. But you'll still be sore afterward!"

"Kate and Al are coming back," Maggie said, hoping Hendrix would decide they'd gone far enough.

"Al's got chores to do."

"See you back at the house, Maggie," Kate called as they trotted past.

Maggie waved and then urged her horse to go a little faster to catch up to Hendrix. As they neared the base of the hills, he reined in his horse and looked up at a flock of birds wheeling in the sky.

"What's the matter?" she asked.

"They're over Black Adder Ravine," he replied thoughtfully. "Stay here while I take a look-see."

"No. I'll come, too," she answered, not wanting to be left alone.

"Probably a cow fallen into the ravine. We'll ride a ways, then dismount when it gets too steep. You go ahead of me."

The higher they climbed the steeper the ravine fell away on their left side, and Maggie was glad that Angel was very sure-footed on the loose gravel of the narrow trail. She made an effort not to look down. After a while, she stopped and let Hendrix catch up. "I think I'd better get down," she told him.

Hendrix nodded and steadied Angel while Maggie slid down the animal's flank. "We'll leave 'em tethered here." He dismounted, took the reins of the two horses and fastened them to one of the saplings that lined the cliff side of the trail, and they began plodding upwards. Getting as close to the edge as she dared, Maggie craned her neck to get a better look at the top of the craggy mountain that towered over them.

"This trail is literally cut out of the side of the mountain," she said in wonder. "Where does it lead?"

"Old road, more than a trail, ma'am. Leads to an old mine. Hasn't been worked for at least fifty years to my knowledge." For another five minutes he led the way up then suddenly stopped and pointed down into the ravine. "Christ! There's a jeep down there."

Maggie stopped beside him. The jeep was upside down, and a man's body lay on the rocks beside it. She grabbed Hendrix's arm. "We've got to get down there."

"No. We'll go back to the ranch for help. Come on." He turned and ran down the road to where they'd left the horses. "Come on." Maggie followed and when they reached the horses he cupped his hand and helped her onto Angel.

"You go on ahead," she said. "I'll be fine."

"You sure?" And when Maggie nodded, he jumped onto his own horse and raced back down the track and was soon a cloud of dust in the distance.

Saddle sore, she arrived at the ranch a few minutes after Hendrix to find everything in an uproar. Young Al came to help her down from the horse and then led it into the stable. As soon as Kate saw Maggie she ran over to her.

"Maggie. You saw the man. Could it be Doug . . . ?"

"I really don't know, Kate," she replied, putting her arms around the girl's shoulders. "Let's go and talk to Hendrix," she added, leading the way over to where he was giving orders to a ranch hand.

"We've got to get up there." Maggie could hear the trembling in Kate's voice. "Do you really think it isn't Doug?" she asked Hendrix.

"We were too far away to tell. As I said, Kate, I doubt it. But we're sure as hell going to find out. Everything's ready to go." He turned as a ranch hand emerged at the top of the staircase which led to Hendrix's barn loft office. "Bernie, you get ahold of the police?"

"Yep." Bernie shouted back. "They're on their way with the ambulance."

"Kate," Hendrix said, placing a large hand on her shoulder, "why don't you and your friend stay here while we go and find out what's happened?"

"No. I want to be there."

"I'm coming too," Maggie said, pushing all thoughts of a lovely hot soak behind her.

"Then get into the Rover." He headed for the stairs leading to his office. As they clambered into the back seats, Maggie saw that a jack and masses of ropes and pulleys had already been heaped into the rear of the vehicle. Al jumped into the passenger seat and a moment later Hendrix returned carrying a pair of binoculars. "Follow us with the jeep," he yelled at Bernie before jumping into the driver's seat of the Rover.

By the time they had bumped and shuddered over the rough track and reached the steep gravel road that led up into the hills, Maggie was fervently wishing that her maiden voyage on the horse hadn't been such a long one. Every bone in her body ached.

40

Terrified they'd meet the same fate as the jeep in the ravine, she clung to the seat in front of her as the vehicle veered close to the edge, its heavy tires biting into the loose gravel.

"You've been up here before?" Maggie yelled to Kate above the noise of the engine.

"This is where I took those photographs."

When the vehicle came to a sudden, shuddering stop, the four of them scrambled out and peered over the edge. Hendrix, looking through the binoculars, gave a low whistle and silently offered them to Al.

"Let me see." Kate grabbed the glasses from Al and peered down. "Oh, my God!"

Maggie took the binoculars out of Kate's trembling hands, but it took a few moments for her to refocus and bring the jeep into view. What was clearly a corpse was spreadeagled on a flat rock a few yards from the vehicle. Overhead several large birds screamed, wheeling, then darting at the body. "Can't you stop them?"

Hendrix leaned into the Rover, and withdrawing a shotgun let off a few rounds into the air. The birds scattered, protesting noisily as the shots reverberated around the ravine. "How are we going to get down there?" Kate cried when the sound had stopped.

"With these." Hendrix grabbed the gear they had brought with them, then fastened one end of the rope to the winch on the front of the Rover and flung the other end over the treacherous edge. Bernie arrived to help Hendrix slowly pay out the rope as Al clawed and bumped his way down into the deep ravine. Minutes passed before they heard a faint shout to say he had reached the bottom. Hendrix took the glasses from Maggie and trained them downward to watch Al clamber over slabs of granite to get to the overturned jeep. Momentarily, Maggie tore her gaze away from the unfolding drama to look at the arid, dusty landscape and feel the unearthly silence. Even the birds, made wary by the shotgun blast and the activity on the cliff's edge, circled at a safe distance now — waiting. There was another shout from below and, wrenching her eyes from the birds, she saw that Al had reached the body.

"What's he saying?" Kate cried, tears running down her face. "Is it Douglas? Tell me, is it Doug?"

Below them Al continued to yell and wave his arms.

"He's saying it's not Doug," Maggie said, putting her arms around Kate. "It's not him."

"Oh thank God," Kate whispered. "Thank God."

"He wants us to haul him back up," Hendrix said, looking through the glasses. "That poor bugger's had it for sure."

"Who is it?" Kate asked.

Hendrix shrugged. "Dunno."

The wait seemed interminable. Hendrix and Bernie winched Al back up the cliff and there was a collective sigh of relief when he clawed over the edge. He sat for a moment, dusty and bleeding, getting his breath back, then looked directly at Kate. "It's not the boss."

"But if it's not Doug, who is it?"

"Bit hard to tell. He's been dead for a least a couple of days by the looks of things." He stood up as a police car came to a crunching halt just below the Rover. Two RCMP officers got out of the vehicle, walked up to the group and peered over the edge. "You've been down?" the officer in charge asked Al, taking in his dusty appearance.

Al nodded. "The man down there, he's dead as a doornail, officer."

"Can't you do something about those birds?" Maggie cut in. "They're coming back."

Hendrix raised the gun and fired another round into the air. "That should scare them off for a bit longer."

The policeman turned to Kate. "It's not . . . ahem . . . Mr. Guthrie, then?"

Kate shook her head. "No, apparently not," she answered before turning to Maggie. "This is Corporal Brossard. Corporal, this is Mrs. Margaret Spencer, a guest at the ranch."

Hendrix handed the binoculars to Brossard. "Have a look for yourself."

Brossard trained them on the jeep. Then he pointed to the creek at the bottom of the ravine. "Is it possible to drive in from the other direction along that creek?"

Hendrix shook his head. "There's no more'n a track alongside of the stream. It'd take half a day to get the body out that way. He's dead anyway, so in my opinion it'd be best to just haul him up." He put his hand on Kate's shoulder. "Kate, why don't you and your friend go back to the house?"

Brossard turned his attention back to Kate. "As it's not your husband, perhaps that would be a very good idea."

"No, it's not my husband," Kate answered heatedly, "but I'm still staying until I see who it is."

There was a sound of a distant siren. "Will the ambulance be able to turn around?" Brossard asked abruptly.

"No," Hendrix answered. "We'll all have to drive up another couple of miles to the old mine. The road's wider up there," he said, "but even so it's going to be real tricky getting all the vehicles turned so that the ambulance can be in front." He headed for the Rover. "When the ambulance gets here, get him to follow you."

Brossard followed Hendrix and leaned into the open window. "I'd appreciate your help when we all get back here."

Hendrix nodded and started his motor.

Maggie, Kate and Al waited on the far side of the track, their backs pressed against the wall of rock, until all the vehicles had made their way up to the mine, turned and came back with the ambulance and police car leading. Then there was the long wait while Brossard, his assistant, and one of the medics were lowered into the ravine. The two women, taking turns using the glasses, watched the drama unfold below them as the men strapped the body onto a collapsible stretcher. Then began the difficult manoeuvre of hauling the stretcher to the top of the ridge.

Once up, Brossard uncovered the cadaver's face and asked if anyone recognized the deceased. Bernie and Al shook their heads, but Maggie had the distinct feeling that despite his voiced denials,

Hendrix knew the identity of the corpse; she discerned a fleeting look of shock on his face, one that quickly retreated behind an unexpressive mask. Kate's expression was one of relief, but she too confirmed that she had no idea who the victim was.

Before Brossard could cover the body up again Maggie stepped forward to get a look. Her first impression was that the man had not been a drifter. Despite the body having been down in the ravine for at least two or three days, and the man's clothes being in a bad state from the accident, she could tell that he had had expensive tastes: the jacket was a soft tan leather, the jeans were well tailored and the boots hand-tooled. Through the left breast pocket of the jacket was a neat bullet hole. Seeing her interest, Brossard quickly covered the man up and pushed the stretcher into the ambulance. After watching them drive away, the foursome from the Wild Rose Ranch climbed into the Rover and with Bernie following, drove back to the ranch without saying a word.

Maggie went immediately to her room and after a soothing bath, fell into a deep sleep. She was awakened by a light tapping on her door.

"Maggie, there's soup and sandwiches downstairs."

Still drowsy, it took her a few minutes to orient herself to the unfamiliar surroundings. "Give me a few minutes." It seemed like a whole day had passed since she had awakened that morning, but a quick look at her alarm clock confirmed that it was only noon.

CHAPTER THREE

Maggie dug into her handbag and hauled out a steno pad and a couple of pencils to plunk down on the lunch table. "Okay," she said. "Let's have the whole story."

"Do you mean you are going to help me?" Kate asked.

"I'll decide when I've heard all the details. Let's start by you telling me where you met your husband."

"My boss, Ray Teasdale, invited all the staff over to his house for a barbecue. Douglas just happened to be staying with him at the time."

"And you got together?"

"Neither of us had a partner and Ray sort of introduced us and we just stayed together most of the evening." Maggie noticed how Kate suddenly came alive when talking about her husband. "He called me a couple of days later," Kate continued, "and asked me on a date. It kinda went from there."

"You liked him right away?"

"Yes. He was so different. You know . . . older, sophisticated. Not the usual type I'd been dating before."

"And what was your boss's reaction to you dating his friend?"

"Thought it was funny at first, but then he tried to butt in when he realized we were serious."

"Why?"

"He said Douglas was too old for me and that he had been married before and had kids." She paused as if thinking back. "But I was married before too." She went to the window. "He knocked me around quite a bit before it ended."

"How did you feel about that?"

"I was only eighteen at the time. I guess I had it coming to me. You know how it is?"

Maggie couldn't imagine how 'it was.' Harry had his faults, but he was always gentle.

"My father had the marriage annulled," Kate added.

"So you started dating Douglas?" Maggie continued.

Kate nodded. "We were married six months later."

"How did you feel about ranching?"

"Well . . . you see . . . I'm really used to the city. I did find the horses and ranch life a bit much. I'm still a bit scared of the big horses, and it can be lonely out here sometimes," she added in a sad little voice.

"I saw you riding, Kate, and you didn't look scared to me."

"Oh, Al's been a great teacher."

"All right then. So what happened the morning Doug went off to Alberta?"

Kate fiddled with the table mat in front of her. "He got up early and left."

"Just like that. He didn't say goodbye or anything?"

Kate's eyes filled with tears. "He always said goodbye because he knows I hate being left on my own," she continued and dabbed at her eyes. "He said Hendrix would be around and not to worry. Just keep the doors locked at night." There was a fresh flood of tears.

"Anything else?"

"No . . . wait, yes. He asked, did the telephone wake me?"

"You have a phone in your bedroom?"

"No. There's one in the kitchen and in Douglas's den and Hendrix has one in the barn."

"And had you heard the phone ring?"

"No. I sleep pretty soundly."

"What about Doug's kids? Have you told them about their father?"

"Yes. Christine suggested that he just needed a break from married bliss. Jamie said that I should be so lucky and not to worry because he was sure to turn up, like a bad penny."

"Jamie doesn't get on too well with his father I take it?"

"Jamie's fun, always kind of ironic, you know, but a bit of a drifter so Douglas got him a job with a friend of his."

"What kind of job was that?"

"He works for some company that deals with mines and things like that."

"Financing them?" Maggie asked.

"I don't really understand what. Anyway, I think Jamie resented his father butting in."

"Understandable. Doug have other family?"

"His mother. She's in a retirement home in Vancouver."

"What about his ex?"

"Oh, she got married again. Lives down in Seattle."

Maggie snapped her notebook shut. "I can't promise my boss will let me take this on, you understand. And to be honest, I don't know what I can really do to help you." She slipped the book back into her bag. "I don't know this area at all, and the police have now agreed to look into it — although that doesn't always mean very much, I've come to know."

"Well, suppose your boss turns me down?" Kate's eyes filled with tears again. "You've got to tell him I need you. Please, Maggie, I don't know what to do any more!"

"Let me think about it, Kate."

"Can't you call him now? Please?"

A sudden banging on the front door startled her up from her chair.

"Hel-lo! Anyone at home except the chickens?"

Before Kate could get to the door leading to the front hall, it opened with some force and in strode a tall, bronzed woman dressed in beautifully pressed jeans and tailored shirt with a loosely tied, multi-colored scarf around her neck. Maggie thought to herself that all that was needed to complete the scene was a white Stetson and a horse named Buttermilk. But the woman's resemblance to Dale Evans stopped at the neckline. Her cold green eyes were taking in Maggie's appearance as she walked and her expression was one of obvious disapproval.

"Maggie, this is Vivienne Harkness," Kate said. "She and her husband live on the next ranch."

"I didn't realize you had a guest," Vivienne said, cooly extending a manicured hand. "I should have called first. But when I heard the ambulance, and what with Doug missing and all, I just had to come."

"Maggie's going to help me find him," Kate said confidently.

"And how do you propose to do that?" Vivienne asked, turning to Maggie.

"She's a private investigator," Kate blurted out.

"Investigator?" She looked Maggie up and down. "That's an odd sort of job for a woman, especially a woman of your age. But perhaps it's a hobby?"

Maggie, wishing that Kate had kept her mouth shut, smiled sweetly back at Vivienne.

"No. I do it for a living, actually. And as I've only just agreed to help Kate, I'll start by asking you a question, Mrs. Harkness. How long have you known Mr. Guthrie?"

Vivienne gave a brittle laugh. "You surely don't suspect me of abducting Doug? I've known him since I was a child. He's like a brother to me." She turned back to Kate. "Did you two quarrel?"

48

"No, nothing like that." Kate answered in a tight voice.

"There, there, pet," Vivienne added blithely. "Knowing Doug like I do, I'm sure it will all blow over."

But Kate, ignoring Vivienne's condescension, was already off on a new tangent. "Did you hear about the dead man that Hendrix and Maggie found in Black Adder Ravine this morning? That's why the ambulance was here."

Vivienne turned her attention back to Maggie. "Well, you have been a busy little girl, haven't you? What were you doing up there?"

Kate answered before Maggie could open her mouth. "Hendrix was giving Maggie a riding lesson."

"And who is this dead man?"

"We don't know," Kate said. "Hendrix called Brossard at the RCMP. and they brought in some extra equipment with the ambulance and hauled him out on a stretcher."

But Vivienne was still focused on Maggie. "That must've given you quite a shock."

"Wasn't exactly my idea of a start to a peaceful vacation," Maggie agreed with a grim smile.

"But I thought Kate said you were here to investigate Doug's disappearance. I'm not quite sure I understand."

"Busman's holiday, really. I try to get away from work but work finds me anyway."

"And Hendrix is giving you riding lessons. First time on a horse?"

Although it had been a few years since Maggie had even looked a horse in the face, she was not going to admit this fact to Vivienne. "Just needed a few tips on range riding. The terrain I'm used to is so completely different."

"But I thought you. . . ." Kate began.

"Point-to-point's very popular on the west coast of England," Maggie quickly cut in. Actually it was Maggie's sister Penelope who was the horsey one of the family, but one little white lie wouldn't hurt.

49

"But. . . ." Kate looked completely baffled.

Maggie had a fleeting twinge of conscience until Vivienne answered, "Range riding is far superior." She turned to Kate. "I'd better go or Jerry will start to think that I've been abducted, too." She placed her hand on Kate's shoulder. "Call if you need my help, dear."

With relief, they listened to the front door closing.

"Has she really known your husband that long?"

"Yes." Kate gave a sly grin. "I think she had great plans — but I sort of ruined things when I came on the scene."

Maggie laughed. "Jerry is her husband?"

"Her long suffering one," Kate answered. "He's in a wheelchair. Fell off his horse and broke his back. Must put a crimp in their, well, you know. . . ."

Maggie stood up. "Do you have a survey map of the area?"

"What for?"

"Just to get my bearings."

"There's one in Douglas's den. Come on."

"This is great!" Maggie said later as she spread the well-worn map out on the table.

Kate stood next to her, bending over the table to point at a line on the map. "I'm not very good with maps, but I think this is the road that runs in front of our property. Yes, there's the lake on the far side. And this is the bridge we crossed last night. It's a mile or so from there to our house."

Maggie shook her head. "I was too tired last night to notice much of anything."

Kate continued, "And there's the road that turns left at the bridge and follows the river till it gets to that green spot. I think those wavy lines there mean mountains." She straightened up, satisfied that she had explained everything quite clearly to a very mystified Maggie.

"Do you know where your property line is?"

Kate thought for a moment. "Douglas said something about the river road."

Maggie looked closely at the map and could see that a red pencil line had been lightly drawn following the river and the road until it reached the green area, which Maggie concluded must be a forest. At that point the road turned away from the river which continued through the trees and into a clearing before wandering around the base of a mountain, and then snaking its way north. She turned the map and read the words "Beaver Mountain" and "2462'."

"Now I get it," she exclaimed. "When the road leaves the river, it continues up to meet this track right here." She marked the spot with an X. "That must be the track we were on yesterday?"

"Yes. That must be it." Kate sounded relieved. "I'm glad you understand it." She peered closely at the map again. "So this is the road up the mountain then." She put a finger on the black line that ran part way up Beaver Mountain. "The one up to the mine."

Maggie nodded and refolded the map. "In the morning I'm going to take Angel out on my own. This map will be of great help."

"On your own! Don't you want me to come with you?"

"No. I'll be fine. But I will need a good night's sleep. You need one too, Kate. Problems always seem more manageable after a proper night of rest."

But it was Al who greeted her the next morning. It was his father's day off and he had been left in charge. "Sure you're up to going out on your own?" he asked.

Maggie wasn't at all sure, but she needed to get away from the house and be completely on her own to think things out before calling Nat and committing the agency to the task of trying to locate Doug. "I won't go far."

"Well, okay," he answered, brightening up. "Pop's left me so many chores to do. . . ."

"I'll be fine. Just help me saddle up."

The morning air was crisp and Angel, greeting Maggie with a friendly whinny, was fresh and eager to get going. Maggie even managed a quick look back to see the trail that the horse was leaving through the dew-covered grass. She pressed her heels into Angel's flanks and headed her toward the distant hills, and it seemed no time at all before she reached the junction where the river road met the road from the ranch house. She stretched her arms above her head, and then reached down into the saddle bag for the two apples and the map she had stowed there. While Maggie peered at the map and took a bite out of her apple, Angel happily chewed hers whole, the juice foaming out of her mouth. Maggie raised her head to gaze across the vast ranch lands. *There's the river.* She could see it in the distance, glinting in the morning sun. "Come on, Angel," she said, giving the horse her apple core. "Let's get down there and have a look at the water." Pointing Angel's nose down the incline, she pressed her knees firmly into the horse's flanks and felt a thrill as the animal responded with a gentle trotting. "Take it easy, old girl," she murmured to her.

Angel quickened her pace as they neared the gurgling river, and when she reached it, stopped suddenly and bent her head to drink, causing Maggie to cling precariously to the saddle.

The dogs seemed to come out of nowhere. One moment Maggie and Angel were alone and the next, three huge German shepherds were rushing at them, snarling and baring their fangs. Trembling with fright, Angel reared back and then plunged headlong into the forest with Maggie clutching onto the saddle for dear life. The dogs kept pace with them, snapping at the terrified horse's legs. Suddenly, there were a couple of shrill whistles, and as quickly as the dogs had appeared, they were gone.

The track, as it ran between the river and the trees with their low hanging branches, was narrow and rutted. "Whoa! Whoa!" Maggie screamed. But Angel, nostrils flaring, her ears laid back, was beyond hearing. She had but one thought, and that was to get as far away as possible. Petrified, Maggie clung to her mount's neck as the tree branches whipped and slashed at horse and rider. Head bowed, she had no way of seeing or ducking the low cedar branch, and it sent her flying backward to land breathless on the dirt track. Angel, now free of Maggie's weight, bolted onward and out of sight.

For a while Maggie lay on her back and caught her breath before daring to assess the damage. But apart from a lump quickly forming on her forehead and a dull pain in her back, there seemed nothing seriously wrong. She pulled herself to a sitting position but then had to wait several minutes for the wave of nausea to pass. Crawling over to the river bank, she bathed her face in the icy cold water.

"Angel?" Maggie called out, but heard nothing. She got shakily to her feet, whimpering as her bruised back protested, took a deep breath and willed herself to lurch forward. The trail was difficult and Maggie could see the broken branches that the panic-stricken animal had left in her wake. She just prayed Angel had stopped running before she hurt herself seriously.

The sun never penetrated through the dense foliage here, and the stones in the shallow river were green and slimy, the mosquitoes and blackflies numerous. As she stumbled along, batting at the insects that were making a bid for her blood, she realized what a precarious position she was in. Her head and back were throbbing, no one knew where she was, and she wouldn't know what to do for Angel if she found the horse badly hurt. She had to steel herself not to give in to self-pity. "Pull yourself together," she said out loud. "You've got yourself into this mess, now get yourself out of it." She followed in Angel's wake for almost half an hour before she saw sunlight ahead, and with renewed effort she slogged toward it and out into the open.

Angel, covered in sweat and pulling at the reins that had become tangled in a thorn bush, was only about fifty feet ahead, but as Maggie approached, the horse whinnied and reared back in fright. "Easy, girl, easy." she said with as much calm as she could muster, then put out a tentative hand. "You're okay," she continued in a soothing voice. "Just let me untangle you and we'll go back."

The horse whinnied again, the sound sending a flock of birds wheeling into the air. As Maggie watched their flight toward the steep cliffs, she realized where she was. "Black Adder Ravine!" Quickly she untangled Angel's reins and tethered her to a tree near the stream's edge where she could crop the grass. Then she climbed up on a boulder to survey the area ahead. It was a lonely, quiet place, covered in huge rocks, scrub trees, bushes and a few stunted firs. She couldn't help thinking that the place could live up to its name and that there really were snakes hiding among the sun-warmed rocks. *So where's the jeep?* She would have to clamber up the side of the ravine if she wanted to locate it. Gritting her teeth against the increasing pain in her back, she forced her reluctant legs to climb, sending sand and pebbles skittering to the bottom. *There it is!* It was only another hundred yards ahead.

"I'll be back, Angel," she called.

Approaching the vehicle, she realized that it was not completely upside down but was tilted slightly off the ground by a huge slab of stone. Her mind returned to the previous day when she had looked through the binoculars and seen the dead man spreadeagled on the rock beside it. The weather having remained dry, the blood-stains were still visible on its surface. Climbing around the jeep, she spotted a flap of rubber on the front left tire. *I wonder. Of course it could have been cut on a rock on the way down, but I bet there's a bullet in there. Unless the cops have already found it.* She pushed her fingers down until she could feel the slack inner tube but there was no sign of the expected bullet.

She returned to the driver's side, and kneeling on the ground, managed to wriggle herself up into the interior of the vehicle to run her hands over the leather seats. By the look of the ragged hole in the driver's seat back, she realized that the bullet that killed the man must have gone right through him and into the upholstery. She reached a hand around the seat and felt along the back of it until she found a corresponding hole, then scanned the area behind the seat. There were pry-marks around a hole in the frame. *The police definitely found that one.*

54

Before backing out she noticed a short length of leather thong dangling from the space beneath the driver's seat, and reaching up, she tugged on it. When it wouldn't come free, she reached beyond the edge of the seat, and her fingers closed over a small soft object caught in the coil springs. She tried to pull it out but it took several minutes before she was able to get it untangled and she could hold it in her hands. Then sliding out from under the vehicle, she examined her find — it was a small leather pouch. As her fingers went instinctively to undo the metal press studs, she heard the rattle of falling stones and looked up toward the road high above the ravine. A deer? There was a sudden glint as if the sun had shone on a piece of glass.

Thwack! The sound made her jump. Thwack! *My God! Someone's shooting at me!* Pushing the pouch into her jean's pocket, she dived down in front of the jeep. *But who would be shooting at me?* She crawled to the far side of the jeep. Thwack! This time the bullet was nearer to its target. She scuttled back to the front of the vehicle. Whoever was doing the shooting knew that she was pinned down. *He must have a telescopic sight to be so accurate. Okay, Nat, what do I do now?* She leaned back against the radiator to assess the situation. There was nothing for it — she had to get over to the base of the cliff and out of the line of fire. She peered around the vehicle again to see what cover there was. Whang! This shot hit the metal rim of the right back wheel, leaving it slowly rotating from the force of the bullet. *If I can crawl down the left side and over to that large boulder. . . .* She risked taking another quick peek and again saw the glint as the sun hit the telescopic lens. *Ah, yes. Got you. You must be hiding up there in those bushes, you son-of-a-bitch.* She started to crawl along the left side of the jeep toward the flat rock where the body had lain. *If I can make it to the other side of that. . . .* Heart racing, limbs trembling, she counted. . .one . . . two . . . three . . . and lunged. The next bullet sent slivers of razor-edged rock flying into the air, making her cry out in pain as a splinter buried itself in her arm, but her lunge had taken her to the sheltered side of the rock. Again bending into a crouching position and keeping her head down, she sprinted for the thicket. Landing face first in the tangled brush, she hid there only a moment before scuttling along the base of the cliff, expecting to feel a bullet in her back at any minute. The rifle did crack again, its sound reverberating around the walls of the ravine, but the sniper had lost sight of his target. Stooping low, she raced over to where Angel was pawing and snorting at this new terror.

"Easy, easy." Grabbing the horse's reins, she ran back to the track through the woods, the horse trotting skittishly behind. Once they were safely hidden, she found a rock to stand on, put her foot in the stirrups and painfully hauled herself up. "Home, girl. And this time, carefully."

She held the reins tightly as Angel picked her way back over the track and after half an hour saw sunlight ahead where the forest petered out. "Whoa, girl." Whoever had been sniping at her would have had time to come around the mountain and be waiting here for her. Cautiously slipping off the horse's back, she risked taking a peek. There was somebody waiting for her, but to her relief, the somebody in question was Al, sitting astride his mare at the junction of the two tracks and peering through binoculars in the opposite direction. Leading Angel, Maggie urged her out into the open and started up the incline toward him. "Al!" She had to scream his name a second time before he finally saw her.

"I've been looking everywhere for you," Al yelled as he rode closer to the bedraggled pair. "My God! What happened to you?"

"Angel was spooked . . . by some dogs . . . she bolted," she gasped.

"Dogs?"

"Angel ran into the forest . . . and a tree branch hit me . . . It wasn't her fault."

"What kinda dogs?"

"German shepherds. They were vicious."

"Jock Macleod's. Dad's warned him about those damned dogs.

Come on, let's get you back to the house." He swung off his mount and cupped his hands to help her up onto Angel.

"Did you see anyone coming down the mine road?" she asked.

"No. But I just got here."

"He must still be up there then," she said fearfully.

"Who?"

"The man with the gun." She hesitated. "I had to go right through to the ravine before I caught Angel. And . . . and someone was on the road above . . . with a gun."

Al shrugged. "Probably somebody deer hunting out-of-season. Come on, let's get back."

But the out-of-season prey was me! She decided not to enlighten him, for the time being, anyway.

Kate greeted her when she finally arrived back at the house with a smile that quickly turned slack-jawed. "What happened to you, Maggie? Are you hurt?"

"A branch knocked me off the horse." She hobbled across the kitchen. "I'll tell you all about it after I've patched myself up and changed."

Maggie pulled her jeans and shirt off, letting them fall on the floor, then staggered into the bathroom. Too tired to shower, she washed the mud off her face and hands, struggled into clean clothes and then, lying down on the bed, closed her eyes. The tapping on the door awakened her.

"Maggie, lunch is ready."

"Coming right down. Thanks, Kate." She bent down to scoop up the dirty clothes from the floor and felt the lump in her pant's pocket. The pouch! And pulling it out of the pocket, she sat down on the side of the bed and popped open the metal press studs. "My God!" The bills — old ones by the look of it — in denominations of $1000s, $500s and $100s, were all rolled up and squashed inside it. She laid them out on the bed and counted them. *There's eight thousand dollars here. Why was it hidden under the seat?* Carefully she pushed the money back into the pouch then stowed it in the top drawer of the dresser. *So that's why I was shot at. Somebody didn't want me finding the money.* "I've got to talk to Nat."

"You look a lot better," Kate remarked when Maggie reappeared downstairs. "Al told me about Jock Macleod's dogs. We'll tell Brossard about it when he comes in the morning."

"Brossard!"

"I think he's taking Douglas's disappearance more seriously now that a body's turned up."

"Kate, I haven't told you everything that happened this morning."

"You said Angel was spooked and. . . ."

It was obvious Kate didn't want to hear any more bad news, but Maggie knew she had to tell her the rest of the story. "I was shot at."

"Shot at! You must've been mistaken."

"No. There was no mistaking those shots." She recounted all that had happened, except finding the money pouch.

"I don't understand," Kate exclaimed when Maggie had finished. "Why would anyone shoot at you? Maybe somebody thought you were a deer. . . ."

"Not a chance," Maggie said. "I think whoever it was didn't take kindly to me looking over that jeep."

Kate slumped into a chair. "I don't suppose you'll want to help me now?"

"Why not? It probably has nothing to do with your husband's disappearance. Someone just wanted to frighten me off." Gingerly she sat down at the table, grateful that the chairs were padded. "But I still have to talk to my boss."

"I don't know what your rates are, but I'll pay whatever it costs."

"All right. I'll phone Nat today and discuss it," Maggie answered.

"We're on a party line," Kate said. "Our signal is two longs and a short."

"A party line? Does that mean that people can listen in?"

She nodded. "But you can usually tell if someone's listening. It's sort of echo-y. The best time to call is late at night. You're more or less safe then . . . unless someone has insomnia."

"I don't think I'll want to wait that long. But I will want privacy. Can I borrow the Rover to take a quick trip into Williams Lake?"

Kate nodded. "I'll come with you."

Maggie pulled a note pad out of her pocket. "Before we go," she said, "I want to go over a few things. First, have you a photograph of your husband?" The silver-framed photograph that Kate produced showed a tall, dark-haired man, sporting a beautiful tan, a boutonniere and perfect white teeth. He had a protective arm around the diminutive Kate in the picture, who was dressed in some gauzy fabric that blew prettily in the wind.

"Your wedding?"

"Yes," Kate answered. "We were so happy," she added wistfully.

"We'll find him," Maggie said in a firm voice. "Now while I go upstairs and grab my handbag, I want you to take this pad and make a list of your husband's friends, acquaintances and family. Anyone and everyone you can think of."

"Do you want Ray Teasdale and Nordstrom and Kraft's addresses too?"

"Who are Nordstrom and Kraft?"

"Jamie's bosses. Albert Nordstrom's known Douglas for years."

"He's the one that deals in mines and things?"

"I think it's something to do with money," she answered vaguely.

"A brokerage firm?"

"Something like that."

"He sounds like a good one to contact. Just write all the names down." And she left the room.

CHAPTER FOUR

The Rover had travelled less than a half mile along the lake side road when a car driven by Vivienne Harkness sped toward them, sending spumes of choking dust into the air as it passed. Momentarily blinded, Kate edged the car off the road. "Wonder why she's in such a hurry?"

As the dust settled, Maggie turned in her seat to look back. "Funny," she said, "there's no sign of her on the road now."

"Probably turned into our place," Kate answered.

"But she can see you're not there!"

"Oh, she won't be coming to visit. You see, the lake's kidney-shaped. We're on the southern bulge and the Harknesses are on the northern one, so it's much shorter to cross our land than follow the lake road."

"You don't mind?"

Kate shrugged. "They've been using the back road way before I came on the scene," she answered, putting the jeep into gear.

The only public telephone in the town was located outside the post office, but Maggie was lucky as there was no one using it and she was through to her boss straightaway.

"A missing husband?" Nat said, when she'd finished telling him about Guthrie's disappearance. "You're supposed to be on vacation, Maggie. It doesn't sound all that dramatic, husbands go off on a tear all the time. If you're so determined to stay up there in the wilderness why not find another place to stay? A lodge or something."

"It's not quite that simple, Nat."

"What do you mean?"

"There's another problem. I — we sort of found a body. Up in a ravine."

"A body?" he exclaimed. "How could you 'sort of' find a body? What's going on, Maggie?"

"I was out riding and we found a jeep that had gone over a cliff. . . ." The line was so quiet that as Maggie related what had happened she thought he'd hung up. But when she got to the bit about watching the police haul the dead man up the side of the cliff, she heard an audible sigh of relief.

"Well, it sounds like the police are on the case, can't you leave it alone?"

"Well-l-l, not quite," she answered.

"Don't tell me. There's more?"

"We still don't know who the dead man is. Then there's the business of me being shot at."

"Shot at!" She held the phone away from her ear until his spluttering stopped. "What do you mean, shot at?"

She filled him in on her frightening escapade.

"What did the police have to say about this?"

"I haven't told them yet."

"Bloody hell, Maggie! Call them right away and then pack your bags and get back here."

"Can't do that. I've promised to help Kate."

"How do you propose to help anyone if you're dead?"

"The reason I was shot at has absolutely nothing to do with Guthrie's disappearance."

"How did you work that out? Women's intuition?"

Maggie decided to let that one pass. "No. It's because of the money."

"What money? You didn't mention any money. Please, Maggie, let me hear all of it!" His voice seemed to be reaching fever pitch again.

"I found some. Quite a lot, in fact. Large bills, too. I'm not sure what it all means yet" Then before he could butt in again, she continued. "I told Kate I had to talk to you first before we took the case. After all, you're the boss."

"Sure sounds like it!" He paused. "You're not licensed, Maggie."

"That's why I'm calling," she answered in her best patient voice. "To put the investigation on a business basis so you can contact a couple of leads I've developed."

"Then what?"

"You can join me up here. A break will do you good, Nat."

"But who's going to look after the office? And don't say Henny!"

"Couldn't you put things on hold for a few days so that she only has to answer the phone and take messages? I really need you with me." She paused for a moment to give him time to think.

"I don't know, Maggie. Who do you want me to see down here?"

"You could call on Ray Teasdale, that's where Kate met Guthrie. Then on to Nordstrom. According to Kate, he's known her husband since way back. Also," she continued before he could interrupt, "he's Douglas Guthrie's son's boss."

"Whoa. One thing at a time." He listened while she went over the list again. "Now," he said. "What about this Kate? Is it possible for me to talk to her?"

"She's just outside. I'll get her."

When Kate came on the line, Nat told her, "I've just listened to Maggie but I think our agency is too far away from the Cariboo area to be of much help, really. Are you sure there's no one closer to where you live?"

"Williams Lake's a very small town, Mr. Southby," Kate answered. "I've had little help from the police, and our ranch manager, Hendrix, insists that I'm paranoid and worrying for nothing. If you can't help me," she ended tearfully, "I just don't know what I'm going to do. "

Nat wasn't very good with tears. "You understand that it would have to be on a business basis?"

"Yes, anything. I'll be happy to pay your fees. After Maggie was shot at . . . I'm so scared. . . ."

"Probably nothing to do with your husband being missing. Put Maggie back on," he mumbled gruffly. Kate handed over the phone. "Okay," he said, "I'll start on it. But I'm not agreeing to anything final until I've investigated Teasdale and Nordstrom and you've spoken to the police. And Maggie, for God's sake, try not to find any more dead bodies for the time being, will you?"

∼

Monday morning brought misty rain and RCMP Corporal Brossard to the ranch. Kate showed him into the kitchen.

"You haven't heard anything new, have you?" she asked.

The two dogs jumped out of their baskets and greeted the corporal with considerable drool and enthusiasm. He pushed one dog down and then the other. "Nothing to report. I'm sorry. It's as you said. Your husband seems to have disappeared without a trace." He stood just inside the room, the dripping from his raincoat making a widening pool of water on the floor.

"What about the railway station? Did you check there?" Maggie asked from her place at the breakfast table. "Or look for his car? Surely someone must have seen him?"

Surprised, Brossard looked at Maggie. "You're a friend of the family, I take it?"

"No," she answered him, shaking her head. "As Kate told you, I'm one of her paying guests."

"Mrs. Spencer is also a private investigator from Vancouver and she's helping me find Douglas." Maggie's warning glance didn't reach Kate in time to stop her from babbling. "And she was shot at yesterday. When she went riding—"

"An investigator?" Brossard's voice cut in sharply. "But I think we'll take the shooting first, Mrs. Spencer, if you don't mind filling me in on the details?" he added coolly, fishing a notebook from an inner pocket.

Maggie reluctantly went through the episode again.

"Have you any idea why someone would shoot at you? Any enemies in this area?"

"I've only been here three days," she answered. "So there's hardly enough time for that. But it could've been the money I found."

"What money is that, now?"

"You didn't say anything about finding money, Maggie" Kate said.

"I didn't want to worry you," Maggie answered. She turned back to Brossard. "I found a leather pouch full of large old bills, caught in the seat springs of the jeep. I'll go and get it." She returned a short time later, her face ashen. "It's gone! I put it in one of the drawers in my bedroom but . . . it's gone!" Trembling, she sat down at the table again. "Good Lord! Corporal Brossard, there was $8000 in that pouch. I counted it myself. . . ." Her voice faltered, then she continued in a very subdued tone, "That . . . that means that someone's been in my room. . . ."

"Are you sure you didn't imagine that money?" he demanded.

"Corporal Brossard," she replied icily, "I held that money in my hand."

He shrugged. "Well, you don't have it now, do you? Now, about you being an investigator. I take it you have a licence to operate in this province?"

"Not as yet," she answered truthfully. "I'm an assistant to Nat Southby of Southby Investigating in Vancouver. I'm up here on vacation. Kate asked me to help find her husband when she found that she was getting nowhere with you."

"And just like that, you're going to wave a magic wand and abracadabra, make him appear?" He smiled sardonically. "Does your boss know you're moonlighting up here?"

"I've brought him up to date."

"And he's ready to rush up here and find Guthrie, show us ignorant locals how to do it."

Keeping a firm grip on herself, Maggie looked Brossard straight in the eye. "If necessary, Corporal Brossard, yes." She stood up from the table. "Now if you'll excuse me, I've things to do."

"Not so fast," Brossard put out a hand to stop her. "I want to warn you that I won't, I repeat, I won't stand for any interference in this investigation. This is a police matter. Do I make myself clear, Mrs. Spencer?"

"Perfectly clear, Corporal Brossard."

Brossard turned back to Kate who had been nervously following the exchange. "Now, Mrs. Guthrie, are you absolutely sure you don't know who the dead man is?"

Kate's answer was to burst into tears. "I already told you I don't know him. Why don't you believe me?"

Brossard's face reddened. "I have to ask," he said in a more gentle tone. "It seems too much of a coincidence that your husband goes missing and then this body turns up."

"Do you know who he is?" Maggie asked suddenly.

Brossard nodded reluctantly. "His name is Lewis Sarazine. Lived over Alexis Creek way." Tucking his notebook into his pocket again, he turned toward Maggie. "I strongly advise you to return to Vancouver, Mrs. Spencer, or," he added, "stick to horseback riding close to the ranch. Stay away from trouble."

"Who could've taken that money?" Maggie exclaimed, after Brossard had left. "I swear I put it in the top drawer of the dresser."

"It had to be the person who shot at you," Kate replied fearfully.

"But how? We've been in all the time. . . ." her voice trailed off. "Except when we went into Williams Lake yesterday. Did you lock the doors?"

Kate's face paled. "No. I never do. Douglas is always after me to lock the doors during the day but I always forget."

"That means," Maggie said slowly, "that whoever shot at me yesterday has been watching the house for an opportunity to get the pouch back."

"Oh, Maggie," Kate grabbed her arm, "I'm so frightened."

"We'll just have to make sure we lock up in future." But it's a bit like locking the stable doors after the horse has bolted, Maggie thought. "Come on. Let's take a cup of coffee into the den and have a look through your husband's files."

"Whatever for?"

"We won't know till we find it."

A short time later the two of them were sitting cross-legged on the floor surrounded by a stack of beige folders, the entire contents of one drawer of Guthrie's desk. At first, the files seemed to contain only invoices for running the ranch, covering everything from cattle feed to horses to harnesses and leather polish. All appeared to be up-to-date and fully paid.

"I still don't understand what we're looking for." Kate said.

"Anything unusual," Maggie answered, picking up a folder and scanning the contents. "Like this, for instance." She passed the file over to Kate. "What's this bill from Johnson and Spiegel's detective agency for?"

Kate took the paper from Maggie. "It doesn't say what it's for. Why would Douglas need the services of a detective?" She sat staring at the invoice for a bit and then pointed to a small note at the bottom. " 'See file on L.S.' What could that mean? It's dated January 30th this year."

"Hang onto that one," Maggie said, opening another drawer and removing its contents. The deeper she dug into Guthrie's files, the more his personality came through: it was all perfectly neat, everything strictly under control. The second drawer contained business correspondence, contracts for the ranch workers and several letters regarding his take-over of the original ranch from his father, as well as the agreement for the purchase of an additional 1000 acres from a man called Mike Rooney. Most of the remaining folders contained information on the farm's employees both past and present, but the last one was unmarked. "I think I've found our L.S.," Maggie announced. She took the single sheet of paper out of the folder. "It's the report from Johnson and Spiegel."

"What does it say?"

Maggie read it through before answering. "It appears that whoever L.S. is, he came into a lot of money, and for some reason Doug got the detective agency to find out where it came from. It says here . . . " she continued, reading from the paper, " . . . 'I could find no trace of the subject inheriting any sudden wealth or any business transaction that would account for increased funds.' " Maggie tapped the folder "L.S.," she mused, "L.S. . . . Could be Lewis Sarazine."

"But why would Douglas be interested in where that man got his money?"

Maggie shook her head, moved over to the window and stretched. The gentle rain had stopped and everything outside had a clean, washed look. It was such a peaceful-looking lake, nature incongruous with the messy human affairs she was now, she feared, getting into more deeply than she had intended. "I didn't realize this was a sliding door onto the deck," she suddenly exclaimed, pushing it open, feeling a need to move and not reply to Kate's question.

"Why don't you go out there for a while and I'll bring you some lunch?" Kate suggested, sensing Maggie wanted to think for a while. "We can tackle the rest of Doug's papers later on."

After a summary lunch spent in silent meditation they returned inside the house reluctantly to investigate the contents of the last desk drawer. "What a wonderful name," Maggie said.

"What is?"

"Shadow Lake Mine. It's on this contract."

"That must be the name of the old mine . . . you know . . . near where the jeep overturned."

"But there's no lake up there, none that I could see." Suddenly she rose and ran upstairs. Minutes later she was back with the map that Jodie had given her of central British Columbia She spread it on the coffee table. "Look, Kate," she said, "there's a Shadow Lake north of the Horsefly River."

"But what about the mine near the ravine?"

"Hendrix told me that to the best of his knowledge it's been closed for fifty years or so. What did Doug say it's called?"

"He never talked about it to me. Just said it was an old mine and to stay away from it because it's dangerous."

Maggie reached for the contract on which she had found the mine's name. "It seems this Shadow Lake Mine was started in 1945 — fourteen years ago — and there were six partners. They're listed here at the end of the contract."

At that moment they heard the crunch of tires on the gravel driveway, and the dogs began barking furiously. "Wonder who that is?" Kate said. She returned immediately, followed by Corporal Brossard, his assistant Dempster, and the two drooling Labs. "Down, Jasper! Get down, Mellow." She pulled the two dogs away from the harassed Brossard. "Into the kitchen, the two of you!"

Brossard carefully brushed the dog hairs off his uniform as he eyed the piles of paper on the desk.

"I see you're going through your husband's files, Mrs. Guthrie. We'll need to see them too."

"What do you expect to find?" Maggie asked.

"A link with Sarazine, perhaps," Brossard answered, not noticing the quick look between the two women. "Your husband disappears, then Sarazine gets shot. . . . As I said this morning, it seems too much of a coincidence."

"You can't possibly think my husband's disappearance is linked with that poor man's death!" Maggie could see Kate was once again having trouble keeping control of her emotions, and she put a hand on her arm.

Brossard nodded curtly. "We'll be as quick as we can, Mrs. Guthrie." He walked over to the filing cabinet, and then turned back to them. "I'll call if I need clarification."

As soon as Brossard's and Dempster's backs were turned, Maggie picked up the Shadow Lake Mine folder from the chair and followed Kate into the kitchen. The two dogs, chastened, merely thumped their tails in greeting. Kate picked up the kettle and filled it. "I'll make us some tea."

"Just what the doctor ordered," Maggie approved, spreading the file on the table.

"What's that?" Kate asked.

Maggie put her finger to her lips. "Sh-h-h."

"Is it the file about the mine?" Kate whispered.

Maggie nodded. "I want to look at it before Brossard gets his hands on it."

Kate remained silent while Maggie carefully read through the document. "Shadow Lake is apparently a gold mine, and the six men involved in it were your husband, Jack Chandler, George Fenwick, J.L Macleod — my God, I wonder if that's Jock Macleod who owns those vicious dogs! — V.M. O'Connor and Lewis Sarazine."

"The man in the jeep," Kate said excitedly.

"Yes," Maggie repeated. "The man in the jeep." She took a sip of tea. "This was signed in April, 1945."

"Douglas never ever mentioned it to me. I wonder why?" Then hearing a sound in the hall, she added, "Is that Brossard leaving?" But to her consternation, the RCMP man appeared again in the doorway to the kitchen.

"There seems little of interest in the files, Mrs. Guthrie. Do you know anywhere else we could look?" His eyes lit on the file spread on the table. "Is that from the filing cabinet?"

"We were just going to give it to you," Kate twittered nervously. "Weren't we, Maggie?"

Brossard walked to the table and picked up the folder. "After your investigator here had looked it over, I suppose." He scanned the document. "So why didn't you tell me about this mine, Mrs. Guthrie?"

"Because she knew nothing about it," Maggie answered. "We've only just found out ourselves."

"M-m-m. I see that Sarazine was one of the partners. Who are these others?" he asked, directing the question at Kate.

"I don't know. Douglas never mentioned the mine or any of those names to me."

"This appears to be an indisputable link between your husband and Sarazine, Mrs. Guthrie." He stared accusingly at Kate.

"Corporal Brossard," Maggie cut in, "Kate can't possibly have anything to do with any of this."

"How so?"

"Because she and Doug have only been married a year. That contract was signed back in 1945. He was still with his first wife then."

"Oh." Brossard looked discomfited. "I see." He stopped abruptly.

"Perhaps you should track down the others on that contract," she suggested ironically.

"I fully intend to do so and, I hope, without your interference." He closed the folder, placed it under his arm and stalked out. A short time later they heard the front door slam and the police car wheel away from the ranch house.

Maggie's mind went back to the leather pouch. Who could have taken it from her bedroom? Perhaps it was one of the men mentioned on the contract . . . Jock Macleod . . . or that O'Connor fellow whoever he was . . . or Vivienne?

It was nearly midnight before Maggie reached Nat on the phone, and despite her party line concerns she immediately launched into an account of Brossard's visit, finding the mine contract and the bill from Johnson and Spiegel's detective agency.

"And this Lewis Sarazine mentioned on the contract, he's the man found in the ravine?"

"Looks like it. I'm more and more convinced the two events are related after all."

"Could be, Maggie, could very well be." He was quiet for a moment. "This RCMP officer. You said his name's Brossard "

"Do you know him?"

"No. But I'll ask Sawasky about him." Southby and George Sawasky, his partner from his Vancouver police days, still kept in touch. They had an enduring friendship and helped each other out when needed. "How did he treat you?"

"Very curt! Asked for identification and immediately became aggressive when he found out that Kate had asked for our help."

"Kate wasn't familiar with any of the names on the mining contract?"

"No. Why don't you run them past Sawasky, too?"

"Good thinking. I've made an appointment with Teasdale for the morning, and if I've time, I'll look in on Nordstrom as well. I'll call you tomorrow night and fill you in." Then before hanging up, he said, "I miss you, Maggie. Please don't take any needless risks."

"I miss you too, Nat." she replied softly, but with a delectable smile on her lips. "How's our Henny, by the way?" The spluttering noises coming from the phone answered her question more than adequately, and quietly satisfied with his response she replaced the receiver without saying another word.

71

CHAPTER FIVE

The Teasdale Advertising Agency was on the eighth floor of one of the new glass towers on Georgia Street. Nat was glad when the speedy elevator trip came to an end as it had left his stomach down on the ground floor, but his feeling of disquiet persisted as the doors opened onto plush blue carpet, electric blue walls and huge, bizarre abstract paintings. Nat, who was of the old school of figurative art appreciation which demanded that paintings should resemble life and not multi-coloured puzzles, eyed the modern art with distaste as he walked along the corridor. The polished teak reception desk inside the Teasdale agency was manned by an equally polished brunette in patent leather pumps and an off-white silk shirt and marine skirt. Large tortoise-shell glasses were perched on her elegant nose. She turned and stood as she noticed Southby's entrance. A gilt-edged nameplate on the desk announced that she was Miss Catherine O'Neil.

"May I help you?" she asked with a mild pout, taking in Nat's crumpled suit with some obvious personal distaste.

"Southby," he said, handing over one of the new cards Maggie had insisted on ordering for him. "Nat Southby. I'm an investigator. I'm supposed to speak with Mr. Teasdale."

The apparition consulted her appointment book, nodded to herself and indicated a line of empty chairs. "Please take a seat, Mr. Southby. Mr. Teasdale is running a little late this morning."

"How late might that be, Miss O'Neil?" he asked. He didn't relish sitting around in this blue nightmare for longer than absolutely necessary.

"He should be able to see you in about a quarter of an hour. Would you care for some coffee?" She indicated a self-serve electric coffee percolator on a nearby table.

Nat poured himself a cup of the tepid, tasteless brew. "Have you worked here long, Miss O'Neil?"

She drew herself up primly at that. "I beg your pardon?"

"I only wondered if you knew Kate Guthrie when she worked here. I don't know her maiden name."

"Kate Guthrie? No, I can't say as I did." Catherine O'Neill returned to her perfunctory posture behind the desk.

"Apart from Mr. Teasdale, do you know of anyone who would have worked with her?"

"I couldn't possibly say," she answered frostily. The telephone on her desk rang and she was soon engrossed in conversation with the caller. Blatantly dismissed, unwilling to sit twiddling his thumbs on a chair, Nat put the cup down on the receptionist's desk and walked around the office looking at the art in more detail. He was doing his best to make sense of one particular painting executed in vivid shades of red, blue and purple which seemed to portray three breasts, two thighs of undetermined gender and the bottom half of a man's torso with a purple eye peeping out of its navel, when a voice behind him said, "It's Henri Boodle's Adam and his Three Eves. He captures everything, doesn't he?" Nat swung round to see a man in his mid-forties extending a manicured hand. He was dressed in a grey silk suit with an open-necked shirt in the palest of pinks. "Ray Teasdale," the man said. "You've come about Douglas Guthrie, I understand." He led the way into an office of teak and glass and indicated an angular blue chair for Nat to sit on. "You said on the phone that he was . . . missing?" He sat down behind the massive desk and fingered Nat's business card.

Sitting tentatively on the edge of the chair that he was convinced was going to tip over at any moment and land him on the thick, piled carpet, Southby opened the interview uncomfortably, through tightened lips. "Guthrie's wife has engaged us to find him. I believe he is an old friend of yours?"

"Well, I don't know if you would exactly describe him as a friend, ever since he took our little Katie away." He laughed in a deprecating way.

"Has Kate called you?" Nat Southby asked.

"No. Was she supposed to?"

"Dunno. I just wondered."

"I find it hard to believe that Doug Guthrie could be missing, Mr. Southby," Teasdale mused. He pushed a cigarette into a gold holder and after lighting it, took a long drag. "He's far too sensible for that. Perhaps he's just mislaid, " he added, laughing at his *double entendre*.

"When was the last time you saw him?" Southby asked, ignoring the play on words.

Teasdale drew on the cigarette again, the smoke wafting gently over to his visitor's nicotine-starved body, and leaned back into his chair. "Let me see. It would've been about a month ago. He was in town to see his mother and those two brats of his."

"Was Kate with him?"

"Not that I know of. It seemed to be one of those duty visits. We got together for dinner as we occasionally do when he's down this way."

"Could you possibly give me the exact date?"

Teasdale leaned forward and punched a button on the speaker-

74

phone. "Yes, Mr. Teasdale?" the receptionist's voice answered.

"Catherine, be a dear and look into my appointment book and see when Douglas Guthrie was here last. Sometime in May, I think." He turned back to Southby. "How long has he been missing?"

"Over two weeks."

"M-m-m. That's not like old Doug. I suppose Katie's beside herself?"

"You suppose right. And he hasn't called you at all?"

"No."

"Perhaps your secretary could have taken a call from him while you were out."

"She'd have taken a message if he had." The speaker-phone buzzed. "Yes, Catherine?"

"Monday, May 12th, Mr. Teasdale" she answered. "I made reservations for you at Oscar's Steak House for dinner."

"Yes. I remember now. Doug's favourite dining spot. Oh, by the way Catherine, has Mr. Guthrie telephoned here during the past week or two?"

"No, Mr. Teasdale. I would have mentioned it if he had," she replied.

"Thank you, dear." He turned back to Southby. "Well, there it is. Sorry I can't help you more than that."

"Just a few more things. When you last met, did he seem worried? Tense? Anything unusual?"

"No, he seemed perfectly okay to me. Apart from being angry about his two kids being so anti-Kate — you knew he was married before? — he was in a very relaxed frame of mind."

"Do you know any of his other friends or acquaintances?"

"A few from the old days. Doug and I went to high school together. That was before he went to the States and made his pile. And then he went completely mad and took over his dad's ranch."

"Have you been there?"

"I flew up a few times in my Cessna when Doug and Deb were

still married," he answered. "Wild Rose Lake has an easy approach, it was always a pleasant trip. But I haven't been there since he and Katie got hitched."

"His first wife didn't like the ranch, I take it."

"She hated it. Deb's a real city girl." He looked at his watch. "I'm sorry to have to hurry you along, Mr. Southby," he said suddenly, "but I have a meeting in ten minutes."

"When you last saw him," Southby asked, trying to get out of the chair without tipping it, "did he mention meeting with any of his old friends while he was in the city?"

"No. But he's been living in the Cariboo for at least twelve years and most of his recent business dealings were up there." He started toying with the surface of his already tidy desk. "In fact I seem to recall he went into partnership with some fellows in a gold mine up there."

"A gold mine?"

Teasdale nodded. "And before you ask, I don't know who the other partners were." He walked around his desk and held the door open.

"I'd appreciate a call if you think of anything."

Teasdale nodded. "Tell Katie how sorry I am. Ask her to give me a buzz."

As Southby exited the building, he drew in a deep breath of air. "Welcome back to the real world, Nat old son," he said to himself quietly. Stopping beside his car, he put another nickel in the parking meter. He would walk the few blocks to Nordstrom and Kraft's office. Do him good.

Granville Street was lined with ground level shops of all kinds and no end of cafés, with office buildings towering overhead. The owners of several jewellery stores, obviously concerned by the rash of robberies that had broken out all over the city, had installed heavy iron grills that covered both doors and plate-glass windows, making it hard to properly see the glittering merchandise offered for sale. But there was nothing to impede Southby's view of the

76

wacky gadgets on display in the Krak-a-Joke Shop display cases, and he spent a happy ten minutes looking at all the ridiculous inventions in the window, laughing to himself and almost wishing he'd had kids.

When he finally located Nordstrom and Kraft's office, it turned out to be located over a double-fronted furniture store which was displaying cheap but serviceable walnut- and pine-veneered bedroom and dining room suites and brightly coloured arborite kitchen sets. Ignoring the "Buy now, pay later" banners plastered all over the place, Nat pushed on.

The door to the upstairs offices was on the side of the building and opened directly onto a small stone-tiled lobby. Next to the elevator was a glass-fronted board listing all the occupants in individually moveable white plastic letters on a black felt background. According to the board, Nordstrom and Kraft were to be found on the third floor, in suite number 303. As the decrepit elevator seemed in even worse shape than the one in his own building, Nat opted for the stairs. He knocked, opened the door into the office, and came upon a small woman, her salt-and-pepper hair curled under in a dated page-boy style, who looked up at him from behind her Royal typewriter.

"Yes?"

"Southby to see Mr. Nordstrom."

Her hazel eyes peered through thick lenses, taking in Nat's appearance. "Oh . . . yes. The detective."

"Investigator," Nat corrected her.

"Please take a seat." She rose from her wooden chair and tapped gently on the door behind her, opened it and disappeared inside. He could hear a muted conversation going on before she returned. "Mr. Nordstrom will see you shortly." She sat and resumed banging on the ancient machine.

While he waited, Nat prowled around the room looking at the pictures depicting mines, freighters and docks. "This company been going long Miss . . . ?"

"Agnes Agnew. Since 1916. Mr. Nordstrom took over from his father, Mr. Albert Nordstrom senior, twenty years ago."

"And Mr. Kraft?" Nat asked, suppressing a smile at the alliterative name.

"Sadly deceased," she answered. "He passed over to the other side a dozen years back."

Nat tried to look suitably sorry. Then, "I guess you've been with the firm a long time?"

"Yes. I joined Nordstrom and Kraft straight from secretarial school. Now, if you'll excuse me, I've work to do."

Temporarily chastened, Nat turned back to the pictures, then swung round again. "Then you must know Douglas Guthrie?"

"He used to be in a lot. Before his divorce, of course." She hit the typewriter keys vigorously.

Nat opened his mouth to ask another question but was forestalled by the inner door opening. A large auburn-haired man sporting a shaggy moustache came out, extending his hand. "Sorry to have kept you. Long phone call. Come in."

Nordstrom returned to his massive leather armchair and placed his hands on the file-littered oak desk. The only incongruous note was a cut glass vase holding two pink carnations. A touch from the devoted Agnes, perhaps? "Take a seat," Albert Nordstrom said, indicating a chair. "Now, what can I do for you?"

"I told your secretary over the phone that Douglas Guthrie hasn't been seen for quite a while and that his wife's asked us to trace him."

"Ah yes, yes. Agnes told me. . . . Doug missing?" He gave a chuckle. "Hard to believe he would leave that new little wife of his behind. Quite a looker." He nodded toward the door. "Agnes really disapproves, of course." He opened a desk drawer and withdrew a pouch of tobacco and proceeded to fill a Meerschaum. "Smoke? Mind if I do?" He glanced briefly at Nat, then without waiting for an answer lit the tobacco. Nat drew in a lungful of smoke as a breeze from the slightly opened window swirled it toward him "No, thanks," he growled. "I quit. When was the last time you heard from him, Mr. Nordstrom?"

"About ten days ago, I guess. It was a phone call."

Southby sat forward in his chair. "Can you be more exact?"

Nordstrom thought for a moment, tapping the stem of his pipe against his yellowed teeth. "It was a Sunday," he said suddenly. "I know because I sleep in on Sundays and the phone woke me up. So it must've been . . . " he consulted his calendar. "June 7th."

"Could you tell me what the call was about? It could help our investigation."

Nordstrom sat quietly for a moment, obviously trying to decide how much to tell Nat. "It was about an old gold mine he and some other men worked nine or ten years ago," he answered cautiously. "He asked for my advice."

"Advice?"

Nordstrom nodded. "The mine went belly up after they'd worked it for four years. My investors were not overjoyed."

"I can understand that. But why bring it up now? Surely it's ancient history."

"Well-l-l. There's more to it, actually." He seemed reluctant to share what more there actually was with the detective.

Nat waited him out in silence.

Nordstrom fidgeted in his chair before finally answering. "One of his partners blew the mine up."

"Blew it up. Whatever for?" Nat asked incredulously.

"Can't really say. Guess he was bloody mad at the time."

"Mad at what?"

Nordstrom shrugged. "Who knows? The unfortunate thing was, he blew up another fella with it."

"Bloody hell!"

"Guy named Fenwick." He sucked on his pipe and blew another cloud of smoke over Nat's head. "A real rough character, drunk most of the time."

"So what happened?"

"Chandler, he's the son-of-a-bitch that set the fuse, was sen-

79

tenced to eight years for manslaughter."

"I would think so."

Nordstrom leaned back in his chair and drew on the now bubbling pipe. "And now he's out."

"Out of jail?"

"You've got it. Called Doug Guthrie and said he was going to get even."

"Even?"

"Yep. Said he was framed."

"Why did Guthrie call you?"

"Been friends for years. Heck, Guthrie's boy even works for me." He stood up behind his desk. "So between you and me, I think Doug's probably just made himself scarce for a while, waiting till Chandler calms down."

"Did you invest in this mine?" Nat said, getting up.

"As I said, a few of my clients did." Nordstrom drew in another lung full of smoke. "They weren't at all happy about the way things turned out."

"Is this the mine located near Guthrie's ranch?"

"No, no. That shaft was sunk before my father's time. Far as I know, it never produced a thing. Doug's mine was near Mirror Lake . . . no . . . that's not it." Nordstrom thought for a moment. "It's been a long time. . . . I've got it. Shadow . . . Shadow Lake Mine. But as I said, it was dynamited ten years ago. There's nothing left of it."

"I see. Well, thanks for your help."

"You said Kate's brought you in on this?"

Nat nodded. "My assistant, Margaret Spencer, is up at the ranch with her now."

"Is that so?"

After making sure Nat was safely out of the office and pounding down the stairs, Nordstrom closed his door firmly, then returned to his desk and reached for the telephone.

While Nat was having his uplifting aesthetic experience in Ray Teasdale's electric blue world, Maggie was out on the range taking another riding lesson with Hendrix.

"Thought you'd shy off having another go on Angel," he said.

"Why is that, Mr. Hendrix?"

"Figured you'd be chicken after she threw you. Most women would."

"Well, then," Maggie replied, "perhaps I'm not like most women."

He grinned. "I guess not. That how come you're a private dick?"

"Who told you I was a private dick, now?"

"Brossard. He figures you oughta mind your own business."

"Hmm. And what do you figure, Mr. Hendrix?"

"I figure we oughta see how you and Angel do at a trot." And he led the way out of the yard.

When Maggie returned to the house at noon, her face glowing with the clear air and the unaccustomed exercise, she found Kate near tears again. "What's wrong?" Maggie asked.

"I had a phone call from Jamie," Kate answered. "Albert Nordstrom's flying both him and Christine up in the morning."

"Oh?"

"That's all I need," Kate said miserably. "Apparently they have decided to take Doug's disappearance seriously, so they're coming to talk to Brossard and Hendrix."

"Why Hendrix?"

"Christine told Jamie that it's obvious I can't manage the ranch on my own, and the family should see how Hendrix is coping." She sighed. "They're staying overnight. I've got to prepare their rooms."

"Give me a few minutes to change, Kate, and I'll help." She paused at the hall entrance. "Has Nordstrom been here before?"

81

"Not since Douglas and I got married. He was a very good friend of both Douglas and Debra."

"I can see how that could be awkward." Maggie moved into the hall, then came back. "Kate, can Hendrix be trusted?"

"Douglas never makes a move without him."

"But how do you feel about him?" Maggie insisted.

Kate was silent for a minute, then she said, "He scares me." She added bitterly, "In his opinion, I'm only good enough to look after the chickens."

That night as Maggie was drifting off to sleep, Kate knocked at her door to say that Nat Southby was on the line.

She took the call in the den. "Hello, boss. What's up?"

"I've interviewed Ray Teasdale and Albert Nordstrom today. Get your notebook, Maggie, and I'll fill you in."

"Well," Maggie said when he'd finished, "things are getting clearer all the time. That phone call Guthrie received could very well be the reason why he's done a disappearing act." She was quiet a few moments, letting the facts sink in. "But, Nat," she continued, "why did Chandler blow the mine up in the first place? And why threaten Guthrie now that he's out on parole? "

"That's bothering me too," he answered. "I'll have a chat with Sawasky and see what he can dig up."

"You realize this is getting quite spooky," Maggie said. "There were six partners. First Fenwick gets blown up, then Chandler goes to jail, now Guthrie goes missing and Sarazine is found dead in the ravine. That's four out of the original six."

"And Chandler's been released from jail and running around with a grudge," Nat added. "Maggie, I'm worried stiff about you being up there on your own."

"What alternative is there?"

There was a moment's silence on the line, then Southby said, "Oh, what the hell! I'm coming up there."

"But what about the Robinson case?"

"They've postponed his court date until September. I'll catch the Monday morning train. You can book a cabin or something for me . . . say for a week."

"Can't stay away from me, eh?" Maggie bantered, although she was in truth relieved that he had decided to join her. "Oh, I almost forgot, Nat, Guthrie's son and daughter will be arriving tomorrow morning. Nordstrom's flying them in."

"You don't say! Nordstrom! I wonder what prompted that? How's Kate taking it?"

"She's more than a bit nervous, actually."

As she replaced the receiver she heard a noise behind her and whirled to see Kate standing in the doorway. "Who was blown up? Who's out of jail? What were you talking about?"

"I didn't realize you were there, Kate" she said, guiding the younger woman to a chair. "Sit down and I'll fill you in."

"But . . . but . . . how did you find all this out?" she asked, when Maggie had finished relating the bizarre story.

"Nat went to see Nordstrom."

"But why didn't Douglas tell me about the mine and it being blown up?"

"It happened a long time ago — 'way before he met you."

"But he could have told me, I'm his wife you know," she blubbered, her eyes filling with tears.

Probably didn't because he couldn't face crying jags like this one. "I suppose he thought you would worry."

"Do you think Brossard knows about the explosion?"

"Hard to say. Still, he's bound to piece it all together sooner or later," Maggie answered.

◇

When Maggie went downstairs to the kitchen early the next morning, she found Kate in the midst of breakfast preparations. "I'm ready for the 'terrible twos' visit," Kate said, trying to make

83

light, but her haggard face told a very different tale.

"How did you sleep?" Maggie asked.

"Oh, not well at all. I kept dreaming that Douglas was being blown up and I was being chased . . . you know the kind of nightmare. . . ."

Maggie nodded sympathetically as she filled her coffee cup. "You said that Jamie resents his father, but what about Christine? Does she have a close relationship with him?"

"Sort of. She would like it to be closer though. Doug told me that after the split the kids moved back to Seattle with their mother."

"They went to school there?"

Kate nodded. "They were up here a lot, though. Used to come up for summer vacations, Easter, Christmas, that sort of thing." She sat thoughtfully for a few moments. "Doug says I imagine it, but Christine really does resent me."

"I suppose it's understandable," Maggie answered.

"Apparently she wanted to quit high school and come and look after her father. But he insisted that she study for a career." Kate placed a plate of scrambled eggs and sausages in front of Maggie.

After breakfast Kate went to feed her chickens and Maggie offered to wash up. She was just putting the last plate in the cupboard when there was a knock on the door followed by the now-familiar heavy footsteps coming down the hall. Brossard and his sidekick had arrived.

The RCMP man looked dourly at her. "Mrs. Guthrie around?"

"Out back. I'll get her for you."

"No, wait. I've something to say to you first, Mrs. Spencer. I've got a suggestion for you and I hope you'll take it in the spirit that it's given."

"Well, Corporal, I've an open mind, you know. What's this suggestion that you're so worried about?"

"I'm suggesting that you go back to Vancouver immediately, to your boss and his . . . ahem . . . investigating services. Make it a nice and peaceful departure, you know." He peered down at her from his

84

six-two height. "I'm sure there are more than enough errant spouses back there to keep you busy."

Maggie felt her face redden. "That's highly insulting, Corporal Brossard." She looked witheringly at the officer. "I'll stay here as long as I'm needed, Corporal. And by the way, where were you at first when Kate asked for help? You wouldn't even give her the time of day. Then I arrive, we find a corpse, and all of a sudden you're hot on the case and now you want to chase me off? I've every right to be here!"

He opened his mouth, clearly agitated, but Kate's return put a stop to what was assuredly going to be a rather nasty response.

"It's about this mine," he said, waving the file in his hand. "How come you say your husband never mentioned it to you before?"

"How can she possibly answer a question like that, Corporal?" Maggie cut in, trying to remain as calm as possible.

"Would you please be quiet and let Mrs. Guthrie speak for herself?"

"It's like I said, Corporal," Kate replied wearily. "I never heard of the place until yesterday. I haven't a clue why Doug never talked about it."

"And you don't recognize any of the names on this contract?"

"Why do you keep asking the same questions? It was you who told me about Sarazine, and Maggie who told me about the mine being blown up."

He turned his steel grey eyes onto Maggie "And where did you get that little bit of information, Mrs. Spencer?"

Hell! If only Kate could keep her mouth shut. She realized she'd been neatly cornered. "From my boss. And," she added, "where he got the information is privileged." She wasn't sure if it was or not, but the line sounded good.

"That will depend solely on what's happened to Mr. Guthrie. Surely you know that, Mrs. Spencer, especially as you claim to be . . . uh . . . some kind of a detective." He smirked at Dempster who was trying his best to avoid looking at the two women. "What do you say, constable?" Luckily for Dempster, Brossard didn't wait for an answer. "As it happens, I do know about the mine, the explosion and the subsequent death of a Mr. George Fenwick." He turned back to Kate. "And frankly, I find it very hard to believe you know nothing."

"What are you implying?" Kate answered furiously. "I'm the one who's been asking you for help. I'm the one who's been sick with fear for my husband and all I got from you and Hendrix is, 'Don't worry.' Well, I am worried." She buried her head in her hands, fresh tears flowing.

Once again, Brossard appeared discomfited. "Mrs. Guthrie," he said at last, "I'm sorry if we appear uncaring, but we have to satisfy ourselves that your husband didn't pick up and take off somewhere on his own, perhaps with your knowledge. Or without, of course . . . " He looked over to Dempster for corroboration but the constable was staring fixedly out the window. "Look at it from our point of view, see . . . His disappearance could've been just the outcome of a quarrel between you, for example . . . " His voice trailed off. "But now I realize we . . . I . . . was mistaken."

"Thank you for that at least," Kate answered tearfully.

Maggie, not being a particularly blubbery person herself, was getting thoroughly fed up with Kate constantly bursting into tears. *If she was like this when hubby was around, no wonder he's disappeared.* After the two policemen had departed, she moved toward the back door. "I'm going out back to talk to Hendrix."

To Maggie's dismay, Kate decided to come along and led the way to the red barn where they climbed a flight of rough wooden stairs to the loft where Hendrix had his office. They found him seated at an old wooden table, pecking away on an Underwood typewriter.

"Jamie, Christine and Nordstrom are on their way," Kate informed him. "They want to ask you questions about the ranch."

He nodded.

"I'll need the Rover to pick them up from the dock."

Hendrix nodded again and resumed his typing.

"The police have been here again," she said.

"Now what?" he asked laconically.

"They questioned me about Douglas's disappearance again," Kate answered. "And the gold mine he used to own."

His facial expression never changed, but Maggie noticed a clouding in his eyes.

"Why didn't he tell me about it?" Kate demanded. When Hendrix didn't answer, she continued. "Do you know where Douglas is?"

"Why ask me?"

He turned back to his pecking.

"Damn it!" Kate said angrily. "You're supposed to be his manager. You know more about his business affairs than I do. Who else should I ask, the bloody horses?" She stamped her feet and turned to go back down. She was halfway to the ground level when she paused, realizing she was alone. "Coming, Maggie?"

"In a minute, Kate," Maggie answered, somewhat surprised that Kate was at last showing some spunk. "I have a few things to talk over with Mr. Hendrix."

"I'm busy, " Hendrix said after Kate had left. "So if you're playing detective, make it snappy."

"You knew who the man in the jeep was, didn't you?" Maggie asked.

"What gave you that crazy idea?"

"I saw your face when the sheet was pulled down. You knew him."

Hendrix shrugged. "I just thought he looked familiar. Now that the cops have identified him as Lewis Sarazine, sure, I'd seen the guy around." He turned to his desk again. "Anything else?"

"Why did you discourage Kate from going to the police when Doug first disappeared?"

"I figured he was gonna be sore when he got back and found

out she was carrying on like he'd been kidnaped or something. I told her a guy needs to go off on his own sometime."

"But he's a married man, Mr. Hendrix."

"More fool him. You'd think he'd know better after the first one."

"Have you any idea at all where he might be?"

Hendrix slumped in his chair. "No," he said in a grumpy voice. "At first I was sure he'd just gone off to tie one on. But it's been too long now for that."

"You've been with Doug a long time?"

"Yep. I worked before that for his father, too."

Maggie decided on another approach. "Look, Mr. Hendrix, I know you don't think too highly of women, especially one who is an investigator. But I'm good at my job and I intend to find Douglas Guthrie, with or without your help." That at least elicited a reply as she moved toward the stairs.

"Don't know what good you can do. But maybe Kate can do with a friend anyhow."

CHAPTER SIX

Maggie and Kate stood on the dock and watched the single-engine Otter seaplane lazily circle the lake and then touch down on the calm waters. The pilot throttled back as he taxied toward them and then cut the engine, causing the small aircraft to drift gently shoreward and nose the dock side. A young man in a tweed sports jacket and grey flannels stepped down onto the float and reached over the wing for the mooring line. "Hi, Kate!" he called. With one quick jump he was on the dock and had begun tying the plane up.

Maggie watched as someone inside the cabin handed three overnight bags down to him. Next out was a young blonde in pressed jeans, checkered shirt, and Western boots. She could be Vivienne's daughter, Maggie thought. The auburn-haired man with an exaggerated mustache who followed her had to be Nordstrom, Maggie decided. After making sure the lines were secure, Nordstrom bent, picked up his bag and followed the others up the dock. Jamie immediately put his arms around Kate and gave her a hug, but Christine merely nodded at her.

"Maggie," Kate said nervously, "I'd like you to meet Christine and Jamie, and this is Albert Nordstrom. This . . . this is Maggie Spencer. She's really a detective but is on vacation and. . . ."

"So you're Southby's little lady," Nordstrom interrupted, placing his beefy hand on Maggie's shoulder. "I met your boss yesterday."

"So he told me." She smiled and neatly slipped from under his hand.

"I thought we'd have lunch on the patio," Kate said as they piled into the Rover and headed up the long gravel driveway to the house. "You're both in your old rooms," she added, nodding at her husband's children, "and Albert, you're in the guest bedroom on the ground floor."

"Fine," Nordstrom replied heartily. "Give us a few minutes to wash up and we'll be right with you." Maggie watched the brother and sister quickly disappear upstairs, their muted voices floating down as they talked together in the hallway.

Lunch proved to be an uncomfortable affair, to say the least. Kate tried hard to keep the conversation going, but Christine seemed determined to answer only in monosyllables.

Nordstrom turned to Maggie who was sitting to his right. "Your boss says he sent you up here to help Kate. Any leads so far?"

"It's all got so complicated," Kate cut in before Maggie could answer. "The police are looking for Douglas, there's this man found dead in the ravine, but people keep telling me not to worry. . . ." Her petulant voice trailed off.

Nordstrom nodded sympathetically and reached across the table to place his hand over hers. "Did you know the dead man?"

Kate shook her head. "No, but Douglas apparently did. Brossard says his name was Lewis Sarazine."

Maggie, watching Nordstrom's face for any reaction, asked, "Did you know him?"

"Vaguely. Only saw him once, I think. He was one of Doug's old partners in the mine."

"What could he have been doing on that road, anyway?" Jamie said. "I mean, it doesn't go anywhere."

"What has any of this to do with Father's disappearance?" Christine asked angrily.

"I think it must be just a coincidence," Nordstrom said, still holding Kate's hand. "But we're here anyway, Kate, to give you our support."

"Maggie's been a great help," Kate answered, drawing her hand away.

"But there's nothing like family at a time like this."

Maggie looked at them sitting there en famille, with so much spite in the air, and wondered if a nest of vipers wouldn't be cosier. "What do you all plan to do while you're here?" she asked.

"We'll go over to see Vivienne and Jerry this afternoon, of course," Nordstrom answered. "Old friends," he continued, turning to Maggie. "Have you met them?"

"Just Vivienne," Maggie replied.

"Good people," he replied. "Known them for years." He looked over to Kate. "Why don't you and Maggie . . . " His gaze came back to Maggie. "It's all right to call you Maggie, isn't it?" He carried on without an answer. "As I was saying, why don't we all go?"

"Oh, I don't think so—" Kate rushed in.

"Actually," Maggie interrupted her, "I think that's a darn good idea. I'd love to see their ranch."

"I'll phone them then." Nordstrom rose from the table. "Be good to see old Jerry again."

"I really don't want to go over there," Kate protested.

"Nonsense. Take you out of yourself. Make you feel a hundred percent better," he called back as he went into the house.

"But if Kate doesn't want to go . . . ," Christine began hopefully. Then her voice trailed off and the sentence was left unfinished.

Kate got up and cleared the table, crashing the dishes noisily

91

while Christine sat grim-faced watching her, not lifting a finger to help. Jamie, who had hardly said a word through the whole meal, stared moodily at the lake. What a happy bunch, thought Maggie.

Vivienne was only too glad to see them. They had all squeezed into the Rover again and bumped over the dusty, potholed back road that led to the Shaking Aspen ranch. Vivienne was waiting at the door, and Christine immediately ran over and flung her arms around the woman. "Oh, Aunt Vivienne," she sobbed. "This is just . . . just . . . so frightening. What could have happened to Dad?"

Maggie, seeing Kate's tense face, slipped her arm around her as they watched Vivienne patting the girl's shaking shoulders. "Yes, it's awful, pet. Simply awful." She unloosened the girl's arms and held them while looking intently into her eyes. "Now look here, I'm sure Kate and the police are doing everything they can. I just know he'll show up." She turned to Nordstrom and held out her arms. "Albert dear," she said, in a husky voice. "It's been too long. And you, Jamie. My, how you've grown."

Kate and Maggie stood well back from the effusive welcome until Nordstrom said, "You've met Maggie Spencer, of course."

"Yes, Kate's friend," Vivienne replied cooly. "How nice of you to bring her."

"She's an investigator," he answered abruptly. "Looking into Doug's disappearance."

"Yes, so she told me." She looked Maggie up and down. "How is your investigation going, Mrs. Spencer?"

"Progressing," Maggie answered, preferring to remain somewhat non-committal.

When they entered the house, Maggie's eyes were immediately drawn to the enormous stone fireplace with the requisite bear skin lying in front of it. This one, she was thankful to see, was headless. The sliding door and window that overlooked the northern part of Wild Rose Lake were bereft of drapes, but colored rugs of various textures were scattered on the highly polished wooden floors, giving a warm setting for the six cretonne-covered armchairs. The golden pine of the dining table, eight chairs and massive sideboard at the far end of the room, all of which would have been otherwise overwhelming, blended right into the decor.

"What a beautiful room," Maggie breathed, impressed.

Vivienne acknowledge the compliment with a smile. "Come and meet my husband." She led Maggie to where Albert Nordstrom was chatting with a man in a wheelchair. "Darling," she drawled, "this is Mrs. Spencer, a friend of Kate's, but she's actually a detective."

Jerry Harkness must have been a big, powerful man at one time but now his flesh hung loosely. Maggie looked into his pain-filled eyes as he lifted his feeble hand to shake hers. "No," he said gallantly, "you're much too pretty to be a detective. Well now, sit down next to Albert here, and tell me what you've been detecting."

Nordstrom got up and moving off, indicated his seat. "I'll talk to the others."

"I'm only a small cog in the agency," Maggie explained as she sat down. Somehow she felt she could trust this man. "My boss, Nat Southby, he's the real McCoy. I'm just the advance party. We're trying to establish what's happened to Kate's husband. Any ideas?"

"'Fraid not, though I'm sure he didn't walk out on Kate. Couldn't imagine that." He looked wistfully over at the girl who was now talking to Nordstrom. "Wish I could help."

"She's just learned out about the Shadow Lake mine disaster."

"But that's history now. Who told her, anyway?"

"We discovered an old contract among Guthrie's papers."

He was quiet for a moment, shaking his head. "That certainly was an unpleasant business," he said eventually.

"Did you know Jack Chandler's out of jail?"

He looked startled. "No, I most certainly did not. When was this?"

"He was released about the same time that Guthrie disappeared."

"And you're thinking that's too close to be a coincidence, aren't

93

you? As well might I. What are the police doing about it?"

"They're beginning to take Kate seriously, especially since Sarazine was found murdered."

"It wasn't an accident then?"

Maggie shrugged. "Not unless he shot himself before plunging over the cliff."

"Shot himself?"

"Yes. But the police are being very quiet about that part of it."

"Does Kate know about Chandler's connection to the mine?" he asked.

Maggie nodded.

Jerry shook his head. "Doug should have told her. You know," he continued, "when they ran into financial trouble . . . that was about 1948, I think, just a year after we were married . . . Viv wanted me to invest in that mine. Am I glad I didn't!"

"You mean, money-wise?"

"Yes. I'd have been in a hell of a fix financially, especially after my accident."

"When did that happen?"

He shifted the upper part of his body in the chair and gazed at the lake. "About ten years ago," he began. "I rode out early that morning to locate some strays. We have over three thousand acres, so you can understand that it took me quite some time to locate them. Anyway, I was on my way back in the early afternoon when one of those freak storms moved in." He paused as if to gather the strength to finish. "I was making for a stand of trees when there was a tremendous crack of thunder, and my horse bucked and sent me flying. You'd have thought old Warrior'd been stung by a swarm of bees." His hands clenched the arms of the chair. "He'd never been spooked by a storm before. It was hours before they found me. My back was broken."

"And the horse?"

"Vivienne had him put down right away," he said sadly. "But it wasn't his fault."

"What are you two talking about?" Nordstrom had wandered back to stand over Jerry's chair.

"He was telling me about his accident," Maggie replied.

"Enough of that morbid stuff." He moved behind Jerry's chair, shaking his head in disapproval at Maggie. "We're all going out onto the patio for some cold drinks."

The glass-roofed patio stretched the whole length of the low house, and as Maggie settled into one of the white-painted basket chairs, Vivienne handed her a tall gin and tonic.

"Just on time," Vivienne said, looking at her watch.

"What do you mean?" Maggie asked.

"There's often a short thunderstorm around this time of the afternoon," she explained. "Terrific show. Something to do with all the lakes and mountains in the area." She got up and dabbed roughly at her husband's shirt with a linen napkin. "Jerry dear, do be careful. You're spilling it," she added irritably.

Maggie found it was quite exhilarating to watch the storm clouds move in over the lake, ruffling the calm waters into white-caps that raced across the open stretches. A flock of ducks took off with the next loud rumble, their legs and feet trailing in the lake as they skimmed across the choppy water. The storm lasted no more than fifteen minutes, but the rain and hailstones hit the roof of the patio with such force that conversation was virtually impossible. Then as quickly as the squall had moved in, it was over and a forlorn cry split the sudden silence. "What was that. . . .?" Maggie cried, startled.

"A loon. Look, over there. A pair of them." Jamie, who was sitting beside her, pointed to the birds. She watched in awe as the two long-necked birds took off, leaving a wake behind them. "They're making for that small island."

"So that's the unearthly sound I've been hearing just before dawn," she exclaimed. "I wondered what it was." She turned to look at Vivienne and Christine sitting close together, talking in low tones. Just beyond them Nordstrom seemed to be describing something to Jerry, his hands moving dramatically as he explained some point. Maggie picked up her drink and wandered into the garden.

"So, what do you think of us, Mrs. Spencer?" The question had come from Jamie who had followed her from the patio.

"Can Mr. Harkness walk at all?" she asked, evading the question.

"No. He's paralyzed from the waist down." He paused while they both turned to watch the man in the wheelchair responding to Nordstrom. "He's a real nice guy, though. What a disaster."

"This is a beautiful place, and well-kept." Maggie said. "I shouldn't think they're short of money, at least."

"Yeah, this ranch brings in quite a bit of money," Jamie answered. "And like dad, Jerry's got himself a good manager. And I suspect," he added, "he's done a fair amount of successful speculation in his time because you can bet your boots that Viv wouldn't have stayed around all this time after the accident if there hadn't been plenty of loot."

"Christine seems to get on okay with her."

Jamie scowled. "She's just sucking up to her to make Kate feel bad." Suddenly he turned and went back to the patio. "Hi guys," he called. "What about us getting back?"

"Oh, must you?" Vivienne cried out. "I was hoping you'd stay for a barbecue. I thawed masses of steaks after Albert called."

"I'd love to stay," Christine said, smiling sweetly at Kate. "I'm sure someone would run Kate and Mrs. Spencer back if they want to leave."

"No one's going back," Jerry said quietly and then turned to Kate. "How about you and Mrs. Spencer — can we call you Maggie? — giving me a hand with the salad while Vivienne and the he-men deal with the barbecue?"

It seemed no time at all before Jamie and Albert Nordstrom had the fire in the large, natural stone barbecue pit alight and were standing, drinks in hand, staring at the flames while they waited for the coals to glow. Vivienne, in the meantime, had set the picnic table with a red gingham cloth, cutlery and matching bread plates and cups.

Maggie thought the steaks were the best she had ever eaten. The slabs of meat were huge, cooked to perfection, and served on individual wooden platters accompanied by green salad and hot corn-on-the-cob. She realized that, for a while at least, everyone was determined to forget the problem of Guthrie's disappearance and concentrate on enjoying the evening. Even Kate seemed relaxed as she sat chatting to Jamie about nothing in particular.

After helping clear the table, Maggie and Kate sank back into the wicker armchairs on the patio and sipped their coffee in silence. Christine, who had been dogging Vivienne's footsteps ever since their arrival, had relaxed at last beside Jerry and her brother. "I'm going to sleep late in the morning," she announced, stretching languidly.

"Where's Vivienne?" Kate asked. "She should be out here enjoying the sunset."

"She and Albert went to look over her LPs. She's got a new hi-fi," Jamie answered. As if on cue, strains of Glenn Miller's Moonlight Serenade came out to them.

"I have to find the bathroom," Maggie said quietly to Kate.

"Next to the kitchen," Kate answered. "Can't miss it."

Maggie slipped through the kitchen and into a small hallway. The laundry and bath rooms were directly ahead, and to her right she could see into the living room where Vivienne, dancing and swaying to the music, had her arms tightly around Nordstrom's shoulders, as he, cupping her firm buttocks closely toward him, nuzzled into her neck. They were so engrossed that neither of them saw Maggie as she slipped quietly into the bathroom. *My-oh-my! Vivienne and Albert!* It was obvious that Kate had little to worry about Vivienne's interest in Douglas Guthrie!

As they prepared to leave, Vivienne trailed behind them. "Thanks, Vivienne," Maggie said. "It's been a wonderful visit."

Vivienne nodded, then turned to Nordstrom and held his hand. "It's been such a long time, Albert." He bent and kissed her on the forehead and then waved to Jerry. "See ya around, pal."

Back at the ranch, the five of them gathered in the living room before retiring for the night. "What are your plans for tomorrow?" Kate asked.

"We want to have a talk with Hendrix and see if there's anything we can do to help," Jamie said, then added, "I think you should sit in, too, Kate."

"Oh, I don't want to interfere with how Hendrix is running the place," Kate replied nervously.

"All the same, you'd better sit in."

"I'd like to borrow the Rover and go into Williams Lake," Maggie said. "If that's okay?"

"Can I hitch a ride?" Christine said suddenly. "There's a few things I need in town."

"I thought you wanted to talk to Hendrix? It was your idea," Jamie exclaimed.

"No. You handle it. I'll go with Maggie."

Maggie shrugged. "Sure. But I intend to go early. What about your lie-in?"

"I'll make that Thursday."

"Thursday?" Kate looked surprised. "I thought you were going back tomorrow."

"No, we're staying till the weekend," Christine said with a cat-like smile. "Didn't someone tell you?"

"Well, I'll . . . I'll need extra supplies then. . . ." Kate's face turned from its usual pale to downright waxen.

"Make a list, Kate." Maggie cut in. "I'll get everything for you."

"Will you, Maggie? Thanks."

"What about you, Mr. Nordstrom?" Maggie said, cutting into the sudden silence. "Are you planning a lie-in too?"

"My dear, please call me Albert." He put his hand on her shoulder. "No, to answer your question. No lie-ins for me. I'm taking a canoe out onto the lake."

CHAPTER SEVEN

In the morning the sky was overcast, the wind wet and gusting, but at least the sporadic rain helped to keep the dust down on the gravel road leading into town. "When was the last time you saw your father?" Maggie asked Christine as the jeep bumped over the potholes.

"He was down to see my grandmother in Vancouver a month ago. Jamie and I went out to dinner with him."

"How did he seem? Worried? Tense?"

"He seemed okay to me, considering he's living with that woman."

"You don't like Kate?" Maggie asked.

"For crying out loud! She's only a few years older than I am."

"I think she could do with a little sympathy from you and your brother."

The girl shrugged. "She won't get it from me. She's just after Dad's money."

"Something tells me you're very close to your mother," Maggie observed.

"Not since she married again. But at least he's the same age, for Pete's sake." She shifted in her seat. "What are you going into town for?"

"My boss is coming up Monday. I have to pick up a few things for him. And of course, Kate's supplies. I shouldn't be much more than an hour."

"Do you know Williams Lake?" Christine asked as they drove into the small town.

"No. First time."

"I'm just going to mooch around," Christine said. "I'll meet you for coffee in the Ranch Hotel when you're finished. Okay?"

"Where's that?"

"Just across from Al's Variety. See . . . over there." she said, indicating the restaurant with a vague gesture.

After Maggie had let Christine out, she drove along the street until she found the general store. Used to shopping in her big-city supermarket, she was amazed at the old-fashioned way the goods were displayed and sold up here. She walked down the uneven, wooden plank floor peering into various sized barrels. The first containers were filled with flour, oats, dried peas, several types of beans, dried fruit, brown sugar, and white sugar. In the hardware section on the other side of the store the barrels contained nails, screws, spikes and other objects of different shapes and sizes, many foreign to Maggie and for which she could hardly imagine a use. Behind the counter were numerous wooden drawers, all neatly labelled, some having a sample of the contents nailed to the front. The back part of the store was taken up with crates of soft drinks.

While she waited behind a Chilcotin mother with several children for her turn to be served, Maggie couldn't help grinning as she watched the children arguing over whose turn it was to take a gulp from the putrid-coloured bottle of soda pop they were sharing. Their lips, tongues and ragged clothes were all covered in the same vivid orange. After Kate's list had been filled by the clerk and carried out to the jeep, she returned to the store and bought some of Nat's favourites: chocolate biscuits, soda crackers, cheese and pop — though not the orange kind!

She was lucky enough to find a parking spot in front of Al's Variety Store and slipped in to buy a flashlight, spare batteries and a pair of strong twill work gloves. Everything stowed, she walked over to the hotel to meet Christine but had to wait for over half an hour before the young woman turned up, accompanied by Vivienne.

"Maggie," the latter drawled. "Nice to see you again."

"Thank you for letting us barge in on you yesterday," Maggie answered.

"I enjoyed the company," Vivienne answered. "I was tired out from being on the range all morning."

"Riding?"

Both Vivienne and Christine laughed. "No," Christine answered. "Vivienne's a crack shot. She means the shooting range."

"I was competing in the Cariboo lady's finals."

"You shoot competitively?"

"Shooting's her passion," Christine answered proudly.

"And did you win?"

"Of course."

Well! How about that? Maggie beckoned the waiter over. "Coffee for three," she ordered.

The return trip to the ranch seemed much shorter. Christine talked incessantly about Vivienne and how wonderful she was and how talented, and why couldn't her father have married her instead of a sissy like Kate. Maggie was relieved when the journey was over.

Christine was first out when the Rover pulled up at the front of the house. But as Maggie reached into the back for the first box of groceries to hand to her, she discovered that the girl had already disappeared into the house. She had at least left the front door open, and Maggie picked up her own purchases and stomped into the house in search of Jamie's help.

Nat was sitting in his office hiding from his new Girl Friday when the door suddenly flew open and Henny entered, balancing a cup of coffee in one hand and a sticky cheese Danish on a paper napkin in the other.

"Mr. Nat, you see my note?" She kicked the door shut behind her.

He nodded as he surveyed the sticky bun oozing icing and the overfilled coffee cup which she had deposited on his notepad.

"Thank you, Henny," he said, moving the offending delicacies to a safer spot, but the cup had already left a wet ring on the paper.

"*Ja.* Maggie told me you like that kind," she said, happily moving the Danish back in front of him. "There is man to see you. Posh? Is that what you say?" She beamed.

Nat checked the flip day calendar in front of him. "I'm not expecting anyone." He looked reprovingly at her. "Did you forget to tell me again?"

"No, no. I did not forget. He is new one. I go and get him."

"Wait. Did he give you a name?"

"Oh, *ja*. I get him."

"But. . . ." Nat had started to rise to his feet when the door banged open again and in charged Harry Spencer.

"What do you mean letting my wife go off to a place like that?" he shouted, advancing into the room brandishing a rolled-up newspaper. "She told me she was going on vacation and all the time she was just doing your dirty work!"

Nat looked at Harry in utter astonishment. "For God's sake, man, calm down. What are you talking about?"

"I can read, you know," Harry spluttered, his ginger mustache quivering. "It's in all the papers! Woman out riding at dude ranch finds dead man in overturned jeep! He was shot! Shot! And you sent my wife there. . . ."

Nat interrupted the tirade. "I didn't send Maggie anywhere,

she went up there on vacation and just happened to find that body. That's all there is to it."

"Mr. Nat . . . I. . . ." Both men had completely forgotten Henny who was standing in the doorway with mouth agape as they yelled at each other across the desk.

"Not now, Henny. Not now!"

After Henny had left, Harry returned to the fray. "She's still my wife, Southby, and she's needed at home. And what do you do? You send her up to this . . . this . . . " He opened his newspaper to find the name. "This Wild Rose Ranch to find dead bodies!"

"Spencer, how many more times do I have to tell you that I did not, I repeat, did not send Maggie up there."

As though he hadn't heard a word that Nat said, Harry continued his rant. "It was bad enough when you nearly got her killed right here in Vancouver, but to send her off to the wilderness at a time like this, when she should be here with her family. . . ."

"What do you mean — at a time like this?" Nat demanded. "Has something happened to Midge?" Nat felt a flicker of fear, knowing Maggie and her second daughter were very close.

"My daughter Mildred is fine."

"Barbara, then?"

Harry drew himself up. "It's my mother. She's in hospital and at a time like this, a man needs his wife beside him," he finished melodramatically.

"Is it serious? I mean, is she . . . uh . . . dying?"

"Serious enough. She's having surgery tomorrow morning."

"Oh, I am sorry." Nat suddenly felt like a heel. "What's wrong?"

"She's having a bunion removed from each foot and will be crippled for weeks. That's why it's imperative that Margaret returns home to take care of her." He held out his hand. "Now I'd like a phone number at this ranch where I can reach her."

Nat looked at the attorney with undisguised loathing. "Mr. Spencer, I would suggest that you get some professional help to take care of your mother. Maggie is still on vacation. I'm sure she'll

103

be in touch when she returns." He drew his yellow pad toward him. "Now, if you don't mind. . . ."

"If you or that imbecile outside won't give me her phone number," Harry spluttered, "I'll find out another way." He turned toward the door. "Margaret will have it on her conscience for the rest of her days if anything happens to Mother."

Nat looked stupefied as the door banged shut. "Bloody hell! The man's a nut case." He buried his head in his hands.

"Mr. Nat." Henny came in and stood uncertainly by his desk. "He is saying that he's Maggie's husband. He is making that up, *ja?*"

Nat looked up. "No, Henny, he's her husband alright."

"I thought she was . . . uh . . . divorcee?"

"No," he answered grimly. "In this country, the only grounds for divorce is still adultery. And Maggie would never consent to that."

"Oh, I see." Henny nodded wisely and retreated, closing the door quietly behind her.

It was getting close to lunch time when he heard a light tap on his door. "Yes, what is it?"

Henny opened the door a crack and peeped round the edge. "Sergeant Sawasky here. I tell him you are busy, but he say that is okay." The door opened wider and George Sawasky strode in.

"It's lunch time, Southby," he said, handing Nat his hat. "I thought we'd go dutch at the Aristocrat."

"Great idea," Nat answered, taking the hat. "Let's get the hell out of here."

They were shown into a corner booth at the bustling restaurant, noisy with the lunch-time crowd, and after quickly perusing the specials, ordered the meat loaf, carrots and green peas with coffee up front from a somewhat harried waitress. "How's Maggie doing up there in the sticks?" George asked while they waited for their order to be served.

"Haven't spoken to her for a couple of days. Why?"

Sawasky took a sip of coffee. "Like I promised, I've been looking into a few things."

"And?" Nat prompted.

"I hope that gal of yours is being careful, Nat. Who told you Chandler was out of jail?"

"Albert Nordstrom. He's an old pal of Douglas Guthrie's."

"I see. But what this Nordstrom probably doesn't know — or didn't tell you — is that Chandler's disappeared too."

"You think he's in the Williams Lake area?" Nat said in alarm.

Sawasky nodded. "Chandler always insisted he was framed." He stopped talking while their plates were set down in front of them. "He's supposed to communicate with his parole officer every week," he continued after the waitress left, "as a condition for early release. But there's been no contact for almost a month. He's in a lot of trouble." He speared a square of the meat loaf and contentedly began chewing. "You know, Nat, it's one helluva coincidence that they're both missing. Hard to believe it's just happenstance."

"I've a bad feeling about this Guthrie," Southby replied. "Could you run him through your system too?"

"I'll give it the old college try, Nat. But Farthing's in line for inspector and he's now my boss, always looking over my shoulder. And you know how much he loves you?"

Nat did know. When he had retired from the force five years previously, Farthing, who had always been jealous of Nat, had taken over his old job. Since then, he'd risen in rank but incomprehensibly, still harbored ill feelings. "Well, look, do your best, will you? I'm worried about Maggie. I've told her to play it cool, but you know she has a mind of her own."

Sawasky reached into his pocket. "Here's a mug shot of Chandler." The photo showed a dark-haired man in his late thirties with a cleft chin and a long scar over his left eye. "You're planning on going up, I guess?"

"Next week. I've told Henny not to make any new appointments for me."

"The sooner the better. Keep me informed, eh?"

Maggie was also just finishing her lunch. The skies had cleared somewhat, and rising from the table, she announced, "I'm going for a ride on Angel."

"You're a devil for punishment," Nordstrom exclaimed. "Kate told me she threw you a couple of days ago."

Maggie's hand went instinctively to the bruise on her forehead. "You know what they say— you have to get right back on." She laughed. "I think my pride was hurt more than my backside."

"You couldn't get me near one of those animals, personally. Except if I've a bet on it," he told her with a grin.

"What about you, Jamie?" Maggie asked.

"I'm like Albert," Jamie answered. "I'd rather just watch'em win."

"I can't spare the time," Kate said quickly.

"There's no need for anyone to come," Maggie said. "I like going out on my own, anyway."

Kate shrugged. "Well, if you're sure."

Al helped her to saddle the horse. The weather was still warm and partially overcast but there were some black clouds now looming in the west.

"Shouldn't stay out too long," Al said, pointing to the clouds. She waited until he had returned to the stable before stowing her new flashlight and gloves in the saddle bag. Good-natured Angel waited patiently while Maggie struggled to swing herself into the saddle, and she felt quite proud of herself for the near-expert way she accomplished this feat.

She turned Angel's head toward the riding track. Feeling much more confident on the horse this time, she made the trip to the start of the mine road in under a half hour. Then she headed up the hill, stopping on the way to look down into the ravine to where the wreck of the jeep still lay. But she noticed that not only had the tires been removed from the jeep; there were other visible signs that the police had been there. There were official markings on the two saplings between which the vehicle had plunged from the road and also around the site below. Nudging the horse, she rode further up the road to where she estimated the sniper must have hidden, then dismounted to search the boulders and bushes on the side of the road, looking for tell-tale signs that he — or she — had been there. But either the sniper had been very careful not to disturb the bushes or yesterday's storm had wiped out all traces. Taking hold of Angel's reins, she continued walking up the hill until she came to the end of the road. The mine entrance was completely hidden by brush and alder, and after tethering Angel next to a broken-down shed, she removed the flashlight and gloves from the saddle bag. When she had pushed her way through the brush, she found that the mine opening was much smaller than she had imagined it would be, and it seemed to burrow straight into the side of the mountain. Apart from the gentle snuffling from Angel, everything was quiet and still, but she experienced that same eerie feeling as on her last visit to the area. She shone the flashlight through the rotting, wooden slats that covered the entrance but nothing reflected back. There was just the deep blackness and a damp, musty smell. Baffled, she pushed her way back through the brush and replaced the flashlight in the bag.

There's no way in. So it wasn't the mine that brought Sarazine up here. But there had to be a reason for him to come. And who knew that he was here? As she prepared to put her foot into the stirrup, she looked at the slope of the mountain as it rose in tiers above the mine entrance. *I wonder what's up there?*

Re-tethering Angel, she pulled on her new gloves and pushed her way back to the mine entrance. Beside it she found a narrow track leading upwards through the bushes and stunted firs, and taking hold of a clump of sagebrush, she started to climb. *At least my hands won't be scratched this time.* Stopping every now and then to catch her breath, she clutched and pulled her way up through the thick tangle until she was out in the open on the first plateau. The mountain still loomed above her but if the mine tunnel did go straight back into the mountain as it had appeared to, she estimated that she must be directly above it at this point. Maybe there was another entrance to it up here. The slab of stone she was standing on was at least eight feet square and was surrounded by boulders, sage and thorn bushes. Not knowing what she was looking for, she peered and poked among them. After about ten minutes searching, she was on the verge of giving up when she hit pay dirt. Well hidden under the scrub and covered by loose grass and small pebbles was a wooden trap door about three feet square. Preparing herself for a tough struggle, she grasped the metal ring and pulled. But it was much lighter than she expected, and she fell backwards abruptly. Brushing herself off, she approached the opening again warily and stared down into inky blackness. *Why didn't I bring the flashlight?* A wooden ladder was fastened by cleats into the rock at the top of the hole, and as she stared down she could just make out its rungs disappearing into the void. Thoughts of snakes, spiders and bats decided her against trying to descend without a light of some sort. *I'll have to go back for it.* Scrambling over the flat rock she made an unladylike, sliding descent back to where Angel was tethered, grabbed the flashlight, pushed it down into the waist band of her jeans, and struggled up the track again.

Kneeling beside the hole, she directed the beam into the depths. The ladder appeared to descend at least twenty feet to what looked like an earth-packed floor. *There's nothing for it, old gal, down you go.* Stuffing the flashlight back into her waistband, Maggie began her descent. The ladder creaked and twisted under her weight and several times it seemed to move away from the damp wall, causing her to stop in fright. After what seemed an eternity, she touched bottom and looked up to the square of daylight. Forcing herself to stop trembling, she stood with her back to the ladder and shone the beam around a small cavern. There were two tunnel openings, one to her left, which she thought possibly went down toward the mine's lower entrance, and the other to the right, burrowing its way deeper into the hillside. *Which way?* She chose the one to the right. Steeling herself, she stooped to enter the dark passage-way but had taken no more than a dozen steps when the tunnel started to slope gently downward. A slight rustling made her freeze in her tracks, and it was all she could do not to turn, rush back and climb up to sunlight and safety. But taking a deep breath, she continued to walk, holding the flashlight in one hand and using the other to feel her way along the wet rocky wall. Twice her feet slipped, but each time she regained her balance. Third time unlucky, they went right out from under her, the flashlight flew out of her hand to bounce ahead, then the beam of light went out, plunging her into sudden inky blackness. Rigid with fright, it took her several minutes to get a firm grip on herself and to begin crawling about, feeling for it. When a complete search all around her revealed nothing, she realized that it must have rolled further down the slope. *I've got to get out of here!* Panic-stricken, she stood and started to turn in what she thought was the direction she had come from. *No! Not when I've got this far.* She turned back. *Take some deep breaths.* Forcing herself to her knees again, she felt her way down the slope through slimy puddles until her hands closed over the errant flashlight. Giving a sob of relief, she pressed the switch. Nothing! "Please, please!" Trembling, she twisted the end and then gave it a jiggle. A powerful and reassuring yellow beam shone upon the wet walls.

The tunnel had opened into a cavern no bigger than the living room of her basement suite. Playing the light over the shored up walls and roof, she could see evidence of mining activity. Rusty picks and shovels and wood for shoring were piled up against one of the walls, and on the floor was an old wooden keg and several boxes, all covered in a whitish, slimy mould. They appeared to have been there for years. Against the far wall was a mound covered by a tarpaulin. *More boxes?* She lifted one end of the tarp. A metal Coca Cola chest! Cautiously she opened the lid. Inside lay a brown leather briefcase with the initials L.S. stencilled in gold.

Crouching, she flicked the clasp and opened the brief case. Inside were several papers, buff folders, a lined note pad and the usual pens and pencils. In the wavering light she read the heading on the top paper: Leonard Smith & Sons. The name was strangely familiar, and she stared at it for several minutes before folding it and slipping it into her jacket pocket. Leaning the briefcase against the open lid, she trained the light on the rest of the contents. Whatever it was had been carefully wrapped against the mine's dampness in a nylon sheet. She reached down and slowly unwrapped the sheet. Gold? Silver? Drugs? But it was none of these. It was bundles of cash! Picking one of the packets up, she riffled through the notes. All used $20s. She reached for another bundle — $100s, yet another — $500s! She sat back on her heels. *What does it all mean?* She replaced the bills and carefully refolded the nylon sheet over them, then reached for the briefcase. A sudden sense of urgency made her replace it quickly and re-cover the chest. *It's got to look as if it hasn't been touched.* But it took several agonizing minutes until she was satisfied with her work.

Before retracing her steps up the tunnel, she flashed her light around the cavern once again, this time noticing an old hurricane lamp standing on a wooden crate. The lantern was filled and ready to go. *Next time I'll bring matches.* The sudden fear that someone might have seen her entering the mine made her want to run, but the journey up the tunnel was too slippery and dangerous for that and she had to content herself with slowly fumbling her way. While she had been exploring, the threatened rain had started, and it poured down on her as she climbed the ladder, but that didn't stop her from taking great gulps of fresh air as she climbed out of the escape hatch.

Although her uppermost thought was to get down to where the horse was waiting, she forced herself to scatter loose grass and sand over the trap-door in an effort to erase all signs of her having been there. Then she ran over the flat rock and down the track to the waiting horse.

"Not a word to anyone, Angel," she whispered into the horse's ear. Angel blinked her long eyelashes and graciously accepted one of the apples that Maggie had stowed in the saddle bag. "Okay," she said, putting her foot into the stirrup to haul herself up, "let's go."

Angel, head down against the sudden downpour, picked her way daintily over the slippery gravel and through the rivulets that were already coursing down the road. Then, as they passed the section where the jeep had gone over, a skittering of small stones glanced off the rock face and landed on the road before them, and both Angel and Maggie raised their heads. When more stones came cascading down all around them, Maggie urged the horse to go faster, though as she leaned over the animal's neck she could feel her uneasiness. "Take it easy, Angel," she pleaded. But a stone hitting Angel's flank made the horse rear up in panic. Maggie was determined to hang on this time. "Whoa! Angel! Whoa!" she demanded as the horse began racing down the hill to get away from the tumbling stones. At the bottom of the hill Angel veered left onto a dirt track leading into a stand of aspen. With scenery flashing by like a jerky movie as she clung to the horse's neck, Maggie was only dimly aware of a bearded man running into the horse's path and making a grab for the bridle. Moments later Angel came to a shuddering stop, but it was a full minute before Maggie could pull herself together and slide off the animal's back. Meanwhile, the man made soothing noises, stroking the horse until it had calmed down.

"Rock slide," Maggie gasped. "Back there."

The man, his Stetson cascading water, shielded his eyes and looked up the steep mountain road. "What the hell were you doing up there in this weather?"

"It wasn't raining when I started out," she answered.

"It's been pouring for almost an hour."

"I tried to take shelter under a tree," Maggie improvised, "and wait till it was over, but the rain got too heavy. How can I thank you?"

"By not telling anyone you saw me." He handed the reins over to Maggie. "I'm sort of trespassing and Guthrie doesn't like me around. Do you want a leg up?"

"No thanks," she answered. "I'll walk a ways and let her calm down." She turned Angel and started to retrace their steps. "Thanks again," she called. "I won't tell the Guthries." He nodded and waited until Maggie had hobbled back to the trail that led to the ranch. When she stopped at last to mount, she saw him climbing into a battered white truck parked under the trees, start the engine, and head up the mountain road that led to the mine.

The rain had settled into a drizzle that soaked both horse and woman to the skin so they were thoroughly miserable when they plodded wearily into the yard and through the stable doors to where Al was busy saddling a horse. "I was just coming to look for you. What happened this time?"

"Rock slide," Maggie said as she slid down. "Angel got hit on the rump," she added.

"Rock slide? Where did you go?" Al ran his hands over the trembling horse. "She seems okay now."

"Went up the mine road a little way. Then Angel got hit by a rock," she answered with a shiver. "I had to walk her back to calm her."

"Where did you say it happened?" he asked again.

"The old mine road. It's the only trail I know," she added with a shaky laugh. "I think it's time you showed me some new ones."

When she got back to the house, Kate was more sympathetic. "You're soaked. What happened?"

"Got caught in the rain and nowhere to take shelter," she answered. "I'll be fine after I've changed."

After dinner, Kate went to bed early. Maggie wandered into the den to find a book to read and came upon Jamie staring into the fire. "Where are the others?" she asked, sinking down in an armchair.

"Gone up to their rooms." He sat looking morosely into the

112

fire. "Do you think something bad has happened to my father?" he asked suddenly.

"I don't know, Jamie. I certainly hope not"

"I can't help being sorry for Kate," he said, leaning forward to throw another log on the fire.

"You don't share Christine's feelings toward her?"

"Not really. She's a bit young for the old man, but heck, if she makes him happy. . . . Christine's just a mite jealous."

"What kind of mood was he in the last time you saw him?"

"He was fine — and very happy that I'd got a job at last."

"With Albert Nordstrom?"

"In the accounting office. Bottom of the totem pole." He smiled at Maggie. "Actually, Dad got me the job. He's known Albert from way back."

Maggie's inner antenna started to kick in. "How far back?"

"Long before Dad took over the ranch from my grandfather. Dad trained as an assayer when he was young."

"Assayer?" Maggie asked. "What exactly does an assayer do?"

"Analyses metal compounds. You know, to see if the ore is of standard purity."

"I see. It must've been helpful when he went into partnership on the Shadow Lake Mine."

"I guess so. Also Nordstrom and Kraft is an investment firm for all kinds of mines, so Dad's done the odd job for them, too."

"Does your father still do the odd job for them?"

"Occasionally, I suppose."

"You like working for Nordstrom?"

"It's okay, I guess. I've always been good with figures." He gave a sudden grin. "Numbers, I mean."

They sat in companionable silence for a few minutes, then Maggie asked, "Are you staying until the weekend?"

"No. Albert's planning to leave tomorrow afternoon and I want to go and visit with my Mom. I think she should be told about Dad."

113

"She's American?"

"Yes. Both Chris and I were born in Raymond, Washington. That's right on the coast."

"So you and Christine have dual citizenship."

"Yes. It helps a lot when you have parents living in different countries." He laughed. "Do you have a family?"

Maggie nodded. "Two daughters."

"So how do they feel about having a private eye for a mom?"

"Midge, the younger, thinks it's wonderful, but Barbara isn't so keen."

"Tell me about them," Jamie insisted. So for the next thirty minutes, Maggie did.

I like that young man, Maggie thought as she let herself into her bedroom later that night.

CHAPTER EIGHT

Friday was another dull and rainy day in Vancouver and the grey building housing Nordstrom and Kraft matched the weather to a T. Nat strode into the reception area and found Agnes Agnew, grey and drab as the weather outside, banging away on her Royal typewriter.

"Can I help you . . . Oh, it's you . . . Mr. Southerly, isn't it?"

"Southby," he corrected her. "Nordstrom in?" he asked, hoping the man hadn't made a quick flight back.

"He's away."

"Any idea when he'll be back?"

Agnes Agnew pursed her lips. "No, sir. He left Wednesday and said he'd probably be away for the rest of the week."

Nat Southby drew up a chair. "Where'd he go?"

"He didn't inform me of his destination, Mr. Southby."

"That must make things very difficult for you," he answered sympathetically.

"I'm afraid Mr. Nordstrom is not like his father," she answered, pouting. "Mr. Nordstrom senior, now he always kept me informed."

"He should have more regard for such a faithful secretary like yourself," Nat commiserated. Agnes drew herself up, and he wondered for a second if he'd laid it on a bit too thick. Then she gave a thin smile.

"I see you appreciate a good assistant, Mr. Southby."

Nat glanced at the large clock on the wall above Agnes's head. "It must be near your lunch time," he said. "Can you possibly take pity on a lonely bachelor and join me for a meal?" He felt quite a heel when he saw Agnes's eyes fill with tears.

"That's very kind of you," she answered. "I'll get my coat."

Later, when they had arrived at the coffee stage of their lunch, and Nat had been filled in on Agnes's lonely life since her father had passed away and how she couldn't live without her two cats, Mindy and Mandy, Nat led the conversation back to her job with Nordstrom and Kraft.

"I think you told me that you went there straight from secretarial college."

"I was just seventeen," she answered. "Both Mr. Nordstrom senior and Mr. Kraft were so nice to work for."

"You must know a lot of Nordstrom's clients and friends then."

"Oh my, yes."

"Mr. Guthrie?"

"He's one of my favourites. He calls me Aggy, you know. Always joking." She paused reminiscing. "Even when he's in a hurry . . . like the last time."

"You tend to remember people like that," Nat answered encouragingly. "And when was the last time you saw him?"

She thought for a moment. "I know it was a Tuesday. I do my filing on Tuesdays and he made some joke about the box files. They're so awkward to use," she explained.

"You don't remember which Tuesday, I suppose?" Nat asked.

"No, but I can tell you when we get back to the office," she said, a tell-tale blush going up her thin neck. "I always make a note on my desk calendar when he comes in."

Nat could hardly contain his impatience for the waitress to bring the bill, and it was all he could do not to rush poor Agnes out of the door and along the road back to the Nordstrom building. But once they were back inside the reception area Agnes seemed to forget about Guthrie.

"Thank you very much for lunch, Mr. Southby," she said politely, removing her jacket and sitting down behind her desk. "But now I'd better make up for lost time."

"Oh, the date," Nat prodded. "You said you'd look up the date."

"So I did." She reached over to her daily calendar and flipped the pages back. "Here we are, Tuesday . . . see, I was right . . . 9th of June." She looked a bit abashed. "Mr. Nordstrom doesn't know about my little notes."

"Your secret's safe with me," Nat winked gallantly, almost wanting to kiss her. "No need to tell Mr. Nordstrom I called in either," he added. "I'll get in touch with him another time."

Southby was jubilant. "Got you!" he said aloud, banging on his steering wheel once he was back in the car. "Got you!" He turned the ignition key and gave a self-satisfied grin. "Ray Teasdale's next. And there's no time like the present." He rammed the old Chevy into gear. If he'd bothered to look up to the third floor of Nordstrom's building, he would have seen Agnes looking out of the window at him with a wistful look on her face.

As usual, it was difficult to find a parking place in the center of the city. "There are too many cars," he muttered to himself on his second time around. "Something ought'a be done about this." Then a parking space miraculously opened up in front of the Teasdale building, and with a wild grin, he beat a shiny new Ford into it. *Either you have it or you don't, pal!* Totally ignoring the beeping horn and the shaking fist of the Ford's owner, he nudged the old Chevy into the spot and then bounded into the building.

Teasdale's receptionist was behind her desk, filing her nails, and frowned as she recognized him

"Yes?" she asked.

"Mr. Teasdale, please."

"I don't believe you have an appointment?"

"No, I don't, but it's important I see him at once."

She got up languidly, walked a few paces and knocked on Teasdale's door. "Mr. Southby would like a word."

"Now what?" Teasdale asked. "Oh, very well, show him in," he added, obviously annoyed, then changed his mind. "No, wait, I'll come out."

"Mr. Teasdale, are you absolutely sure that Guthrie didn't come into Vancouver last week?"

"Look here, Mr. Southby, as I told you the other day, I haven't seen the man since early May."

"Yes, well, I'm sorry to be a nuisance, but I have received information that he definitely visited his mother around June 9th. That's two days after he supposedly left for a trip to Alberta."

"Then your informant must've been mistaken. He would've called me." He turned to go back into his office. "Anything else?"

"No, I suppose not. Thanks for your help."

Teasdale walked back into his office, firmly shutting the door.

Nat gave one of his lop-sided smiles to the receptionist, had another peek at Adam and his Three Eves, and shaking his head, left.

Although it was after two o'clock, Henny was still in the office when he returned. "I thought you'd be gone by now," he said, throwing his hat at the stand. He bent and retrieved it from the floor and hung it up. It just wasn't the same without Maggie.

"Going now, Mr. Nat," she replied. "Have made camomile tea for you."

"I don't think I like. . . ."

"You drink. Good for nerves." While she was talking, she carefully buttoned up her beige raincoat and then, pulling a beige and green rayon scarf out of one of the pockets, tied it over her head.

"Going to rain," she added. "Typing on desk."

"There's no need for you to come back after lunch, Henny!"

"*Ja*, there is. Lots to do if you go to be with Maggie on Monday."

Seeing it was no good arguing with her, he waited until she had left before tipping the offending beverage down the sink in the washroom. Then he sat behind his desk, an unlit cigar in hand and pulled Henny's third effort — a wrap-up on a forging scam — toward him to see if she had at last obeyed his instructions and taken out her own comments as to how she thought this particular case should have been handled. She had done very well, considering. Her latest advice was just handwritten and attached by paperclip: 'I do not think he is telling truth, Mr. Nat. Don't trust man who wears lots of gold rings.' He couldn't help smiling as he signed the document. *Maggie, my girl, I sure need you back here.*

～

Maggie and Kate watched the Beaver float plane take off, Maggie wondering if she should have asked more questions from the three visitors, and Kate thankful that they were at last gone. As the plane rose from the lake and dipped its wings in a last salute, the two women drove back to the house and collapsed into the lounge chairs on the deck.

"Thank God that's over," Kate said.

"Did you have your meeting with Hendrix?"

"Yes. Albert came too, and he kept insisting that Hendrix bring Jamie up to date on the affairs of the ranch. And you know, Maggie, it really isn't any of his business."

"Did Hendrix oblige?"

"Not really. He sort of hedged and insisted that everything was running just fine. He's of the opinion that we should just carry on as we are until we hear further from the police."

'What was Jamie's reaction to that?"

"I'm sure Jamie doesn't want to get involved with the ranch affairs at all. Anyway, he agreed with Hendrix."

Stretching lazily in the warm afternoon sun, Maggie closed her eyes and mentally ticked off all the recent events. *Guthrie's missing, Sarazine's dead, somebody stole that money pouch I found in his jeep, and there's all that cash in the mine. It's all connected somehow. But what's the link? And where does Nordstrom fit in?*

"Maggie." She opened her eyes to see Kate standing beside her, smiling again. "The sun's over the yardarm, and I think we both deserve a drink." She placed a glass at Maggie's elbow.

"Thanks, Kate. This is just what the doctor ordered." As she reached for the glass, she felt something crackle in her pocket — it was the piece of paper that she'd taken from the brief case. Her first impulse was to haul it out and read it, but remembering Kate's inability to keep anything to herself, she just took the glass from Kate's hand and smiled thanks instead. Time enough to read it when she reached the safety of her bedroom. Then she settled back in her chair and listened to Kate re-hash her woes once more.

~

Southby only had Agnes Agnew's word to go on that she'd seen Guthrie on June 9th. But who else would he have visited? His mother, perhaps? With Henny off to lunch, he looked through the filing cabinet himself. Henny certainly kept the records straight, he was forced to admit, and it was only minutes before the new Guthrie file was open before him and he had located the address of the nursing home.

It was nearly two when the old Chevy rolled to a stop in front of the Princess Margaret Retirement Villa on Queens Road. The four-storey, wooden-faced building hardly lived up to its grandiose name, though the builder had added a pseudo-stone entrance and etched the home's name in cement over the lintel. A set of wooden double doors led into a square foyer where several of the building's occupants sat on faded cretonne-covered settees and arm-chairs that were grouped around a fake fireplace. As one, they looked up hopefully and eyed Southby approaching the semi-circular receptionist's desk, but then sensing he was not a real visitor, went back to their passive staring. The desk name plate said Miss Ethel Gouge. Dressed in a starched white uniform with an impossible hat pinned to her upswept hair, she turned her fixed smile onto the detective. "May I be of help?"

"Yes, Miss . . . Gouge. I would like to see Mrs. Sara Guthrie, please."

She looked Southby up and down before consulting an appointment book in front of her. "Is she expecting you?"

He held up a box of chocolates in lieu of a reply. "A surprise gift. From her son," he added.

"Oh, how nice," the nurse replied, a smile now on her no-longer wooden face "She will be pleased. He isn't very good at visiting, you know." She turned the book around and handed the detective a pen. "Perhaps you'd be so good as to sign in. Then take the elevator over there, just to your right. Suite 308."

Nat tapped on the door of 308, but it was several minutes before it was opened by a frail lady in her late eighties. "You don't know me, Mrs. Guthrie, but I've heard of you through your son and grandchildren. Can I come in?" He thrust the box of chocolates into her hands.

She opened the door wider then, less hesitant, and the musty smell of ancient furniture, old clothes, moth-balls and neglect engulfed him.

"Chocolates!" She exclaimed loudly. Clutching the box, she led the way inside and pointed to one of the deep armchairs beside the narrow window. Her voice, excited now, rose in intensity. "Who did you say you were?" she yelled.

"Nat Southby." The detective raised his voice to match her decibel level. "I've been trying to locate your son. Have you seen him recently?"

She sat down in the chair opposite and wrestled successfully with the cellophane on the box. "Black Magic. My favourite." She stuffed a chocolate into her mouth with astonishing dexterity. "Do you want one, boy?"

"No. No thanks, Mrs. Guthrie. But I do need to find your son. When did you see him last?"

"Blast?" She leaned forward and looked out of the window, then back at Southby, appearing somewhat disappointed. "I didn't hear any blast. Where was it?" She slipped another chocolate into her mouth. "Ugh! Marzipan!" Out it came as quickly as it had gone in, and she put the offending candy back into its paper doily, selecting another in its stead.

"When was the last time you saw Douglas, Mrs. Guthrie?" Nat shouted once more.

But now her hearing had apparently made a remarkable recovery.

"No need to raise your voice, young man. I'm not deaf, you know. It's time he came and visited his mother." Carefully she selected another chocolate. At this rate, the whole box might be gone before she spilled the beans. "And those grandchildren of mine." She bit energetically into the candy. "Might as well be dead for all they care." She looked at the gilt clock on the overcrowded dresser. "You'll have to go now. It's time for my program." She struggled out of her chair and over to the 12-inch black-and-white television, turned it on and then fiddled with the rabbit ears as the snowy image on the screen rolled over and over vertically. "Cheap! My son bought it." She pushed the ears up and down, vainly trying to obtain some stability. "Damn thing's always jumping." Sensing an opening, perhaps his last chance, Southby leaned over and carefully adjusted the rabbit ears until the picture became clearer and stabilized.

"When was that?" Nat shouted over the volume. But his chance had passed, and the old lady had settled down to watch *As The World Turns*, her attention riveted on the now flickering but at least visible image on the screen. He sighed, knowing he wouldn't get any more from her, and let himself out. As he was closing the door he saw Sara Guthrie extract a half eaten caramel from her top dentures and put it in an ashtray beside her. She didn't even notice that he'd left.

Back in the lobby he handed one of his business cards to the receptionist. "Mrs. Guthrie's son hasn't been seen for a while, Miss Gouge," he explained. "His wife has hired me to look for him. Is it possible that you can tell me when he was here last?"

She took the card and read it thoroughly before handing it back. "I'll look in the book." Nat waited impatiently while she sorted through the pages. "June 10th. That's when he brought that television for his mother."

"You keep records of all visitors?" he asked, surprised but pleased to at least be making some headway.

"We've had some unfortunate thefts. People here are very gullible," she added by way of an explanation. "They'll let just about anyone in."

The detective nodded, but as he turned to leave, he had another thought. "Do you have a phone number to call, you know, for emergencies?"

She ran her finger down the book again. "There's his home number in Williams Lake. Oh, just a minute, there is another reference to—. I'll just check." She reached back to the shelves jammed full of buff files and selected one. "Here it is. He gave us a local number as well in case of emergency. I suppose it won't do any harm to give it to you." She wrote the number on a slip of paper and handed it over.

"You wouldn't by any chance have the person's name to go with the number?" he asked hopefully, as he tucked the paper into his wallet.

"I'm sorry, Mr. Southby. That's against our policy. I shouldn't have even given you the number, but since there are extenuating circumstances. . . . In any case, you're a detective, aren't you? Surely if anyone can find that out . . . " She let the sentence die, and Nat hurried out in case she had a change of heart and demanded the slip of paper back.

Back at the office Nat sat quietly looking at the paper. I've seen that number before. But where? No better way to find out! Reaching for the telephone, he began to dial. "Teasdale Agency." There was no mistaking the voice in his ears, even over the phone.

"Teasdale Agency," Catherine O'Neill repeated. Swiftly replacing the receiver, he rose from his desk and opened his office door.

He found his Girl Friday thrusting papers into buff folders and happily humming an off-key version of Elvis's *Love Me Tender.* "Henny."

She looked up from her work. *"Ja,* Mr. Nat."

He sat on the corner of her desk. "You want to do some real detective work for a change?"

"Me? You want me to do detecting?" She grinned at him. "You must be yoking, eh?" Her 'j's still came out as 'y's.

"No, Henny, my girl. I'm not yoking." He pulled up a chair next to her. "Now listen carefully." He outlined what he wanted her to do, then repeated it twice more to make sure she understood. "Okay," he said at last. "You're ready. Dial the number." Then he slipped into his own office, opened the door wide so that he could watch her. As soon as Henny reached the agency, she gave him the nod and he quietly picked up his own phone.

"Teasdale Agency. Can I help you?"

"Ja," Henny answered. "This is nurse from Princess Margaret home."

"You sure you have the right number?" Catherine O'Neill asked.

"Ja. Teasdale Agency. Your number is given for Mr. Guthrie. His mother live here. It say on card, call Mr. Teasdale for emergency."

"An emergency! Oh, dear. I'll get him for you straightaway." Nat could hear the receptionist talking excitedly to her boss, even if the words were difficult to distinguish. Then Teasdale came on the line.

124

"What's wrong with her this time?"

"Mrs. Guthrie she is in bad state. We can't reach her son so we call you."

"He saw her last week, for Christ's sake," Teasdale replied, obviously irritated "And he's out of town."

"Can you give us number to call?" Henny asked.

"I told you. He's out of town," Teasdale said, by now quite irascible. "Can't you people deal with it? Isn't that what you are paid for?"

"Can you pass message on?" Henny improvised. "She is very upset."

"Oh, damn the woman. Look," he said, "I don't know where he is. Call his home number." He paused for a moment and then asked, "Are you her nurse?"

"Ja. Sometime."

"What do you mean, sometime?"

"Sometime I'm her nurse," Henny looked up at Nat in alarm. He quickly shook his head and made a cutting motion across his throat.

"Someone calling me. Got to go, sorry." She replaced the receiver and leaned back in her chair, her face flushed, "I'm not used to telling lies, Mr. Nat."

"In this business, Henny," he replied sadly, "it is sometimes necessary."

After Henny had left for the day, he went over the conversation between her and Teasdale again. *It doesn't sound as if he knows where Guthrie is. But he could be covering up for him.*

There was only one other thing he had to do before leaving for the Cariboo, and that was talk to Guthrie's ex and that posed another problem he was not anxious to deal with. Agnes Agnew! "My God! What a name!"

"How can I help you, Mr. Southby?" Agnes gushed when she heard his voice.

"Is your boss back?" he asked casually.

125

"He came in this morning but has left again. Have you found dear Mr. Guthrie yet?"

"No, but you could go a long way in helping me find him," Nat said.

"Me! How?"

"I need to get in touch with his ex-wife, Debra."

"I'm afraid I can't help you there," she answered sadly. "I haven't seen her since the divorce."

"But doesn't Guthrie's son work for Mr. Nordstrom?"

"Oh, yes. Such a nice young man. Takes after his father."

"Then wouldn't you have his next-of-kin on his personnel files?"

"Oh, but those files are privileged, Mr. Southby."

"But they might help us locate Douglas Guthrie."

"Oh dear. I wish Mr. Nordstrom was here to advise."

"I can assure you he would agree, Miss Agnew. After all, Guthrie's his friend, too." He crossed his fingers. Five minutes later, feeling pleased with himself if just a little seedy at his manipulating Agnew's feelings he sat back in his chair, the information he needed before him. Douglas Guthrie's first wife was now a Mrs. Eric Wright and she lived in Seattle.

The third ring was lucky, and a pleasant-sounding Mrs. Wright picked up. After introducing himself, Southby asked if she knew that her ex was missing.

"Yes," she answered. "Jamie called and told me. It certainly is worrisome."

"He hasn't contacted you?"

"Why on earth would he do that?" she replied. "We'd gone our separate ways long before we finally split up."

"You weren't keen on the Cariboo, I take it," Nat persisted.

She laughed. "That's an understatement, Mr. Southby. I don't like horses, I don't like ranches and by the time I left Douglas, I didn't like him either."

"Do you mind telling me why?"

126

She was quiet for a moment. "He was a good father to the kids. Christine adores him and blames me for the break-up, but he has quite a roving eye. Have you met Vivienne Harkness?"

"No, not yet."

"Well, watch out. *Femme fatale*, or she thinks she is." She chuckled in a very pleasing husky voice. "Anyway, from what Christine's told me, he's dumped Vivienne and got himself a wife young enough to be his daughter."

"Kate," Nat answered. "She's the one who hired us to find him."

"Jamie said she'd hired someone." She paused for a moment. "Going back to your query, Mr. Southby, it wasn't just his women I objected to. It was that bloody gold mine. He left me on my own for weeks at a time, and the men he was in partnership with . . . well, they were a pretty rough crowd. Gave me the creeps, if you really want to know."

"I've heard about the mine," Nat answered. "Wasn't there some kind of explosion?"

"Yes. Doug swore that he had nothing to do with it, but it still left a nasty feeling. If you get my meaning." She didn't wait for an answer but went straight on. "Actually, George Fenwick was the nicest one of the whole bunch."

"But according to Albert Nordstrom, Fenwick was a rough character and a heavy drinker," Nat said, somewhat surprised at her information.

"George liked his beer. That's true. But rough . . . no, sir."

"I understand he and Chandler wanted to go on mining when Douglas closed shop?"

"Well, yes, of course. They needed to. They'd put everything they owned into that mining venture," she answered. "Without it they were dead ducks. George used to talk to me quite a lot," she explained.

"But then he got himself killed," Nat said quietly.

"Yes," Debra Wright answered. "George was literally a dead duck, Chandler went to jail, and that just left the other four." She paused. "That's when I got out."

127

"Did you know that Sarazine was killed in an accident last week?"

"No, I didn't." She stopped abruptly. "Look Mr. Southby, I think I've said enough. My husband wants me to put all that stuff behind me."

After replacing the phone, Nat drew his yellow pad toward him. He and Maggie were going to have a lot to discuss when he saw her on Monday.

∾

Maggie spread the yellowed sheet of paper out on the bed. It appeared to be the first page of a contract dated September 10th 1950, to buy Friendly Freddie's Used Cars, a dealership in North Vancouver. But it was the name of the law firm that jumped out at her. Snodgrass, Crumbie and Spencer. *Harry's firm!* Quickly she read the rest of the page. *I need to go back and get the rest of those papers.* But the thought of returning to the old mine by herself made her flesh crawl. *I'll wait until Nat gets here.* Then a new thought came to her. *Harry can tell me about it! I'm sure he must remember.*

She waited until that evening to place the call.

"Margaret. Thank God. You got my message then?"

"Message, Harry? No."

"Where are you, Margaret? I told that . . . that . . . Southby person that there was an emergency. . . ."

"Has something happened to one of the girls?" she asked in alarm.

"No. It's Mother. She's having an operation on her feet."

"Oh, nothing serious. Well, that's a relief. Now Harry, the reason I'm calling. . . ."

"Nothing serious? Nothing serious? I'm talking about my mother here, Margaret!"

"Yes. Well, you'll need to get a nurse to stay with her. Now listen Harry, do you remember having a client years ago named Leonard Smith?"

"What are you talking about, Margaret?"

"You had a client named Leonard Smith," she repeated slowly. "You negotiated the purchase of a car dealership for him."

"You can't expect me to remember clients from long ago! And in any case, you of all people you should know better, Margaret. I can't divulge any information on clients, past or present. Especially if it's for that man you work for." She heard him take a deep breath and waited for it. "And your attitude toward my poor suffering mother, is . . . is absolutely uncalled for."

"I'm sorry if she's in pain, Harry. I really am." Maggie felt a bit of a heel. "Well, how's Emily?" she added, trying to move away from the source of the dispute. But Harry was no longer with her; the line had gone dead.

I guess I'll just have to wait until Nat gets here. There was no way she was going to call him and broadcast everything she had learned about the mine, the money and Leonard Smith over the party-line phone.

CHAPTER NINE

The train was three hours late and with all the waiting and no news, by the time it chugged into the station in the gathering darkness and disgorged its passengers Maggie had convinced herself that Nat had missed it anyway. She was turning away, bitterly disappointed, grimly preparing to drive back to the ranch alone when she heard his voice. "Maggie, Maggie!" Whirling around, she saw him jump from the train. "Fell asleep," he explained, taking her in his arms and giving her a fierce hug. "God, it's good to see you."

"I've so much to tell you, Nat," she said, pointing to the Land Rover parked under the street lamp outside the station, "but you look so tired."

"I'm just about all in," he replied. "There was a huge rock slide just before Squamish. Took the crews some time to clear it away. It's been one hell of a journey." Automatically he opened the driver's door of the vehicle. "Don't you want me to drive?" he asked to his surprised assistant

"Typical man," she laughed, moving him aside and slipping into the driver's seat. "No, dear. Just sit back and grit your teeth. It's a bumpy road." She waited until they were out of the town and heading toward the Horsefly road before she began telling him all about her visit to the mine, her descent to the underground cavern, finding the old cooler and the money.

"You went back up there on your own," he said angrily, "after I asked you not to?" He paused for breath. "Maggie, suppose you'd had an accident? Or someone took another shot at you? Did you think about that? How would we have been able to find you?"

"Calm down for Heaven's sake," she answered, gripping the wheel, miffed despite realizing he did have a point, or possibly because of it. "I didn't have an accident, nobody plugged me, and besides, I had to find out what was up there." She felt in her jacket pocket and withdrew the folded paper she had taken from the briefcase. "Read this."

He turned on the dash light and leaned forward to read, then sat back thoughtfully. "Where have I heard that name before?"

"Think back some years. Harry wouldn't tell me anything, or couldn't remember, but there must be a connection some—"

"Jeez! Of course." Southby gave a low whistle, slapping himself on the forehead. "My God! The Leonard Smith abduction. Maggie, my girl, what have you stumbled onto?"

"When I noticed that Harry's law firm was acting as attorneys for Smith, I called him. . . ."

"Wait. Let me guess. All he wanted was —"

"To talk about his mother. Just went on and on about her poor feet."

"Ah yes! The bunion file." He paused, then continued carefully, "Harry called on me, Maggie. Harangued me. Wanted to know where you were staying up here."

"You didn't tell him, I hope? " she asked in alarm.

"D'y think I'm nuts? I told him you were working on a case,

couldn't say where you where. Can't say he was too happy with me. Now about Smith," he continued, gripping the door handle as they rounded a bend a little too fast. "Easy there, Maggie. As far as I can remember, Smith owned car dealerships, food marts, and that sort of thing. I think he got his start buying up scrap metal before the war."

"And he was kidnapped," Maggie said.

"Yes. From the parking garage in the basement of his office building. The ransom money — $750,000 I think — was paid, but Smith was never returned." Carefully he refolded the paper. "I was on the force at the time, and there was one helluva stink because the abductors not only got the ransom money but disappeared without a trace."

"And now I've come upon his briefcase in the old mine and by the look of it what's left of the ransom money." She drove in silence for a few moments. "I wonder if his body is somewhere in that mine too."

"Possible, I suppose," Nat finally said, "We never even got a whiff of a lead. He just seemed to have vanished into thin air."

"Do you think Douglas Guthrie's disappearance has anything to do with the kidnapping?"

"Mm-m. Nine years ago. That's just about the time his first wife was leaving him and they closed the mine at Shadow Lake."

Maggie slowed to make the Horsefly turn-off. "You'd better hang on. This road's really full of potholes. What have you been up to since I spoke to you?"

"Ow!" The Rover had found a pothole.

They were almost at the ranch before he'd finished telling her about his phone call to Debra Wright, his visits to Nordstrom, Teasdale and Guthrie's mother. She laughed so hard at the graphic details of his visit to Sara Guthrie and of Henny playing detective that she had a job to concentrate on her driving. "From what you've just told me," she said, slowing as the headlights revealed another pothole, "there certainly appears to be another side to

Douglas Guthrie. And it seems," she added, "to be one that Kate doesn't know anything about."

"Well, this is it," she said as they turned into the Guthries' drive. "You'll feel much better after a shower and some food. Kate said she'd keep some supper for you."

"I thought I was staying in one of the cabins."

"You are. But Kate insists you eat with us in the main house."

"But when do I get to see you alone?" he asked plaintively.

"I'll come and tuck you in," she answered with a laugh. She showed him to his cabin and left him to unpack and have a cleanup. "Be as quick as you can." Maggie gave him a light kiss. "Kate's anxious to meet you."

"Have you found out anything new, Mr. Southby?" Kate asked, as soon as the introductions were over.

"Just a little," he hedged, sitting down at the table. "And please, call me Nat. But I need to be brought up to date on everything that's happened here first."

"I don't think the police are any further ahead," she answered sadly. "I'm just hoping that you'll have more success."

"Well, the first thing I need," Nat said, hungrily helping himself to the food Kate had put in front of him, "is a good night's sleep. Then I'll be able to tackle anything." He gave a tired smile to Kate. "I hope you don't mind if we talk in the morning." Having been warned by Maggie that Kate was a blabbermouth, he was not about to tell her anything she didn't need to know, and while they ate, she rambled on, rehashing all the events to date.

Afterward, Maggie accompanied him to his cabin. "Just look at those stars, Nat! Let's sit outside for a while," she said, guiding him to the porch swing. "Do you think I should've told Kate what I found in the mine?" she asked, snuggling down beside him.

"No, not yet. Are you sure no one saw you go in?"

"The only person I saw was the man who stopped my horse,

and he wasn't anywhere near the mine. In fact, he—"

"Which man who stopped the horse?"

"Didn't I tell you about the rock slide? I had so much to tell you," she said, "I guess I completely forgot. The slide spooked poor Angel into bolting and all of a sudden this man ran into the road and grabbed her reins. I don't know what would have happened if he hadn't."

"Rock slide. How did it start, for chrissake?"

"It must've been the rain. How would I know?"

"What did this man look like?"

"Taller than you. Dark with a straggly beard. Wore one of those big western hats. I can't remember anything else." She thought for a moment. "Oh, yes. He had an old white truck parked in the trees and he drove off in it afterwards."

"Did he look anything like this?" He took Chandler's photograph out of his wallet and passed it to her.

"A bit. But the man I saw had a beard. I suppose it could be him."

"Anything else you haven't told me?" he asked, returning the mug shot to his wallet.

"No. Except he made a point of saying I wasn't to tell anyone that I'd seen him." Maggie stood up. "What's the agenda for tomorrow?"

"Well, after I've spoken to this Hendrix, what say we visit the mine?"

"Fine," Maggie said. "I'd better get back to the house."

"Aren't you coming in for a nightcap?" he asked, taking the key out of his pocket and unlocking the door. He pulled her inside the room.

"I thought you were absolutely all in and couldn't wait for a good night's sleep."

"I can't think of a better way to make sure I sleep like a baby, can you?"

It was pitch black when Maggie finally slipped quietly, and happily, into the house and tip-toed up to her room.

At breakfast the next morning, Kate was anxious for the three of them to have a sit-down discussion, but Nat put her off. "Before we do that," he said, "I need to familiarize myself with the ranch, have a talk with Hendrix and possibly the police, and see for myself where that jeep accident was." He'd decided not to tell Kate about his growing suspicions that Douglas might have been seen in Vancouver. "By the way, I met your mother-in-law a couple of days ago," he said.

Kate gave a little giggle. "She's quite something, isn't she? She doesn't think much of me, of course."

"She's much older than I expected," Nat added.

"That's because Douglas was a late-in-life baby," Kate said. "She dotes on him. No woman is good enough for her boy. Even Debra didn't come up to scratch, and she even provided the old biddy with a couple of grandchildren."

"She really loves that television set your husband gave her," Nat said. "She's already hooked on the soaps."

"When did he give her that?" Kate asked, surprised.

"A few weeks ago, according to the nurse on duty."

"No, that can't be," Kate said firmly. "We both went to see her on our last visit. He didn't give her a TV then."

"Perhaps he had it delivered," Maggie cut in. "Any appliance dealer would be only too happy to oblige, to make the sale."

"Y-e-s," Kate went on slowly, obviously thinking over events as she spoke. "Perhaps that's it. But why didn't he mention it to me?"

"I'm going over to talk to your manager, " Nat said, getting up from the table. "I've a couple of questions to ask, then I want to borrow one of the jeeps. Maggie's going to show me where the accident happened."

They found Hendrix in his office and after introducing Nat, Maggie left them to it.

"You've been with Guthrie a long time," Nat began.

135

"Yup. But before you start, I don't know where he is."

Unperturbed, Southby continued, "Kate told me that on the morning Guthrie disappeared, she heard the two of you talking outside the house." Nat was sitting on one of the rickety chairs next to the desk. "Can you recall what the conversation was about?"

"How the hell do you expect me to remember a conversation that happened . . . what . . . over two weeks ago?" Nat was at once interested by the sharp reaction to his question.

"It was the last day that Guthrie was here. You'd remember."

"Nothing special, I guess. As far as I can recall, it was just things he wanted done while he was away. Run-of-the-mill."

"Did you ever have anything to do with the mine?" Nat asked suddenly.

"The old mine up there? No, it was closed fifty years ago. Ain't nothing up there."

"No," Nat said calmly. "I mean the Shadow Lake Mine."

Hendrix looked startled. "Shadow Lake! Not me. I was too busy keeping the ranch going to get involved with that."

"You did know the co-owners, though?"

"Yeah. Sure. They were all here at some time or other."

"But now Mrs. Spencer tells me you didn't recognize Mr. Sarazine when you helped haul his body out of the ravine."

"Nobody would recognize you either, Mr. Southby, if you'd been lying dead for at least three days in that ravine." He gave a hoarse chuckle. "This area is still pretty uninhabited and there are plenty of wild animals around scavenging." He paused. "Even grizzlies," he added dramatically. "Now, if you'll excuse me, I've work to do."

"We need to borrow one of the jeeps. Mrs. Spencer's going to show me where the accident occurred."

"You can take the one that's out front. It's been gassed up."

Nat was impressed with the vastness of the Guthrie range. With Maggie driving, he had a chance to enjoy the spectacular scenery that seemed to change with every added mile. Just before

136

they started up the mine road, Maggie showed him the trail that cut through the forest to end in the ravine and the dirt track where she had encountered the bearded man. She stopped the jeep beside the site of the accident and they climbed out. The police labels still flapped in the gentle breeze, and Nat put a protective arm around her shoulders as they peered down into the ravine. He realized how easy it would have been for the sniper to have killed her from this vantage point. So the intention must have been to only scare her off. Climbing back into the vehicle, they drove up to the mine.

First Maggie indicated the boarded up entrance to the mine and then, leading the way to the side of it, showed her boss the track up to the top. "Have you got your flashlight?" she asked, before starting up. Nat nodded. "Okay, let's go." As she climbed the familiar path, she could hear Nat puffing away behind her.

"But where's this trap door?" he asked, when they reached the flat stone above the mine.

"Over there, behind those little evergreens," she said with a gesture. "Come on, I'll show you."

A minute later they were standing beside it, and bending down, Maggie grasped the iron ring and yanked the trap door open to reveal the gaping hole.

Nat looked down, aghast. "Bloody hell! You went down there on your own?"

"It's not so bad once you're down there," Maggie lied.

"That so? Well, as the senior investigator in this case, you'd better go down first and hold the ladder for me," Nat said. Though it had apparently been installed long after the mine was closed, it still looked a bit frail, and he didn't like to admit that he was uneasy about climbing down into the pit, plus a mite claustrophobic when it came to caves or other small, dark places.

When he joined her at the bottom, they stood for a few moments letting their eyes adjust to the blackness before entering the tunnel that led to the cavern. Maggie, going first, could hear

137

her partner-in-sleuthing stumbling and cursing behind her, but at least this time with two flashlights, they could easily see where they were going.

He flashed his beam round the small room, noting the ancient keg, boxes, picks and shovels that Maggie had described. In the meantime, Maggie had moved over to the tarpaulin-covered chest. "Over here," she called as she folded the tarp back and opened the lid. "Oh my God!"

"What is it?" He moved quickly to stand beside her.

"It's gone. The money's gone!" Her voice had sunk to almost a whisper. "Nat, the money was right there with the briefcase." She lowered the lid.

"You understand what this means?" he replied, as he helped her to re-cover the cooler. "Someone saw you on Thursday."

"But there was no one. I'm sure I would've seen them."

"What about the man who stopped the horse?"

"No! He was too far away. It would have been impossible for him to have seen me here then run down the mountain road to where he stopped Angel."

"How long were you down here?"

"I don't know. I suppose about twenty minutes."

"That's quite a long time."

"Yes, but . . . he would've had to follow me up the road in his truck. And Nat," she added, "I had to go back to get my flashlight from the saddle bag. I would surely have seen him then."

"Let's get back up top," Nat said. "This place is giving me the willies."

They clambered out, and Maggie watched Nat lower the trap door. "Oh damn!" she said. "I was in such a hurry to show you the money that I forgot to see if the sand and grass I'd scattered over the trapdoor had been disturbed."

"Well," Nat answered seriously, "too late now. Besides, if the money's gone, then it must've been." As they stood on the flat rock surveying the area, he pointed further up the mountainside.

138

"Someone could've easily seen you from up there."

"And I was down there alone." Sickening waves of remembered fear swept over her.

"Yes," Nat answered, "and its likely that the rockslide was another deliberate attempt to frighten you off." Sobered by that realization, they climbed down to where they had left the jeep.

"What now?" Maggie asked. "Corporal Brossard?"

"I suppose," he replied, letting the jeep into gear. "But let's stop at that rockslide on the way down." When they reached the area, they hopped out of the vehicle and gazed upward. "You know, Maggie, I just can't see any reason at all for these rocks to have come down on their own."

"Why not? There's plenty of them up there."

"No, look," he said, pointing upward. "The rock face is smooth for a good thirty feet or more and then the wooded slope goes sharply back at a steep angle." He stepped back, closer to the edge, to get a better look. "I know you said it was raining, but there aren't any stream marks up there to explain such a big rock slide."

"But something caused it. Look at them all."

"No, what's obvious to me is that this slide was deliberate. Someone saw you enter the mine, I'm sure of it."

"Poor Angel," Maggie said sadly as they got back into the jeep. "I remember I had been thinking how difficult it was for her to keep her footing on the wet gravel, and then the rocks just started coming down."

"Poor Angel, nothing! Suppose one of those rocks had hit you?" Nat put the jeep into gear again. "Show me where you saw the truck."

"Down there," Maggie said, pointing to the narrow track. But when they reached the area, the only sign of the vehicle was the tread marks where it had been parked.

"I suppose we'd better go and see the RCMP," Maggie said again, as they neared the ranch.

"No, let's wait till I've spoken to Sawasky. He's running a check

139

on Guthrie and his pals." They parked the jeep and while Nat went into his cabin to clean up, Maggie continued on to the house.

"So what did Nat have to say about the ravine?" Kate asked when she arrived in the kitchen entrance.

"He was horrified," Maggie answered.

"Did you go down there?" Kate asked. "You're covered in dirt."

"We hunted around the mine entrance," Maggie improvised. "It's still pretty muddy up there from all the rain. I'll go and change."

"George, do you recall the Leonard Smith abduction way back?" Nat asked, when he'd finally managed to make contact with his buddy.

"Sure do. Why?"

"I think Maggie's stumbled onto a lead. Could you see what you can dig up?"

"That must've been at least . . . what . . . ten years ago? I remember they never found him."

"It was nine years."

. "What's she found out?"

"This is a ten-twelve, George," Nat said, using the code to tell his friend that someone could be listening in. "But it's serious enough that we might have to contact you officially."

"Have you told Brossard?"

"Not yet. We've only just got in."

"Well, you'd better get on to him. Especially if something's happened on his turf."

"I suppose," Nat answered slowly, "we'll go into Williams Lake this afternoon."

"Let me know, what happens, okay?"

"Sure thing, George. I'll call in after the meeting."

After the phone call, Nat wandered into the kitchen. "Okay for Maggie and I to use the jeep again?" he asked. "We have to see Corporal Brossard."

"You'd better call him first," Kate answered. "He has a huge territory to cover and may be out."

But as it turned out, Nat reached Brossard on his first try. The corporal reluctantly agreed to meet with them at three that afternoon.

"I see you've brought in the big guns," he said to Maggie, nodding the couple toward the two visitors chairs. "What's it this time, more money that somehow isn't there?"

"Actually," Nat said, after he'd introduced himself and produced his investigator's licence, "I'm the one that insisted on seeing you. And I think you should listen to what Maggie has to say."

"Mrs. Spencer," Corporal Brossard said sarcastically after listening to her story, "are you sure you're not letting your imagination run away with you again?"

"Believe me, corporal, I saw that money and the brief case," she answered.

"And who did you say was . . . ahem . . . kidnapped?"

"Leonard Smith."

Brossard shrugged. "Never heard of him. And then you said that someone tried to kill you with a rockslide." He gave a tight smile. "It was raining hard at the time, I believe."

Maggie could feel her face redden. "Mr. Southby's sure it wasn't a natural slide," she answered him coldly.

"You an authority on rock slides, Mr. Southby?"

Nat stood up abruptly. "That's it! Corporal Brossard, it's obvious you don't want to believe Mrs. Spencer's story, but I advise you to check into the Smith abduction. Let's go, Maggie."

Brossard stood up and put his hand on Southby's arm. "Okay, okay, sit down. No need to get huffy. Let's go through it again." He turned back to Maggie. "Now, this money. Was it just thrown in the box or was it in stacks?"

"I told you, there were stacks of twenties, fifties, and hundreds. All denominations." she answered. "And the brief case was on top."

"You didn't take any of the money?"

141

"No. I left it there."

"So, if it's gone, you've no evidence of this . . . uh . . . ransom?"

"But I do have evidence," she answered witheringly. "This!" And she handed over the sheet of paper that she'd taken from the brief case.

He read the paper slowly. "This is a sales contract. What's this got to do with a kidnapping?"

Margaret looked to Nat, waiting for him to take over.

"How long have you been in British Columbia, corporal?" Nat asked.

"Five years."

"Leonard Smith was abducted about nine years ago. Look at the date on the paper, September 10th 1950." Nat paused. "I was with the Vancouver police at the time. He disappeared about a week later. The case caused quite a stink."

"So Smith was never found?"

"There wasn't a trace of him or the money . . . up to now."

"I'll give you this," Brossard said thoughtfully, "If you're right about all this, and Mrs. Spencer was seen, you could both be in danger." He turned to Maggie. "You recall, ma'am, I did tell you to leave the disappearance of Guthrie to us."

"But," Maggie said with a smile, "if I had followed your advice, corporal, you wouldn't have known about the abduction or the ransom money." She rose from her chair to stand beside Nat.

"I'll have to keep this, of course" Brossard said, indicating the contract. "And I do strongly advise the two of you to return to Vancouver as soon as possible."

"We're here to find Guthrie," Nat answered. "That's what we've undertaken, and find him we will."

Before returning to the ranch, Nat stopped at the town phone booth and put in a call to Sawasky. "As promised," Nat said, when he heard his friend's voice. "Listen, I'll fill you in."

"I've made enquiries about Guthrie, Teasdale and Nordstrom," Sawasky said, after hearing Nat out. "There's nothing so far on

Guthrie or Teasdale, but Nordstrom was questioned on an investment scam about five years ago. Just penny mining stocks on the Vancouver Stock Exchange with a couple of suspicious twists, but nothing illegal could be proved."

"How about that!" Nat answered. "And Smith? What did you find out about him?"

"His sons took over the business after the old man went missing. They told me that just before he was abducted, someone had approached Smith to get him to invest half a million dollars in a mine. The son I talked to said that after getting his lawyers to investigate, Smith declined. Seemed it was too risky even for him."

"Too much of a coincidence. Did they remember who it was that made the offer?"

"He didn't know. Could've been Nordstrom, I suppose. But, as far as I can tell, he's clean as a whistle now. Anyway, I've put in a call to one of my pals down in Seattle to see if they know anything about Guthrie."

"Why did you have to see Brossard?" Kate asked, when they finally got back. "Was it about Doug? Do you know where he is?" She bit back the tears. "I think there's something you're not telling me! Has he been hurt? I've been trying to keep calm but . . . but . . . it's all getting too much."

Maggie put her arm around the younger woman and led her to a chair. "We're still in the dark about Doug, but there have been other developments, Kate. You see, I found another entrance to that old mine. . . ." And she proceeded to tell her all about the cache of money in the mine and Leonard Smith's abduction.

CHAPTER TEN

Al looked Nat up and down, noting his five feet ten inches and taking in his rather rotund figure. "Are you sure you've ridden before?"

It was nine o'clock in the morning, and after a quick breakfast Maggie had led her somewhat reluctant Nat to the stables. She had been determined that he was going to experience the joy of riding, whatever his misgivings, but now she was wondering if her unbridled enthusiasm had been all that wise.

"Uh-h-h . . . sure. Lots of times," Nat replied, sizing up the huge black animal with obvious trepidation.

"When was the last time. How long ago?" Al persisted.

"We-l-l, it's been a while, that's true," he admitted, still looking warily at the horse. But Maggie was already astride Angel, and Nat realized he couldn't put his own moment of truth off much longer.

"This is Satan," Al replied, still looking dubiously at Nat.

"Don't worry, he's not at all like his name. Do you want to use the block to mount up?"

"Don't be ridiculous! I can manage." He'd seen how easily Maggie had swung herself up and wasn't about to be outdone. He grabbed the horn on the saddle, put his foot in the stirrup and strained to lift himself. Satan, not enjoying the detective's fumbling ways, shifted his stance. Then hot urine cascaded in a jet that seemed to Southby like Niagara Falls, splashing off the concrete floor and onto Nat's new jeans and boots. Startled, and jumping back to get out of the way, Nat lost his footing. "A-a-agh!" He floundered backward and collapsed into the steaming pool.

"Bloody hell!"

Imperious, Satan turned his head and the two of them glared at each other. Noting the glint of triumph in the horse's eyes, Nat rose to his feet and grabbed a handful of hay to wipe his jeans down. Then he seized the saddle horn again, determined to be master.

Trying his best not to laugh, but smirking all the same, Al weighed in. "As you haven't ridden for a while, perhaps the block would be a good idea after all?"

Southby looked daggers at poor Al, and was a hair's breadth from a vitriolic rejoinder when he noticed Maggie giggling so hard that the ridiculousness of his situation got the better of his ire and he couldn't help but join in the laughter. "Okay," he said sheepishly. "Okay."

But even with the help of the block it took a lot of effort to get him astride the huge beast.

"I think I better come along just in case," Al said. "Sit tight," he commanded, and headed for his own horse's stall.

"But aren't you going to the rodeo today?" Maggie asked. Kate had told her that there was a small one held in Williams Lake each year, and that all the local ranch hands took part in it.

"Yep, I'll go into town later. It can't possibly be as much fun as last year, anyway."

"Why? What happened last year?"

145

"First off, Princess Margaret came all the way here from England to officially open the event. And as if that wasn't enough excitement, a helluva big Brahma bull went crazy and charged the first aid tent." He chuckled. "Shoulda seen 'em all scatter. It was a real hoot."

"What a shame I missed it," Nat said dryly.

With Al leading, they headed for the trail. Grim-faced, Nat clung for dear life and thanked God that Al was setting a leisurely pace. "Nice Satan." He patted the majestic neck. Satan's reply was a snort and toss of his head, and Nat decided to concentrate on savoring the earthy smells of the range and praying that the trip would be short.

The trail took them through several acres of rapeseed, its tall fronds rippling in the gentle breeze. Al, dropping back to ride beside Nat, told him the cereal was fodder and that it grew so quickly it was almost ready for reaping. Holding on tight, Nat turned his head and took a cautious look, nodded mute agreement. As they neared the foothills, Al took the lead again, leaving the trail and guiding the pair onto a back road that skirted the river.

"This is the trail Hendrix and I took," Maggie called back to Nat. "It follows the river and goes around the east side of the mountain."

When they reached the river, Nat watched Maggie slipping easily off Angel and leading her to the water. "Would you like to dismount too?" Al asked.

Nat shook his head ruefully. "I don't think I'd be able to get back on."

Al laughed. "There's lots of boulders around."

"It's my backside I'm worried about. It's numb." He sat quietly enjoying the sight of the horse nudging at Maggie's pocket where the apples were kept. Laughing, Maggie found the fruit and held one out to her mount and another to Satan. Al's horse, not to be outdone, ambled over for her share. It was so peaceful and quiet that the only sounds they could hear were the three horses chomp-

146

ing, the soft breezes that whispered through the aspens and the birds chirping as they flew from branch to branch. Bucolic heaven.

"You're an old softie," Maggie murmured, stroking Angel's nose. "I suppose we'd better get back." She was about to swing up into the saddle when a glimpse of white caught her attention. "What's that over there?" she said, pointing to a clump of trees upriver.

"It looks like a pickup," Al replied. "What the hell's it doing here?" He led his horse forward with Maggie following on foot and Nat still up on Satan.

"I've seen that truck before," Maggie exclaimed, as they got closer. Then she stopped and lowered her voice. "There seems to be someone asleep inside."

"Sure looks like it," Nat said, from the lofty height of the horse. "But . . ." He urged Satan to get in front. "Keep back, Maggie." he said. "I don't think he's sleeping." But she had gone on and was already tethering her horse beside Al's, and Nat realized there was nothing for it: he had to get off the damned animal. This proved to be a very difficult operation and by the time he had slithered down Satan's flanks, Al and Maggie were peering into the driver's open window. The man was oddly still and — they quickly realized — very dead.

"He's been shot!" Maggie turned her pale face to Nat. "Oh, Nat, he's been shot." She turned away from the window and ran over to an oak tree and held onto the trunk for support. It took several minutes for her to stop retching, her thoughts flashing back to when she first started to work for Nat, and her discovery of the brutally murdered body of Ernie Bradshaw.

"Do you know him?" Nat asked Al.

"Never seen him before." The two men walked around to the open window on the passenger's side and peered in. On the bench seat beside the dead man's outstretched right hand, lay a gun, a couple of half-eaten, dried-up sandwiches, a bottle of unopened Coke and a packet of cigarettes. The bullet had entered the man's right temple and left a jagged hole, his skin burned from the closeness of the weapon.

Maggie straightened and walked over to the two men. "Did he shoot himself?" she asked.

"Sure looks like it," Al said. "We'd better call the cops."

"You said you'd seen the truck before," Nat said, turning to Maggie. "What about the man?"

Maggie steeled herself to have a closer look. "It's the man who stopped Angel from bolting."

Nat pulled a wallet out of his back pocket, extracted the small photo which Sawasky had supplied, and compared it with the dead man. "It's Chandler. No doubt about it"

"The mine partner who was in jail?"

Nat nodded. "Mm-m-m." He walked around the truck to the driver's side again with Maggie following and peered closer at the dead man. "The bullet's gone right through," he said, pointing to the exit wound. "God knows where it is." He studied the angle of the hole. "Probably in one of those trees over there."

"Who's Chandler?" Al demanded.

"One of Guthrie's old partners," Maggie answered.

"Must've been before my time," Al replied.

"He was just released from prison," she explained. She turned to Nat. "How can you tell it's Chandler? This man in your picture doesn't have a beard."

"See that scar through his left eyebrow? It's quite visible in the photo."

"But, why would he kill himself? He's only been out of prison for a few weeks."

"Maybe he didn't." He put the photo into his wallet, then reached into the truck box to flip back the stained green tarpaulin that covered its contents. Aside from a few tools, there was only a suitcase. He lowered the tailgate, pulled himself up into the box, and opened the suitcase. It contained the man's personal belongings — underwear, socks, a couple of shirts and an extra pair of jeans. But under the clothes, neatly folded, was a survey map. He took it out and spread it open. "H-m-m." Jumping down from the truck with the map still in his hands, he opened it out again on the tailgate.

Maggie, looking over his shoulder, suddenly exclaimed, "Look Nat. There's Shadow Lake. Where that mine was located."

"According to this, it's about eighty miles north of here," Nat said as he measured off the distance with his thumb and forefinger. "This certainly bears looking into."

He carefully folded the map up again and slipped it into his inside jacket pocket. "We'd better get back to the ranch and call Brossard. He's going to have a caniption when he hears about this!" Then he looked at Satan and realized that to get back to the ranch he had to get back up on the horse. He took Satan's reins, started to psych himself up, then stopped abruptly and stared at the ground, suddenly deep in thought.

"Now what?" Al asked, looking down, too.

"These tracks. They were made by new tires. Look at the clear tread marks."

"So?" Maggie asked.

"That pick-up's tires are as bald as an eagle. Someone else has been here."

"Soon as you're up on Satan, we'll follow them a ways, see where they lead," Al said.

Southby and Satan eyed each other again. He could almost sense the animal sighing. Steeling himself, he grabbed the saddle and made two unsuccessful attempts to mount up. "This won't work," he grumbled. "Maybe I'll just walk back."

"It's quite a distance, you know," Al chuckled, dismounting. "Let's not give up so fast. Here. Stand on this boulder and I'll help you." It proved to be a struggle, but Maggie held the horse's head steady while Al heaved and pushed until eventually Nat's rear end was in a position that enabled him to swing his right leg over. "I don't think I'm really meant for the cowboy life," he gasped, as he manoeuvred himself into a sitting position. His backside was already sore and he quailed at the thought of the journey back to the ranch.

A quarter of a mile down the tracks led to another road cutting across over a small bridge spanning the narrow river.

"Where's that one go?" Nat asked.

"Harkness ranch," Al replied. "But there's no mystery there. It's much shorter to come this way to visit the Guthries than go by the lake road."

"Those tracks are fairly recent," Maggie said. "It only stopped raining a couple of days ago."

"So?" Al asked.

"Neither of the Harknesses have been over to see Kate this week."

"They could've used the short cut to go on to Williams Lake," Al replied. "Do that a lot."

"You're right," Maggie answered. "That could be it. Kate told me they often come this way."

Al turned his horse around. "Come on now, forget the tracks, let's get back to the ranch."

"I wondered where you'd got to," Kate said as they entered the house. "You look pretty grubby, especially you, Mr. Southby!"

"Never mind that now, Kate. We went for a ride with Al, and I'm afraid we found a man. . . ."

Kate's face paled. "Not Doug?"

"No, not Doug. But another man. He's been shot."

"Shot! Is he . . . dead?"

"Afraid so," Nat cut in. "Kate have you seen this man before?" He held out Chandler's photo.

Kate gazed at the picture and then shook her head. "No. Never. Is he the one that's dead?"

"Yes." He walked over to the telephone. "I'm calling Brossard."

150

"You seem to have an unnatural gift for finding dead bodies, Mrs. Spencer," Brossard said dryly, when later that afternoon they all stood around the truck. He turned to Nat. "And you think this is Chandler?" He peered once again into the driver's window and compared the man to the photograph in his hand. "You may be right."

"It'll be easy for you to find out," Nat answered. "His prints will be on file." Another police car bumped its way over the dirt road toward them. "Here come the rest of your gang."

"Coroner from Hundred Mile," Brossard said, going to meet the new arrivals. "I'll see you back at the house, " he added over his shoulder. Perfunctorily dismissed, Nat could only nod at the retreating police officer's back.

"What about the tracks?" Maggie asked, as they walked toward the jeep. "Shouldn't you have mentioned them to Brossard?"

"Oh, I don't think he needs us to tell him such elementary information. Besides, if he's really as good as he thinks he is," Nat replied, "he'll see them for himself."

"You weren't long," Kate said when they entered the house. "What would you like, tea or a good stiff drink?" They opted for the latter and took their filled glasses out onto the patio. "What does it all mean?" she asked.

"As far as I can figure," Nat answered, "it's all somehow connected to Leonard Smith. That's the only logical explanation."

"The man who was kidnapped?" Kate asked. "You can't possibly think that my Douglas was mixed up in that?"

Nat shot a look at Maggie. "Kate," he said slowly, turning back to her. "I'm afraid we have to face some unpleasant facts. Either Doug found out about the Smith business accidentally and was abducted to keep him quiet," he paused and placed his hand over Kate's, "or he's somehow mixed up in it."

Kate pushed his hand away and jumped up from her chair. "He would never have done anything like that!" There was a note of hysteria in her voice. "I brought you here to find him, and now all you've done is make things worse! You don't know him, he's. . . .he's . . . too kind . . . too honest." She burst into tears and ran back into the house. Maggie shook her head at Nat, then followed Kate in. Outside, Nat drained his glass as he listened to Maggie's voice soothing the distraught young woman.

Later, once Kate had calmed down and the two women were preparing the evening meal together, Nat put in another call to Sawasky. As usual it took nearly fifteen minutes before the operator managed to get a line through to Vancouver, but at least the policeman was in.

"So what's fryin'?" George greeted him.

"I rode a horse today," Nat replied with a chuckle. "Big thrill. First time since I was a kid. And that was on the merry-go-round at Happyland."

"That must've been quite a sight, I wish I'd been there with my Kodak," Sawasky replied. "What else is up?"

"We found Chandler today — dead — with a gun beside him."

"You sure it was Chandler?" He listened while Nat went through the events of the day. "I don't like what's happening up there," he said, when Nat had finished.

"We're thinking about taking a trip up to one of the lakes tomorrow."

"Good idea. Take a picnic basket and make a day of it."

"That's just what we're planning."

The evening meal was delicious, but they all ate in silence, no one daring to break the peace by referring again to the events of the day. After dessert, Maggie and Nat walked over to his cabin and sat down outside. He spread the map of Shadow Lake on the picnic table and they leaned over, studying it in the dying light. "There's two things we've got to do tomorrow," he said, straightening up. "First is to follow those tracks and see if they do end up at the Harkness ranch, and the second is to take a run up to Shadow Lake." He folded the map and stowed it in his jacket pocket. "Now

152

let's go inside. It's been a long, trying day and it's time for some relaxation, don't you think, m'dear?"

~

Next morning, eyes bright and alert after a very restful night's sleep and with a good breakfast in their stomachs, Maggie and Nat went to find Hendrix. "We might as well follow the tracks right now," Nat said. "Let's go get the key for the jeep."

"Where are you two off to this time?" Hendrix asked, handing him the key. "If you're thinking of going back to see the truck by the way, the cops took it and the body away yesterday."

"We're taking the bridge road to visit the Harknesses," Maggie replied.

"The main road's the best way. You won't get lost on it."

"Prettier the bridge way," she answered. As they drove off, he watched them thoughtfully until they disappeared around a bend in the road then entered his own cabin.

The detectives soon arrived at the scene of the latest shooting, but as Hendrix had said, all trace of the truck was gone and the tread marks had been completely obliterated by the many vehicles that had been parked there. They drove slowly on until the heavy tire marks they were looking for became visible again and followed them over the bridge onto the Harknesses' land. The trail ran close to the river for another five miles then branched off, the river snaking its way north, while the trail turned south to where in the distance they could see the Harkness ranch buildings. But the tread marks didn't turn in at the ranch. They continued on to be eventually lost on the gravel road that circled Wild Rose Lake. Nat reversed the jeep and headed back onto the Harkness property.

Vivienne seemed delighted at their impromptu arrival. "Hope you don't mind us dropping in on you," Maggie said after she'd introduced Nat. "It was a spur of the moment idea."

Nat felt himself sinking into Vivienne's deep violet eyes. "So

153

nice to meet someone new in this God-forsaken land," she said, at last letting go of his hand. "Come in and meet Jerry."

"How's the investigation going?" Jerry asked, once they were settled on the patio. Vivienne had left them to make drinks and, catching a high sign from Nat, Maggie had gone to help her.

"You've heard about Chandler?" Nat asked.

"Just heard. The man had done his time. What would make him shoot himself now?"

Nat shrugged.

"Strange bird," Harkness continued. "Didn't fit in here."

"You knew him then?"

Harkness nodded. "Saw him at Guthrie's from time to time."

"But Maggie told me that you weren't part of the Shadow Lake mine venture."

"No, thank God. I'd have lost my shirt on that goddamned mine." He shifted in his wheelchair. "I was tempted, of course. Viv and I'd just got married, you see, and it looked like a golden opportunity to get in on it when they needed more financing." He gave a tired smile. "But in the end I decided it was too risky."

"You've only been married about ten years then?"

"Twelve. We'd both been married before. My wife died and Viv's first marriage was a disaster."

"It must've hurt Guthrie — the mine having to close like that?"

"You bet. He'd used Wild Rose Ranch as collateral."

"How did he get out of that?"

"Never quite knew. His wife Debra had a bit of money, but not enough to bail him out."

"Your accident was sometime around then?"

"Yeh, a few months before Chandler blew up the mine and killed Fenwick. Those were mean times." He turned at the sound of the two women chatting as they came through the door. "Ah . . . Here's the girls with our drinks." He smiled at his wife. "We were talking about my accident," he said. "You were very close to being a rich widow, weren't you?"

Vivienne stood behind his wheel chair and rested her hands on his shoulders. "You shouldn't talk like that. Thank God we found you when we did." She sat down and picked up her drink. "Well, cheers."

"By the way, do you remember the Smith abduction affair?" Nat asked. "Must've been around the same time Guthrie's mine went belly up."

"Remember something about it in the papers," Harkness answered. "He was never found, was he? Why do you ask?"

"There's a possibility he was brought up here to the Cariboo."

"How very exciting," Vivienne said. "Of course, with all the hills, valleys and lakes up here, it could've been happening right here on our ranch lands and we'd never know it!"

"So what did you two talk about in the kitchen?" Nat asked when they were driving back.

"She did most of the talking," Maggie answered. "Telling me how totally bored she is. Apparently his first wife died about a couple of years before they met. I gather Vivienne thought she was onto a good thing until Jerry got hurt."

"Tell me again. How did it happen?"

"He was thrown from his horse when it was spooked by lightning, but he told me he thought he heard a gun shot just before it happened."

"Wonder who'd remember the details?" he mused.

"Vivienne told me they'd only been married two years."

"Yeah. Jerry said it was ten years ago," he said, as they turned into the dirt road leading to the ranch. "It must have been around the time the mine failed. . . ."

"Which was just before the Smith abduction," Maggie added.

"I've only been with the Guthries going on two years,"Al explained, when Nat tackled him the next morning. "You'd have to talk to my dad."

"What do you want to know?" A voice behind him enquired. It was Hendrix.

"Mr. Harkness's accident," Nat said, swinging round.

"Why do you want to know about that?"

"Just curious. Did you help find him?"

Hendrix nodded. "His wife called here for help, so we all turned out. It took us several hours."

"What about the horse?"

"Our first thought was for Jerry Harkness," Hendrix answered tersely. "We could see he was in a real bad way so we strapped him onto a board and got him to the hospital."

"And the horse?" Nat persisted.

"His wife found Warrior next day. Broken leg. She shot him."

"Mrs. Harkness?"

"Yep. Not squeamish, that one." He turned to walk away.

"Before you go," Nat called. "Would it be possible to have one of the jeeps gassed up after lunch? And perhaps a spare can of gas," he added.

"Spare can! We're getting low with all your running around. Tanker doesn't come in till Friday." He was still grumbling as he went off.

"Where do you plan on going?" Al asked.

"To Williams Lake early this afternoon and then Horsefly tomorrow morning."

"That road to Horsefly's pretty bad. I'll check the spare."

CHAPTER ELEVEN

It was close to two o'clock when Maggie and Nat rolled into Williams Lake, heading for the town's one and only public phone booth to call George Sawasky.

"Must be telepathy," George said on hearing Nat's voice. "Got a little something on your missing person."

"Guthrie?"

"Yep. He's not the innocent lamb that your client thinks he is. First off, did you know that his first wife's an American citizen?

"Yes. I spoke to her on the phone. She's living in Seattle with her second. But last time I checked, marrying an American was still legal."

"Sure it is, but get this. She and Guthrie were married in 1934, just after his thriving rum running business came to an end when prohibition was repealed."

"Rum-running! Well, I'll be damned!"

"Yep. Worked in his teens for Archie Gillis. You remember, the infamous fella who owned the Malahat schooner?"

"The Malahat! Do I ever. She was one beauty of a boat. I remember being told that she could carry something like 50,000 cases of hard liquor at a time." Nat chuckled. "She must've made some thirsty Americans very happy."

"Our boy Guthrie didn't actually do any of the dirty work himself. He let others haul the booze ashore from the mother ship, but he was one of Gillis's receivers and arranged distribution around the Seattle area."

"So that explains what he was doing over the border," Nat said.

"He was back in British Columbia shortly after his second kid was born. That's when his father died and left him Wild Rose Ranch." There was nearly 30 seconds of crackling sounds on the line before Nat could make out Sawasky say, "One more thing, Nat. My pal on the Seattle force tells me the timing for Guthrie's homecoming had less to do with the old man's death than with the fact that they were closing in on him for some other racket."

"Did he say what?"

"He didn't have all the information at hand. But he's sending me the details by mail. I'll have them in a day or so and get right back to you on it."

"Does Guthrie have a record here?"

"If he does, I haven't been able to find it so far."

"What about Nordstrom and Teasdale?" Nat asked over a fresh outburst of static.

"Nothing on Teasdale but Nordstrom's another kettle of fish. The more I dig into his business, the more nasty whiffs of investment fraud come over. His father was a regular upright citizen, but little Albert . . . let's just say he's not exactly following in his father's footsteps. There's nothing solid I can pin down yet. But I'll keep looking."

"Does Brossard know any of this?"

"We've been in touch by phone and a report's on its way to him." He paused for a moment. "You and Maggie seemed to have

158

really stumbled onto something nasty, Nat. Just watch your backs, will ya?"

"We will. But I think we'll pay another little visit to Brossard while we're still here."

"Go easy. He's a delicate soul. Don't want any more complaints about you from him, do we?"

"I'll be the soul of discretion, George. You know me."

"Yeh, I do! That's the problem."

Brossard wasn't happy to see either of them. "Have you received the latest report on Guthrie?" Nat asked, when they entered his office.

"How do you know about that?"

"Puts a completely different light on his disappearance, doesn't it?" Nat continued, ignoring Brossard's question.

"It does, I have to admit it. But it's all the more reason for you two to keep completely out of this investigation."

"We're still under obligation to Kate Guthrie to find her husband."

"You do understand it's your duty to report anything you find out?"

"I think you'll find, corporal, we've been doing just that."

"I guess you have," he acknowledged grudgingly. "But I'd still like to know where you get your information."

"That's my business — information — but Maggie and I promise to let you in on anything else that's relevant and that we feel you should know."

After they left, Brossard stood up and hauling back his leg, kicked his waste paper basket into the air and clear across the room.

They stayed to have dinner in Williams Lake so it was close to eight before they turned off onto the Wild Rose Lake Road. The sun was still well above the coastal mountains in the west and a cool breeze blew pleasantly over their faces as they drove with the jeep's top down. "Look," Maggie exclaimed. She pointed to a small plane circling the lake. "It's a bit late for someone to be landing." She watched the plane make its final approach. "Look's as if it's coming down farther up the lake."

"Wonder who that is?" Nat said, trying to drive and watch at the same time.

"Same type of plane as Nordstrom's, I think. But it could be anyone." They drove along the lake road in pleasant silence. "Hey!" Maggie said, "you've passed the entrance to the ranch."

"I know," Nat answered with a smile. "Thought we'd take a drive to a nice spot I noticed yesterday. It's close to the Harknesses' place." He drove until they were a few hundred yards from the ranch turn-off then pulled over into a clump of bushes. "This will do." Taking her hand, he led her through the trees until they were at the edge of a sandy beach. He pulled her down to sit next to him.

"I'm sure we're trespassing on the Harknesses' land, but it's so beautiful here, I don't care," Maggie breathed.

"What the Harknesses don't know won't hurt them." He put his arm around her. "We'll sit here, watch the sunset and forget all about the Harknesses, the Guthries and kidnappings."

"What a wonderful idea." She relaxed, leaning against him. Then she suddenly sat bolt upright.

"What's the matter?" he demanded.

"The dock. I can just see the Harkness dock from here."

"It doesn't matter. They can't see us."

"But," she insisted, "that plane we saw circling — it's moored there."

Nat struggled to his feet, walked further down the beach and peered toward the dock. "You're right," he said, when he returned to Maggie. "Or one like it. You think it's Nordstrom's?"

"We're a bit too far away to be sure. Can't see the markings."

"Then we'll get closer. Come on." Taking her hand and using the bushes that edged the lake for protection, he led her toward the dock. They were about fifty yards from it when Nat pulled her back

160

into the bushes. "Well? Is it Nordstrom's?" he asked.

"I still can't be sure."

"All right. You stay here and I'll slip down and see if there is any way of identifying it."

"But suppose someone comes? You'll be caught."

"Don't worry. I'll be as quick as I can. Just stay well back."

"No. I'll come with you."

"There's no sense in both of us taking the risk. Just sit tight." Cautiously leaving the shelter of the bushes, he trotted along the beach and onto the dock, stepped onto the plane's float, then opened the cabin door and climbed into the pilot's seat.

Maggie was the one who heard the far-off boisterous voices first. "Nat," she whispered as loud as she dared. He didn't hear her. "Nat!" she called again, louder this time, waving frantically to get his attention. She had to get nearer. Moving quickly to the edge of the water, she tried one more time "Nat!" This time he looked up and saw her making an urgent gesture for him to come back, but it was too late. The voices were too close. Scuttling back to the shelter of the bushes, she watched helplessly as he made a quick decision and climbed over the seat back and disappeared into the rear of the plane. *Damn! They'll see him!*

Heart hammering, she listened to the voices, much louder now, accompanied by the sounds of feet scrunching along the gravel road that led from the house to the beach. Crouching down, she quickly retreated further back into the bushes. The wait, knowing that it was inevitable that Nat would be caught, was excruciating. Then, as she watched, the door of the plane opened slightly and Nat lowered a long cylindrical object gently into the water. *What the hell's he doing?* Moments later, a second cylinder followed the first, and the door closed. Maggie didn't realize that she'd been holding her breath until it was obvious that the people walking towards the plane were so busy arguing they hadn't seen a thing.

"Please, I'm sorry. I didn't know!" a woman's voice said.

Kate? That's Kate's voice! Maggie's first instinct was to rush out of the cover of the trees and go to her.

"Oh, grow up." *That's Nordstrom!*

If that's Kate and Nordstrom, who are the others? *Maybe Jerry Harkness has been faking and he can walk!* Then another thought came to her. *Perhaps they're the other partners mentioned on that mine contract.* In any case, Kate seemed to be unhappy about being with them, and Maggie just hoped that Nat wouldn't try to pull a rescue act. Nordstrom was a big man and, by the look of things, had plenty of help.

Terrified that they would see her, Maggie retreated yet further into the bushes and hunkered down before the foursome reached the plane. Although she felt safer, it was now difficult for her to see clearly what they were doing. But she heard a man's voice say, "Here, take your bag."

Oh God, they're getting into the plane! Minutes passed before she peeked out again and recognized Nordstrom's bulk as he stepped onto the float to untie the mooring rope from the strut, and then give the plane a push away from the dock before climbing in himself.

They must have seen him by now! But the craft just bobbed up and down for a few moments, the engine started, and the plane taxied to the middle of the lake. Maggie was about to get to her feet when she realized that one of the people had not got aboard the plane and was still standing on the dock, watching the aircraft take to the air. A good few minutes passed before the figure finally turned and walked back toward the ranch.

Maggie remained in the shadows. *What the hell am I going to do now?* For a brief moment she thought about following the figure back to the ranch, but realized that she and Nat would be in considerable danger if Jerry or his ranch hands were somehow mixed up in abducting Guthrie and now Kate.

≈

Nat, covered by the blanket he had found behind the rear seat, lay huddled there awaiting discovery when something landed heavily on his head. "Ooph!" The sound came from him involuntarily and he waited tensely for someone to yank the blanket from him, but the blubbering coming from the person on the other side of the seat and the roar of the engine seemed to have covered the sound.

"Here, I'll shove these boxes over," Nat heard, and another heavy object was dumped on top of him. "And for chrissake, stop crying." The order was delivered in a voice that Nat didn't recognize.

"But . . . why can't I just stay at the ranch?" *Kate! That's Kate's voice. What's she doing here?*

"I'll explain when you've calmed down," the man answered her.

"This baby feels heavy," the pilot shouted, as he eased back on the stick. "It must be you, Kate. We'll have to toss you out."

That's Nordstrom! Nat thought.

"But I only weigh . . . ," Kate began.

"He's only joking," the other man shouted over the increased noise of the engine. "Must be the air cylinders," he yelled.

"Forgot about them. Anyway, it's only eighty miles to Shadow Lake."

The rest of the conversation was lost to Nat as the Otter started to climb. *Eighty miles! How the bloody hell am I going to get out of this thing?* He spent the next forty-five minutes in strained discomfort, a feeling greatly intensified as they started their descent. *This could be it, Nat old son!* He felt and heard the swish as the floats touched the water and then a steady thrum as the plane taxied a short way before the engine was cut.

"Home sweet home," the man in the passenger seat said. "For now, anyway."

"Why did you have to bring me here?" Kate sounded completely miserable.

"You two get out," Nordstrom said. "I'll pass the stuff out to you."

Not my blanket, please!

Nat felt the plane rock as the two climbed out and Nordstrom began heaving their baggage out after them. "Here, take these," Nordstrom said. "We can come back for the rest later."

"Just give me the briefcase," the other man said. "Don't want anything happening to that!"

"My bag," Kate protested. "I'll need that."

No, you don't, Kate! Nat had managed to move the first bag that had landed on his head, but Nordstrom would have to lean over him to get to it. But to his relief, Nordstrom slammed the door, and Nat could hear Kate's complaints growing distant as the men hurried her away from the plane.

He waited a few minutes before peeking out of the side window. The light was fading so rapidly now that he had a job to make out the trio as they neared the end of a long dock then began climbing a flight of wooden steps set into the bank. Above the steps Nat could make out a cabin nestled in the trees. Beyond it, the land rose toward the mountains. He waited until they had disappeared into the trees, hoping they wouldn't return for the rest of the luggage before he had made his escape.

Once on the dock he realized he had two choices: lower himself into the cold lake water and swim ashore further along or take his chances and follow the trio. The unpleasant thought of cold water and wet clothes made the decision easier. As he quickened his pace moving toward the shore, his foot caught on an iron ring set in the rotting planks of the floating dock and he just managed to prevent himself from overbalancing. *Damn!* Rushing, he realized, could be as hazardous to his health as being caught by Nordstrom and his friend. He could have ended up taking a swim in that cold, clear water, after all. *That's all I need!*

Knowing there was nowhere to hide if one of the men came back to the aircraft, he made up for walking slowly along the dock by running up the wooden steps toward the cottage above, and by the time he reached the top, he was panting so hard that he was sure someone would hear his rasping breath. But his luck held, and he sank into the shadows of the surrounding brush, taking great gulps of air before looking for a better hiding place.

"We'll only be a few minutes." The door of the cabin opened, and Nat caught a glimpse of Kate before it was shut again. He held his breath as the two men passed within feet of where he crouched, but he waited until they had descended to the dock before slipping over to peer through the cabin window. Kate, still huddled in her coat, was filling a big enamel coffee percolator with water. He was considering tapping on the window to attract her attention, but realized the two men were returning, with Nordstrom leading the way carrying a box of groceries while the other man lugged Kate's suitcase in one hand and a roll of bedding under his other arm.

"You couldn't have put them in," the other man said. Nat managed to catch a glimpse of the man as he passed close to his hiding place. He was a good head taller and slimmer than Nordstrom, and by the way he had bounded up the stairs carrying the suitcase and bedding, in better physical condition.

"I already told you I didn't," Nordstrom answered testily. "I gave them to Jerry's ranch hand to stow." Nordstrom put the box on the ground while he opened the door.

"They couldn't have walked off by themselves," the other man said angrily. The door closed with a bang behind them.

Nat couldn't help smiling. *No they didn't. Those compressed air cylinders are swimming in the lake near the Harkness dock!*

∼

After watching the plane disappear, Maggie waited to be sure the fourth person had really gone before she started to move stealthily through the bushes to where they had left the jeep. Once the cry of a loon split the silence and she paused momentarily, her heart pounding. When she reached the jeep she climbed in, so tense that even the sharp barking of one of the ranch dogs made

165

her jump. *If I can hear that dog, they can hear me from the ranch when I start the motor.* Twice her hand reached for the ignition key and both times she pulled it back. Then the air was suddenly rent with the high-volumed, gloriously exuberant tones of Glen Miller's *In The Mood.* Someone in the ranch house had turned on the hi-fi and was playing it full blast with the windows wide open, and under cover of the music Maggie started the jeep. Although it was now dusk, she resisted using her headlights as she drove back to the Guthrie's ranch, relying instead on the light of the watery moon which made occasional appearances amid the increasing cloud cover.

Nat's cabin was just as he had left it, unlocked and with the drapes wide open. After closing them, she walked to the table. *Where the heck have they taken you?* She stared down at the map that he had left spread out and ran her finger first south and then north from Wild Rose Lake. *Shadow Lake, of course!* Her finger moved back to Wild Rose Lake then followed the road north. It was a lot more than eighty miles by road, she decided. That just made her more determined to set out as soon as possible. After re-folding the map, she slipped it into her jacket pocket.

At the house, the dogs greeted her ecstatically, and after giving each of them a biscuit from the crock on the counter, she shut them in the kitchen and made her way to the second floor. The four upstairs bedrooms were joined by an open balcony which over-looked the living area. Kate's room was at the opposite end to Maggie's with two other guest rooms and a bathroom in between. Pushing Kate's bedroom door open, she saw clothes closets wide open, drawers spilling undergarments, and discarded items flung across the bed and chair. The look of a hasty departure and the silence of the house suddenly got to her and she ran out of the room and down the stairs to the kitchen where the dogs thudded their tails on the floor in greeting. *What am I going to do? Call the police?* But Nat hadn't been kidnapped. In fact, he was a stowaway, an illegal and unwanted passenger on the plane. Brossard would probably fluff her off, anyway, since he had warned the both of them not to meddle. No, she had to take care of this alone, and as far as she could see, there was absolutely nothing she could do until morning light, when she could at least have an even chance of not getting lost on the unmarked dirt roads. *What I really need right now is a stiff drink. But I'll settle for hot chocolate.* "And you two beauties," she said to the labs as she waited for the kettle to boil, "are going to sleep with me upstairs tonight." But although a comfort, the dogs took up too much room on the bed, and she only managed to doze off now and again as her sleep was fitful with worry about her boss, her friend, her lover.

~

Nat in the meantime had waited until the soft glow of an oil lamp was shining from the kitchen window before he began looking for a place to sleep. He moved stealthily up the hill, past the side of the cabin and around to the back of it where the shape of a shed loomed out of the dark. *Just what I'm looking for!* But the sound of the back door opening and the wavering beam of a flashlight made him freeze in his tracks, then melt into the shadows as the carrier of the light reached the out-building and lifted the wooden peg out of the hasp on the door. Moments later Nat scuttled further back into the trees as the earsplitting noise of a generator filled the air. *Bloody hell! That was a bit too close for comfort.*

Waiting a good five minutes after the man emerged again from the shed and re-entered the house, Nat slipped over to the hut and, quietly removing the peg, slipped inside, immediately colliding with a pile of small logs that had been stacked under the window. The noise as the top row tumbled down onto the earth floor made him freeze again. But nobody came rushing out to confront him. It was at that moment that a watery moon, peeping through the overcast sky, shed its dim light through the window and onto the contents of the cluttered construction. Knowing the moonlight would go as quickly as it had come, he quickly re-stacked the wood and then stumbled over to where a small, wooden, square-ended dinghy was leaning against the back wall and slipped in behind it. As he leaned back, his thoughts went to Maggie, and he wondered what she'd done after seeing him disappear into the Otter. There was no way for her to know where the plane had flown to. Would she go to Brossard? *Somehow, I don't think so.* Then, even though the generator was extremely noisy, he found himself nodding off.

The sound of the door being opened and the beam of the flashlight bouncing on the walls of the shed brought him to. Holding his breath and hoping that no part of his body was visible, he listened as the generator was turned off and the man departed. Crawling out of his hiding place, he stretched his cramped legs and then scuttled back to spend the long, uncomfortable night dozing and worrying about Maggie.

CHAPTER TWELVE

It was the sound of heavy rain on the shed roof just before dawn that awakened Nat. *Where the hell am I?* Then the sight of the dinghy extending over him brought it all back in a rush. He squinted at his watch in the faint light. *Nearly four thirty.* Struggling to his knees, he crawled out from behind the boat. *Let's hope they're all late sleepers and don't want to start up that blasted generator again.* "I'm meant for comfort," he muttered, as he reached out to the generator to assist him onto his feet. Once upright, he stretched his sore and aching limbs. "And I need my morning coffee!" Luckily for Nat, the door hadn't been re-fastened by the unknown man the night before, and he was able to push it open a crack. He was met by a curtain of rain. Confident that he was the only early riser, he turned up his jacket collar and made a dash for the protection of the overhanging eaves on the blind side of the cottage, then moved around the corner and peeked through the kitchen window. There was no sign of anyone up yet.

Although the cottage had been built on a flat shelf overlooking the lake, the tree-covered land behind it sloped sharply upward. Wishing he had Chandler's map with him, Nat tried to remember the Shadow Lake Mine area on it. *I'm sure it showed a road on the north side of the lake with a side road leading to the mine. There must be other cottages along the lake, maybe if I just show up I can catch a lift back to civilization. Still, have to come up with some reasonable explanation for being here.* In any case there was no way he was going to risk his neck by hiding in the plane for a return journey.

He retraced his steps to his final hiding spot of the night before and found that the gravel path continued up the hill. Padding quietly up the narrow path, he cursed the persistent rain that trickled down from his bare head and into his upturned collar each time he had to push his way through the overhanging branches of dripping firs and cedars. Out of breath, he reached the top of the property to find the path had widened into a driveway, and just as he had hoped, straight ahead was a gravel road. *So this cottage is the end of the road.* To his left was a ramshackle garage, looking as if the next gust of wind might topple it. When he attempted to open one of the double doors, it scraped on the earth floor, but inside he found a red flatbed truck with makeshift plywood sides. Walking around the vehicle, he gave each tire a kick. Two of them needed air, but apart from that, the truck looked serviceable enough. Climbing into the cab, he saw the key was still in the ignition and there were two rifles fastened behind the driver's seat. "Well, well! How about that?" he said out loud. "I wonder if I've found Maggie's sniper?" The distant hum of the generator starting up made him pause. *Nat old son, you got out of there just in time. Now do I get this thing going and get out of here or stick around and see what that trio's up to?* He decided on the latter. Using the trees as cover, he was making his way back toward the cabin when he heard voices. Two men were now standing by the shed.

"You couldn't have shut the door last night," Nordstrom said.

"I did, I tell you," the other man answered. "I remember distinctly. Anyhow, you're getting paranoid. Who would break in here?"

"You never know," Nordstrom said edgily.

"Here? Come off it."

"Fine for you to say. But too many things have gone wrong lately," Nordstrom answered. "Is the truck ready to go?"

"I think we've got slow leaks in a couple of the tires. Wish you hadn't forgotten those air tanks. Now we'll have to use that damn hand pump."

"I didn't forget them," Nordstrom snarled. "Anyhow, I wanted them to make a dive to repair the dock floats, not fill flat tires. The point is, will the damned truck get us to the mine?"

"Oh, sure. Anyhow, we'll take the pump with us. And we've got the spare."

The mine! I wonder if that's where they've got Guthrie?

The rain had penetrated right through his jacket and he had begun to shiver violently with the cold when around him wafted the delicious smell of frying bacon. What with the dampness seeping into his bones, his stomach craving hot food and that wonderful first cup of morning coffee, he began to feel it might be worth his while to knock on the door and ask for a handout. He couldn't help smiling when he pictured the look on their faces if he did just that. Instead he retreated further up the path, melting into the brush, willing away his hunger before the smell of the food made him do something rash.

A half hour passed before the door opened again, and he heard Nordstrom call out, "Hurry up, Kate. Don't take all day." Minutes later the trio emerged from the cottage, Nordstrom leading, Kate in the middle and the other man bringing up the rear.

"Why do I have to come?" Kate said.

"You said you wanted to see the mine," Nordstrom answered. "Now's your chance."

"But, I . . . "

"Stop whining, Kate, and get a move on." The man in the rear gave her a little push up the path then suddenly came to a standstill. "You two carry on," he said suddenly. "I've left the flashlight on the table."

Nordstrom went on up the path, but Kate stopped and turned to watch the man go back to the cottage before slowly continuing after Nordstrom. Taking a chance, Nat moved partially out from behind a large cedar. "Kate," he whispered, as she drew level. "Kate." But her startled expression made him quickly put his finger to his lips. "Sh-h-h."

"Wha. . . ."

"You say something, Kate?" Nordstrom turned to look back at her.

"No . . . a . . . a branch hit me."

Nat heard the sound of the cottage door banging shut and slipped back behind the tree. "What's going on?" The other man had caught up with Kate. "Why did you stop?"

"I walked into a branch."

"Is that all? Move it, then, we can't take all day."

There was something ominous about the studied calmness of the two men that deeply disturbed Nat. And then it hit him. Oh my God, what if they've tricked her into going to the mine so they can kill her? He stepped impulsively out onto the path, then just as quickly retreated. *The guns!* He slipped well back into the bushes. *They could blow me away in a second!* Feeling helpless, Nat watched them through the trees as they disappeared into the garage. It was at least twenty minutes before he heard the cough of the truck's engine and knew that they were finally on their way. *Dry clothes and something to eat. Then I can decide what to do.*

To his relief, the cottage door was unlocked. He had no problem finding a sweater and a rain slicker, but locating a pair of pants that fit turned out to be impossible. One pair of jeans, which he took to be Nordstrom's, were huge while the only other pair in the place wouldn't meet around his middle. He'd have to settle for a dry top and damp bottom. Finding food was easier. Quickly he made two sandwiches of thick slices of bread and cheese, one to eat then and one to take with him, and drank a mug of the tepid coffee left in the big enamel percolator.

Luck was with him when he searched the desk in the kitchen. There were several maps, one very similar to Chandler's, showing the lake, the roads and the track that led up to the Shadow Lake Mine. The lake's about fifteen miles long, Nat thought as he measured it by eye against the scale at the bottom of the chart. And the north road that edges it stops after about ten. That X at the end of the road must be this cottage. He walked to the window overlooking the lake where he could see a watery sun trying to break through the clouds. *Yes, this cottage is definitely on the north side.* He went back to the map. He could hike back to civilization to get help, but who knows how much time that would take him, and Kate could be dead by then. No, he would have to follow them up to the mine on foot. He squinted at the map. *The turn-off to the mine looks to be about five miles back along the road, and it's next to a stream! It should be easy to find, and I can be there in an hour if I walk fast.*

Minutes later, his sandwiches in one of the big patch pockets of the slicker and the map in the other, he stepped outside. But before starting up the path, he quickly stowed his wet jacket and shirt behind the boat in the shed.

～

Maggie had slept very poorly, only drifting into deep sleep toward dawn, and when she awoke it was already seven thirty. The morning was dull and grey and threatening rain at any moment, and she was no nearer to a serious plan for how to find Nat or Kate. She showered, packed her bag, then went downstairs to feed the two dogs and let them out in the yard before making herself a quick breakfast. It was not quite eight o'clock when she arrived at the stables.

Al was mucking out and looked up in surprise. "Thought you were leaving early."

"Change of plans. Is your father around?"

"Probably still at the barn."

"Thanks." She met Hendrix coming out of his cabin.

"Thought you'd be gone by now," he said.

"Mr. Southby stayed overnight in Williams Lake," she improvised. "He's meeting with Brossard this morning. I'm to meet him later. Have you any idea where Kate's gone?"

"Riding."

"But. . . ." she stopped herself in time.

"Yup. Went out real early."

"But Ginny's still in her stall. I saw her."

Hendrix shook his head. "You must've been mistaken." He tipped his hat and started to walk toward the stables, then stopped and turned back to her. "I thought you said you and your boss were going to Horsefly?"

"Changed our minds. I'm picking him up in Williams Lake and then we're driving down to Hundred Mile House to follow up a lead."

"Hundred Mile House?" Hendrix sounded surprised.

"I wanted to tell Kate that we'd need the jeep for a couple of days."

Hendrix slowly stroked his chin. "Can't see that'll be a problem. I'll tell her when she gets back."

"Thanks." She felt his eyes on her as she walked down the gentle slope to where the cabin complex was partly hidden in the stunted pines. Once inside Nat's cabin, she packed his suitcase and toilet gear, then walked back up the slope to stow them in the jeep. A piece of paper fluttered in the breeze under the windshield wiper:

**GET OUT OR DEATH CAN
BE ARRANGED FOR YOU TOO**

She felt herself go cold as she re-read the message. *How did it get here? And when?* Crushing the note in her hand, she climbed into the vehicle and drove to the front of the house. *Was it meant for me? Does that "you too" mean they've killed Nat and they're letting me know?* But she had watched them leave in the plane, and she knew they would have had to wait until daylight to take to the air again, and she hadn't heard a plane come in this morning. Maybe they sent a message back by radio phone to whoever it was on the dock. She slipped out of the jeep, her thoughts going back to the deaths of Chandler and Sarazine. Maybe the "you too" referred to them and not Nat. *What am I going to do?*

Purposefully, she marched into the house. Kate had left a picnic hamper out for Maggie and Nat to take on their proposed trip to the lake. All Maggie needed to add was food. Rummaging in the fridge and pantry shelves, she soon had enough snacking food to keep herself alive for a couple of days, then filled a thermos with the left-over breakfast coffee. Next she found blankets and an extra flashlight. Making room for the picnic basket and her other supplies, she had to move a coil of rope from the back of the jeep. About to throw it on the ground, she stopped. "One never knows," she muttered and put it back.

Maggie had one last thing to do before leaving. She knew that all the party lines would jangle when she cranked the phone, but she had to risk it.

"Number please." Maggie gave her office number and waited to be connected.

"Thank goodness you are calling," Henny said, when she recognized Maggie's voice. "Your Mr. Spencer, he called in two times."

"What did he want?" Maggie yelled over the sudden crackling noise on the line.

"He says his mother is coming from hospital on Monday," Henny yelled back.

"Hospital! Oh, yes. Harry did say something about a hospital. What's wrong with the old. . . ." She caught herself in time.

"Mr. Nat didn't tell you? She had . . . what did he call it . . . ? Onions?"

"Onions? Wait a moment, this line is terrible. I'm sure you said onions."

"*Ja.* That's right. On her feet."

Then in spite of all her worries, Maggie started to laugh. "You mean bunions, Henny."

"*Ja, ja,* that's what I say. He wants you to look after the old lady. He has real work to do, he says, and he ask for your phone number."

"You didn't give it to him, did you, Henny?"

"No. Mr. Nat said not to, so I don't."

"Good." She paused, phrasing in her mind what she wanted to say. "Henny, listen carefully. I want you to do something important. If I don't call you by midday tomorrow, you must telephone Mr. Southby's friend, Sergeant Sawasky."

"*Ja.* I call Sergeant Sawasky. But tomorrow is Saturday."

"Oh hell! You're right. But you'll find his home phone number on Nat's desk. Now, listen Henny," she carried on, speaking slowly. "I want you to tell him Mr. Southby's going fishing for the missing link at Cloudy Lake. And then say ten twelve. Have you got that?"

"Mr. Nat's got time to go fishing?"

"Just tell him Mr. Southby has gone fishing to find the missing link," Maggie repeated.

"Link? He is golfing too?"

"Listen to what I'm saying, Henny."

"I am listening. I call his friend now. I think boss is in trouble, *ja?*

"No, Henny. I don't want you to call him till tomorrow, please."

"Okay. Not until tomorrow and I say he is gone fishing and golfing and then ten, eleven, twelve. He knows what that mean?"

"Not golfing!" Maggie shouted. "Oh, blast. Listen to me, Henny. Just tell Sawasky that Nat's gone fishing on the lake and say ten twelve."

"*Ja.* Okay."

176

Maggie replaced the receiver. *She's going to get it all wrong!* But she gathered up her things, gave the dogs a last pat — hoping that Hendrix or Al would remember to feed them — and climbed into the jeep. At the open gates to the ranch, she stopped to look across to the Guthrie's dock where several small boats bobbed in the grey, choppy water. *It was so pretty yesterday in the sunshine. But now it looks . . . sinister.* The jeep bumped over the cattle guard, and Maggie swung the wheel to the right to follow the lakeside road to the Harkness ranch. She stopped at a point where she could see their dock. The plane hadn't returned. She put the jeep in gear again and drove on to the ranch house.

"Well, hello," Jerry Harkness said, when he opened the door. "Come in." He wheeled himself backwards. "What can I do for you?"

"We heard a plane last evening and assumed that it landed at your dock. We couldn't help wondering if it was Nordstrom. Nat wanted to ask him something if he happened to be about."

"Vivienne said he called in for a short visit before heading north."

"You didn't see him yourself?"

"I play poker on Thursday nights. Over at Bill Fowler's place." He smiled at the look on Maggie's face. "I can still drive, you know. Hand controls."

Maggie blushed. "Of course. I'm sorry. Is Vivienne around?"

"You didn't see her? She said she was going over to see Kate this morning."

"I haven't seen either of them. What time did she leave here?"

"Quite early. Around six-thirty, I think. I'm sure she said she was calling in to see Kate before going into Williams Lake."

Maggie's thoughts went back to the threatening note. Was Vivienne the one who'd left it? And had she also taken the pouch of money from her room? She returned her attention to Jerry. "Will you say goodbye to her for me?"

"You're leaving?"

177

"Picking my boss up in Williams Lake before heading down to Hundred Mile House for a couple of days." She turned toward the door, then stopped. "Where did you say Nordstrom had gone?"

"Shadow Lake. That's where the mine was. He built a cottage up there that he uses for fishing." He wheeled his chair to the front door and opened it for her. "Hard to get to by road," he said, "but a cinch if you fly in."

"You've been there?"

"Just once. About ten years ago when they were trying to talk me into investing in their mine. Beautiful country."

"I bet it is," she said under her breath as she climbed back into the jeep. "Well, I don't have a plane, so the road it's got to be."

Henny sat looking into space after Maggie's worrying phone call and thought about her boss, Mr. Nat, being in danger. What if Sawasky was going away for the weekend? Then she couldn't get the message to him until Monday and by then it might be too late. She would never forgive herself if anything happened to her boss. She knew that it was up to her to take matters into her own hands. Pulling the Rolodex toward her, she found Sawasky's phone number at the police station and dialled.

"Vancouver city police," the woman's crisp voice answered.

"I speak to Sergeant Sawasky, *ja*?"

"Who's calling?"

"You tell him, Mr. Southby's Henny."

"And what is the nature of your call?"

"What you mean, nature? I have important things to tell him," Henny answered impatiently. "You get sergeant on phone. Please," she added, remembering Maggie's instructions to always be polite when using the phone.

"I'll see if he's in."

"Why do you ask all those questions if you don't know he's in?" She heard a shuddering sigh on the other end.

"Give me your name and number," the icy voice replied. "I'll ascertain if he's available."

"I told you — Henny. Mr. Southby is my boss. Tell him it is very, very much an emergency." The phone went dead and she had to wait another agonizing five minutes before the sergeant phoned back to her.

"What's up, Henny?" George Sawasky asked.

"It's Mr. Nat. He's gone fishing and golfing and Mrs. Maggie said to tell you that it was twelve something and I am very worried because. . . ."

"Whoa! Whoa! Henny. Let's start at the beginning."

"Mrs. Maggie is upset and she is telling me that Mr. Nat has gone fishing at Cloudy Lake. Then she said, tell you ten, eleven something."

"Was it ten twelve?"

"Ja. That's right. Ten twelve. She said you know what it means."

"Yes."

"She says for me to call you tomorrow. But I am very worried so I call today."

"What else did she tell you?"

"Wait, I tell you." She read from her notes. "Tell sergeant Mr. Nat is gone fishing at Cloudy Lake. He is finding link that is gone missing. You understand, ja?"

He was quiet for a moment. "Missing link at Cloudy Lake you said."

"Ja. That is what I say."

Then it came to him. Shadow Lake and the missing link. Must be something to do with Guthrie's disappearance. Or perhaps she meant something to do with Smith's abduction. "How long ago did she call, Henny?"

"Ten minutes. I look at the clock when the phone rings."

"Okay, Henny. I'll try to reach her before she goes." But although he got through to the ranch house in record time, there was no answer. His call to Corporal Brossard took longer and the reception was not very friendly.

"I've enough problems with your two interfering friends without the Vancouver police getting involved," was his answer.

"Hey! Wait a minute, pal. Aren't you forgetting something?"

"What's that?"

"Mrs. Spencer did find that money."

"Which promptly disappeared," Brossard interrupted.

"Then there was Smith's letter," Sawasky reminded him. "And that letter, by the way," he added sharply, "can bring me in on this investigation officially."

"How do you make that out?"

"I was on the Smith abduction case when it went down. It will take five minutes to get my boss to assign me back onto it."

"But finding that letter doesn't prove a thing," Brossard insisted.

"Sure, but it's the first lead we've had in nine years." Brossard made no response and Sawasky added, "By the way, have you managed to find the missing Guthrie?"

"We're working on it."

"Well, it looks to me as if the interfering couple have stumbled onto part of that mystery too."

"What do you mean?"

"Maggie's message to me mentioned a missing link. It can only mean she's onto something with regard to Guthrie or the Smith case."

"I can't go rushing off to this Shadow Lake just on your say-so. What do you think this is?"

"But they may be in danger!"

"Yeah, that's right, and they may be shacking up in some cabin for all you know. They're a pair of goddamned meddlers," Brossard muttered, then gave an exaggerated sigh. "Look, the best I can do is take a run over to the ranch later this afternoon and see what Hendrix knows."

"That may be too late. You should go to Shadow Lake now."

"Hey, this isn't your big city, you know, Sawasky. We don't have planes just waiting around at our pleasure."

"Corporal, please . . . "

"No. Keep your nose out of this, Sawasky. Stay out of it or I'll have to call my superior. Now, if you'll excuse me, I've serious work to do."

Sawasky placed the phone back in its cradle in frustration. "What the hell do I do now?" He called Henny back. "Have you got the Guthrie file handy?" he asked her.

"Ja. Right here."

"Read me the names of everyone Nat contacted."

"Wait." There was a pause while she flipped pages. "Ray Teasdale, Albert Nordstrom. And it say here, James Guthrie is Mr. Douglas Guthrie's son and he works for Nordstrom. And he made a call to Mrs. Debra Wright — that was once Mr. Guthrie's wife. She lives in Seattle. And his mother who is old and is in nursing home—"

"Nordstrom's address," Sawasky broke in impatiently. "Give me that."

Twenty minutes later, he was looking for a parking spot close to Nordstrom's business. It took a while before he found one a couple of blocks away, then he had to run back through the crowds of Friday shoppers to the Capitol Furniture store and Nordstrom's offices. The elevator wasn't working and he was forced to take the stairs. Panting with the added exertion of the climb he came face to face with a startled Agnes Agnew.

"Can I help you, sir?"

"Sergeant Sawasky, Vancouver Police" he said, flashing his badge. "I need to see Mr. Nordstrom urgently."

"That's not possible. He left yesterday. Gone up to his summer place for a few days."

"Do you know where his summer place is located, miss?"

"A place called Shadow Lake in the Cariboo. Do you know it?"

181

Shadow Lake. That clinches it. "I'd like to speak to Guthrie's son, James. He works here, doesn't he?"

"Yes. But . . . but . . I don't know where he's gone." Miss Agnew was obviously thoroughly bewildered.

"Great! That's all I need." He was about to leave when he realized that the woman was very upset. "Was there something else you wanted to tell me, Miss . . . uh . . . ?"

"Agnew. It really isn't any of my business . . . but. . . ."

"It doesn't have something to do with Mr. Guthrie by any chance, does it?"

She nodded. "It was yesterday morning. Jamie and Mr. Nordstrom were having . . . uh . . . words."

"Do you mean arguing?"

She nodded again miserably. "Shouting. I couldn't help overhearing."

"What did they say?" Sawasky pressed her.

"It was about money and something about Jamie's father."

"And then what happened?"

"I heard Mr. Nordstrom say he was going to Shadow Lake and Jamie should go with him."

"And did he?"

"I don't know. Jamie came storming out of Mr. Nordstrom's office and he went down the passage to his own," she said, pointing. "Later I heard him running down the stairs."

"What did Mr. Nordstrom do after the argument?"

"He asked me to get Mr. Teasdale on the line."

Sawasky checked the list of names he had jotted down in his notebook. "He's a friend of Nordstrom's?"

"Oh yes. They've known each other for years."

"I don't suppose you overheard any of his conversation?"

Agnes was shocked. "No, sir! I never listen in on people's conversations!"

"Just a thought." Sawasky shrugged. "Did Mr. Nordstrom fly his plane up?"

"Yes. The road to the lake is terrible, apparently, but it sounds like such a pretty place, doesn't it?" she added wistfully.

"Does he have a telephone there?"

"No. He uses the radio-phone on the plane when he wants to contact me."

"Thank you, Miss Agnew. You've been a great help."

"Have I? I just wish I knew where Jamie was."

So do I! So do I!

Back in his car Sawasky thought the situation over: Nat and Maggie were in danger, Brossard was up in Williams Lake and wouldn't get off his butt, and here he was sitting in his car at least 250 miles away as the crow flies — and at least double that by road. Although he'd threatened Brossard about going up there officially, he knew it would be useless to ask his boss. Farthing would never authorize it, especially if it concerned Southby. For one thing, the scene of the action was way out of his jurisdiction. As well, Farthing hated Nat's guts with a passion. The hell with it! He'd do it on his own time! He put the car into gear and pulled away from the curb. He would go back to the office and see if the package from the Seattle police had arrived, book time off, pack a bag and head for the Cariboo. All he hoped was that his old, rusty-but-trusty Ford would make the trip in one piece.

∾

"How's old Harry doing?" Bella Goodman's skirt was hiked up over her ample thighs as she perched on the corner of Doreen Fitch-Smythe's desk. She nodded toward Harry's closed door.

"Gone to pieces since his wife left him," Harry's secretary answered, keeping her voice low.

"I take it she's really left him for good?"

"He won't admit it," Doreen said with a laugh. "I think he had her trained so well that he didn't even know where his clean clothes came from. But he's certainly found out," she added, with a smirk.

"I saw him coming out of that Chinese laundry down the street yesterday with a huge pile."

"He's such a stuffed shirt anyway. How you've managed to work for him all these years is beyond me." Bella slipped down from the desk. "I'd better go before my boss starts yelling."

Doreen Fitch-Smythe watched her friend walk away. Yes, Harry Spencer was certainly a stuffed shirt, but Doreen had been taking extra care with her clothes and make-up since his wife left him. A lawyer, after all, was a pretty good meal ticket.

The object of their conversation was at that moment staring into space in his office and feeling very sorry for himself indeed. The buzz from the intercom brought him back to the present with a start.

"Mrs. Spencer on the line, sir." His heart leapt as he grabbed the instrument.

"Margaret?"

"Don't be a damn fool, Harry. It's your mother."

"Oh," he said. "What can I do for you, Mother?"

"I'm making sure you don't forget to come and get me on Monday. I've had enough of this frightful hospital!"

"How do you feel?"

"Damn fool question. I'm in pain. That's how I feel."

"Would it be possible for you to stay there a few more days? You see, I haven't found anyone to look after you yet."

"Where's that wife of yours? Still gallivanting all over the country, I suppose? It's high time you put your foot down, son."

"I'm doing my level best to locate her, mother, and I don't need you to tell—"

"Don't you talk to your mother like that, young man. I'm checking out of this place on Monday, and don't forget the wheelchair!"

"But . . ." The line had gone dead. *What am I going to do? That stupid woman in Southby's office insists she doesn't know where Margaret is.* He had tried to get Midge to come and look after her grandmother but she had refused point blank. And it was no good asking Barbara. The new baby took up all her time. *How selfish young people are these days!* He reached for the intercom. "Would you look up a reputable home nursing agency for me, Miss Fitch-Smythe?" he asked.

"No word from your wife, then?"

"She's away on . . . uh . . . business," he replied curtly. "She'll be back soon enough." He didn't care to see his personal affairs talked about among the office staff. "And ask Information for a telephone number for the Wild Rose Guest Ranch. It's somewhere near Williams Lake."

Harry, drumming his fingers impatiently on his desk, waited for the call to the ranch to be connected.

"Wild Rose Ranch," a man's voice answered.

"I would like to speak to Mrs. Spencer."

"Spencer? Oh, you mean Maggie."

"Mrs. Margaret Spencer," Harry corrected.

"She's gone."

"What do you mean — gone?"

"She and her partner went chasing off to Hundred Mile this morning."

"Southby! He's there too?

"Yep!"

"Tell her to call me immediately when she gets back."

"Who shall I say to call?"

"Her husband, of course." Harry slammed the receiver down. What a mess! He looked at his watch — ten o'clock. *If I leave now I could be in Hundred Mile House by early evening. Yes, that's what I'll do. I'll go and get her. I'll make her see that her place is at home with me and looking after Mother.* Having made his decision, he leapt from his chair and wrenched open the connecting door. "Miss Fitch-Smythe?"

"Yes, Mr. Spencer," Doreen Fitch-Smythe said sweetly.

"Hold all calls. I'm leaving for the rest of the day."

185

CHAPTER THIRTEEN

When Nat reached the road above the cottage, he stood for a moment consulting the map to get his bearings. The tread marks from the truck showed that it had turned left, and though worried that he might meet it on its return journey, he started in that direction. The rain had let up and a watery sun was now trying to get through the scudding clouds; he made good progress for the first half hour as the tracks were easy to see and the road fairly straight. But the going got tough as the road meandered up and down, and because the recent rain had filled all the ruts with water, they oozed thick black mud. His new hiking boots, bought especially for this trip to the Cariboo, rubbed his heels sore but he struggled on, slipping and cursing until he came to a small high bridge spanning a stream. Sliding down the bank, he sat on a slab of stone under the bridge and removed his boots. Then rolling up his pant legs, he lowered his feet into the stream and sighed in ecstasy as the cold water lapped at his blistered heels. With the map spread out on his knees, he made a rough estimate of his location. *Another four miles should do it.* But the thought of walking those four miles made him cringe. While he was trying to pluck up the courage to put his boots on and resume his trek, he heard a truck approaching and saw a flash of red as it drove overhead on its way back toward the cottage. From where he sat, it was impossible to tell how many people were in it. Had they already disposed of Kate up at the mine? Would he find Guthrie's body there too? I should have tackled them back at the cottage, he thought. *Why the hell didn't I take one of their guns from the truck when I had the chance?* But even then the odds of them getting him before he got them would have been far too uneven. It was now noon and two hours had gone by since he'd seen the three of them leave the cottage. *At least my sore feet saved me from being seen.* Packing his socks with grass he determinedly pulled on his boots and scrambled back to the road.

∼

For Maggie the driving was slow and hazardous because the gentle rain which had begun as she left the Harkness ranch soon turned into a heavy rainstorm, complete with hailstones. It seemed to her that she hit every pothole that riddled the road and she had to stop frequently in order to wipe the splattered mud from the windshield. The rain was just easing slightly when the engine started to misfire and falter. *Keep going, damn you!* To her relief it smoothed up again, but she was just congratulating herself on its recovery when the motor misfired again. Nothing had passed her in either direction for at least half an hour, and she was terrified that the vehicle would break down completely and leave her stranded on the lonely road. She coaxed the jeep along, successfully willing it to make it to the small town of Horsefly where she pulled into the one and only gas station in a state of nervous exhaustion. Then the rain picked up once more. It was well past noon by this time, and the corrugated tin-roofed building beside the gas pumps seemed deserted. But the faded sign over the small office at least bore a name: Ed Hinkle, Mechanic. *Thank goodness!* It was at precisely this moment that the engine gave one more shudder and died.

She sat listening to the rain drumming on the jeep's roof for several minutes, wondering what to do next, when suddenly a man in greasy overalls appeared at the garage entrance. Maggie rolled down her window. "Didn't hear yer drive up," he said through the curtain of rainwater which cascaded off the bit of sloping roof over the entrance. As he spoke, he lovingly polished a piece of car's innards on an oily rag. "What can I do for yer, fill'er up?"

"The darn thing's died on me," she answered, "and I do need gas."

"Whatcher doing in these parts?" he asked, carefully laying down the car part before stepping out into the rain to lift the hood. "Yer can't be passing through 'cause there ain't nowhere to pass through to." He laughed at his own joke.

"Just touring," she answered. "Can you fix it?"

"Mm-m-m. I'll have to push it into the garage and have a look-see."

"Do you think it will take long?"

He pushed his cap back further on his head. "Can't tell. Come back after yer've et."

"Et? Oh, okay," she said, when she realized what he meant. "Where's the best place?"

"Buckskin Annie's, up the road a piece," he said pointing. "Where yer headin'?"

"Shadow Lake."

"Shadow Lake?" he repeated, shaking his head and letting the hood clang down. "That road's a corker when it's rainin'. Turn yer insides out."

Buckskin Annie's was different from any eating place that she'd ever seen. As she opened the heavy wooden door, she reeled back from the smoke, noise and the heavy smell of cooking oil. While she hesitated in the doorway, a huge woman wearing a fringed buckskin vest bounded up to her. "Jest you?" she asked. Maggie gave a slight nod. "Over here, then." She led the way to one of the three long tables in the room. Four men, already seated at the table, looked up at her as one, then resumed shovelling food into their mouths.

"How are yer?" the man next to her asked, giving her a gappy-toothed grin. She smiled back weakly before looking down at the stained menu. "Pan-fried steak's good," he continued, taking a huge bite out of a wedge of bread. "So's Annie's chicken pie."

Maggie chose the chicken pie which arrived piping hot, smothered in gravy with peas and mashed potatoes on the side. As she broke the flaky pastry with her fork, she couldn't help thinking of Nat and wondering what he was doing for food. *If only you could be here, Nat.* He really enjoyed a well-cooked meal!

"Goin' far?" Gappy-Tooth asked, reaching for his mug of coffee.

"Shadow Lake," she answered.

"Wouldn't try it today," her new friend went on.

"Why not? It's stopped raining."

"That road's a killer after it's been raining." He sucked on a toothpick. "Only last week Klaus, him that works for the Lazy Q, got caught in a mud slide." He paused dramatically. "Took six men to haul him out."

"Out of the mud?" Maggie asked horrified.

"The lake," he answered. "His truck slid in the lake. Ain't that right, Josh?" he said, turning to one of his companions. Josh nodded sombrely and kept on chewing.

"Was he dead?" Maggie couldn't help asking.

Gappy-Tooth laughed. "Dead? Take more'n that to kill old Klaus. Jest wet and yellin' like a bull moose. Don't yer want yer cake? Goes with the dinner."

Maggie, absolutely stuffed with the chicken pie, shook her head. "Mind if I do?" Before she could answer, her dinner partner had reached over and her cake had gone the way of his own dessert. Wiping his mouth on the back of his sleeve, he leaned back and gave a loud and satisfied belch. "Best fer yer to let it dry up a bit. Wouldn't want ter fish yer out of the lake." He was still laughing as Maggie paid her bill and left the restaurant to retrace her steps to Ed Hinkle's garage.

The garage doors were open and the jeep with its hood up was inside. But there was no sign of the mechanic. After walking around the vehicle and then looking underneath, just in case the missing man was under there tinkering, she returned outside and pushed open the door to the small office.

"Yer looking for me?" Holding a huge sandwich in his oily hand, Hinkle was leaning back in a scarred, wooden swivel chair behind the counter.

"Have you found out what's wrong?" she asked.

"Fuel pump." He took another bite of his sandwich and washed it down with a long swig from a thermos. Then cramming the last of his lunch into his mouth, he stood up and ambled out the door. Maggie, at a complete loss when it came to mechanical things, followed meekly.

"Needs a new one," Hinkle proclaimed, his head disappearing under the jeep's hood.

"And you have one in stock?"

"Nope. Phoned Williams Lake. They're sending one up on the bus this afternoon." There was a pinging sound from outside as someone drove over the alarm wire. Hinkle's head re-emerged from the engine, he wiped his hands on a rag and went out to greet his customer.

Maggie watched while he served gas, his free hand gesturing as he made some point or other in the animated conversation. Even after the nozzle had been replaced in the pump and Hinkle had received payment, neither seemed to be in any great hurry. She walked outside and coughed. "What time will the bus get here?"

"Four. Maybe four-thirty," Hinkle said. "She needs a new fuel pump," he said, turning back to his customer. "Going up ter Shadow Lake."

The man shook his head. "Road's bad."

"Is there someplace I can rent a car?" she asked.

"No-o-o," Hinkle said. "Nothing like that this side of Prince George."

The afternoon dragged on, the alarm bell pinging from time to time, and like clockwork, each new customer was told that Maggie was off to Shadow Lake. Each one commented on the state of the road.

∼

It seemed to Nat that he'd walked ten miles instead of four, but he eventually came to another bridge and just beyond it the turn-off marked on the map. He paused to watch the foamy water cascade down under the bridge. The road beside it swung north along the edge of the stream. "This must be it," he muttered. "There's tracks going up, anyway." But although the road surface had dried fast and the walking became easier, it was late afternoon by the time he staggered up to the mine entrance.

Everywhere he looked was devastation. There were piles of rubble and large slabs of stone around the entrance. Rusty machinery, buckled tram lines, wooden carts and other unidentifiable bits and pieces of equipment lay among the huge boulders, so that the place looked like a war zone. He stumbled over the rubble at the entrance and made his way inside. *Damn! Why didn't I look for a flashlight at the cottage?* Although it looked as if a lot of the rubble had been hauled out of the mine — probably when they had been searching for Fenwick's body — there were still mounds of rock partially filling the passageway.

"Guthrie!" he shouted. "Kate! Can you hear me?" But the only sound was the steady drip, drip, drip of water somewhere in the darkness. Taking a few more steps he called again. "Kate! Guthrie!" Again — silence. There was absolutely no way to explore the mine without a flashlight. Outside again, Nat tottered down to the stream and using his hands as a cup, drank the mineral-coloured water. He then leaned back against one of the boulders, took off his boots and socks, and reached for the sandwich he had made for himself at the cottage.

The food revived him somewhat, but though the packed grass had helped cushion his feet, the blisters on both of his heels had broken. As he pulled on his socks again, he thought longingly of the box of bandaids in his medicine cupboard at home. *I bet Maggie has some in that handbag of hers. It weighs a ton.* He groaned as he got to his feet. *There's no way I can walk out of here today.* He climbed the hill again and sat down just inside the entrance. *At least this will give me some shelter if it rains again. And I can take these bloody boots off!*

～

It was after five that afternoon before the bus arrived in Horsefly with the new fuel pump for Maggie's jeep and almost dark before she finally slipped behind the wheel of the repaired vehicle. Looking toward a particularly large mountain north of Horsefly she could see grey, heavy clouds shrouding the top and clinging to the trees that grew thickly up its side. Her instinct was to go looking for Nat immediately, but common sense told her to wait until the morning when she could at least see where she was going. "Is there a hotel or something nearby?" she asked Hinkle before switching on the ignition.

"If yer wants yer comfort, then it's the Cariboo Inn. Jest bin built. Cost yer a mite, though."

"How do I find it?"

"Over that bridge across the way and follow the signs. Yer can't miss it."

She found the Cariboo Inn nestled among firs, alders and aspens on the edge of Horsefly Lake and took a room for the night. *Thirty dollars! Hinkle was right!* After unpacking her toilet gear she went down to the dining room where from her table by the window

192

she watched heavy clouds blot out the last of the daylight and shroud the lake in darkness. In bed later, exhausted by the day's events, she lay listening to the lap of the water against the pebble shore and thought about Nat until sleep finally came.

~

The sun had already gone down when Nordstrom found Nat's wet Harris tweed jacket in the shed. He returned to the cottage with it. "I was getting the dinghy out for a little early morning fishing when I found this," he said. He turned to Kate. "Who does it belong to?"

"I don't know," she answered in a terrified voice.

"It's still wet. It has to belong to someone who's been here recently."

"That explains my missing rain slicker!" the other man exploded.

"I don't know. . . ." Kate began again.

"Who does it belong to?" Nordstrom screamed at her.

Kate's face crumpled. "It's . . . it's Mr. Soutby's . . . "

"Southby! How did he get here?" he asked, his voice suddenly soft and menacing. "And where is he now?"

The other man grabbed her by the arms and pulled her out of the chair. "Answer him."

She struggled to free herself from his grip. "You're hurting me," she whimpered.

"How did he get here?" he shouted into her face.

"I don't know."

"I didn't see a car," Nordstrom said. "Or a boat, for that matter."

"Could he have hiked in?" the other man asked. He threw her back into the chair. "When did you see him?"

"When we were leaving this morning," she whispered.

"Then where did he go?"

"I don't know," she wailed.

There was silence for a moment before the other man suddenly burst out. "I'll bet he's nosing around the mine!" He rushed to the door and flung it open. But darkness, coupled with the wind and rain from a sudden squall, pulled him up short. "We'll never find him at this time of night."

"How would he know where the mine's located?" Nordstrom asked.

"He would need a map," the other man answered, glaring at Kate. "Did you give him one?"

"No, no. I told you. I only saw him on the path."

"We'll soon see," the other man said, striding over to the desk and sifting through the pile of papers. "I left one here," he added, "and the damn thing's gone. He must've taken it."

"Don't worry," Nordstrom cut in. "He won't be going anywhere in this weather. All we have to do is get up there early and flush him out." He reached for his rain coat.

"Where are you going?" the other man demanded.

"To make a phone call, of course. Our partner needs to know about Southby."

"Yeah," the other man agreed. "Right."

Behind him, Kate sobbed.

Nat, dozing just inside the entrance to the mine, awoke to find the wind and rain lashing into his face. Struggling to his feet, he eased himself further back into the darkness. Although no coward in the face of real danger, without the comfort of a flashlight, he wasn't overfond of unknown crawling creatures. He reached into his pocket for a sandwich, only to realize that he'd left the bag down by the stream. *Damn and blast!* He wedged himself against the cold slab of rock and tried to sleep, but he was sure that he could hear rustling and slithering in the blackness beyond. He would head for civilization at dawn, blisters or no blisters.

Sawasky, red-eyed and weary, consulted his map again. He hadn't been able to leave home as early as he wished because Lucille, his wife, had used every trick in the book to persuade him not to make the trip. "Leave it to the Mounties up there," she had said. "That's what they're paid for." And when he'd tried to explain how uncooperative the police were in Williams Lake, she had countered by saying, "You probably rubbed them the wrong way. You know how you hate people interfering in any of your cases." Which of course was true, but he couldn't make her understand that this case was different. Nat and Maggie were his friends, and they needed him.

It had been after six that evening by the time he'd lined up someone to cover for him over the weekend, kissed an icy Lucille, hugged his two kids goodbye and left the house. This meant that dusk was falling as he began driving the terrible, unpaved road that wound through the Fraser Canyon. Several times he had to pull over against the rock face as another vehicle came down toward him on the narrow road, and he whistled to himself to keep his mind off all the hair-raising stories he'd heard of trucks and cars going over the treacherous edge. Sawasky had no head for heights at the best of times, and it was all he could do not to look down into the raging waters of the Fraser River as it rushed and roared over the rocks hundreds of feet below on its way to the sea. Eventually, the road came down from the dizzying heights and the rapids became less turbulent, but it was still a great relief when he eventually drove into the desert-like town of Cache Creek. He stopped for a snack and a couple of hours sleep in the car before tackling the next stage of the trip that would take him up onto the Cariboo plateau.

He breakfasted in the small town of Hundred Mile House. "Funny name for a town," he told the waitress when she returned with his order. "A hundred miles from where?"

195

"Lilloet. That's Mile Zero. There were road houses at the mile points back in the 1800s when the miners came through here on their way to the gold fields. This was the site of one of them."

Sawasky put his mind back to the scanty history lessons he had endured at school. "I thought they came by boat up the Fraser River?"

"Yeh. But if you read under those pictures over there," she pointed to the sepia photographs mounted on the wall, "you'll see that they only went as far as Hope by boat." She deftly refilled his coffee cup. "You must've gone through Hope to get here."

Sawasky nodded. "Oh, yeh. I remember Hope."

"Well, according to them pictures, the prospectors used pack mules the rest of the way after Hope and they stopped at these road houses."

"Is the original road house here still standing?"

"No. Went years ago. But the town decided to keep the name." She slipped the bill in front of him. "Where're you heading?"

Sawasky looked up into her tired face. "Horsefly. Know it?"

"My husband's from those parts. Take the Hundred Fifty Mile turn-off. It's another two or three hours from here."

"Is it paved?"

"Sure, some of it. About time too."

"Is there a gas station nearby?"

"Turn right out of here. It's across from the school. Can't miss it."

Sawasky glanced at his watch before getting into his mud-splattered car. It was already six o'clock! "Thanks. I just hope I'm not too late."

While Sawasky waited impatiently for the gas attendant to finish filling the shiny Chrysler in the other bay, he couldn't help overhearing the raised voice of its driver.

"Hurry up! I haven't got all day." The man had now got out of the car. "You still haven't cleaned my headlights. You can see they're splattered with mud."

"Keep your shirt on, mac. I've only got one pair of hands," the attendant answered back

"And I need a map," the whiny man continued.

"Where you going?"

"I was supposed to meet my wife here, but I've tried all the hotels and she's not here. So now I have to go on to some God-forsaken place called Wild Rose Lake."

"You don't need a map. Take the Hundred and Fifty turn-off to Horsefly. Wild Rose is about ten or so miles farther in."

Odd that he's going to Wild Rose Lake too, Sawasky thought. I guess there must be other houses on the lake.

CHAPTER FOURTEEN

Nat was suddenly wide awake. The breaking dawn provided just enough light for him to see around the mine entrance. He inched himself toward it and listened. He was sure it had been the sound of an engine that woke him. But it had stopped. Scrambling for his boots, he pulled them on quickly, wincing with pain as the hard leather scraped the open sores on his heels, and prepared to make a run for it. The rush of adrenalin made his heart beat faster as he again crept to the opening, but when he saw Nordstrom and his pal, rifles at the ready, already climbing the hill he quickly withdrew into the shadows, then turned to stumble further back into the inky blackness. Then he stopped short. Without a light of some sort, he had no way of knowing what lay ahead.

"He's around here somewhere." It was Nordstrom's voice.

"Give me the flashlight," the other man said. "I'll see if he's inside."

"Here, catch." Nat heard a clatter on the stones outside.

"I told you to pass it to me, not throw it, you stupid idiot."

Pressing himself against the rough wall, Nat held his breath as the man walked a little way inside.

"You've busted the damned lamp. But he's in here somewhere. Look at this."

"Your slicker!"

Bloody Hell! I forgot that. Now as Nat's eyes became accustomed to the gloom of the mine, he began to feel his way further back over the huge piles of stone and rubble, but a sudden sharp bend to the left, shutting out the faint light from the opening, took him by surprise. Instinctively putting is hands out in front of him to grope his way, he felt the soft blackness encasing him and it was all he could do to push back a wave of panic. Get a grip on yourself, he thought. Their flashlight's broken. This cheered him up momentarily. *So they can't see in here any better than I can.* He began to breathe easier. *In fact, they don't even know for sure that I'm in here.*

But they weren't in doubt for long. As he advanced further over the rubble, it was his sudden yell as his feet slid from under him that gave him away. He found himself flying into space.

"Southby just found the shaft!" he heard Nordstrom yell. And then both men laughed. "I think we can safely leave him resting there a while."

"You stay here, " the other man ordered. "I'm going back to the cottage for another lamp and some dynamite. I think it's time we had another little accident at Shadow Lake."

"You mean blow it up with Southby inside?" Nordstrom sounded uncertain. "Maybe he doesn't know anything."

"But maybe he does. We can't be certain and he's too dangerous to let go, at this point. Just the fact that he showed up at all is worry enough for me. Anyhow, no one knows he's here."

"But . . . suppose he told the Spencer woman he was coming here?"

"She'd never figure out that he's in the mine."

"You sure?"

"It'll solve everything. Once the mine blows no one in their right minds will try to dig down inside."

"Okay, but don't leave me here too long on my own. Make it fast."

Nat, his right foot twisted painfully beneath him, heard the men still laughing as they moved away from the entrance. "Murdering bastards!" he muttered. "Got to get out of here before he comes back." Before trying to stand up, he felt cautiously around him, and then stretching out his arms until they touched a wall, he leaned back against it. *Nordstrom had called it a shaft!* Wincing in pain every time he had to move his foot, he inched his way forward on his behind, his legs straight out in front of him. He had only gone a couple of yards before his feet were suddenly dangling in space. Heart beating wildly, he back-tracked to the safety of the wall. *Bloody hell. I must've landed on a ledge.* Too terrified to move in the total darkness, he leaned back against the stony surface again and closed his eyes. "Get up, you coward," he admonished himself. "Those bastards will be back soon." Pressing his back against the wall, he eased himself slowly to his feet. But putting his full weight on his right foot was impossible. Intense pain shot up through his body, bringing waves of dizziness and nausea. Finally he turned to face the wall. It wasn't solid rock, as he had expected, but compacted gravel, and each time his exploring fingers loosened a stone he would wait and listen as it bounced across the ledge and down into the shaft. He found himself counting as he waited for the faint splash when it eventually hit water. About forty feet, he told himself.

Standing on his good leg, he stretched his arms as high as possible until he could feel the rim of the shaft. He was slightly under six feet, so he estimated that the top was about seven and a half feet above the floor of the ledge. Although it sloped very slightly away from him, it was too steep to climb without footholds. If he just had some kind of tool! But his pockets were empty. Sinking down to the floor again, he considered his predicament. The other man would be back well within the hour. He would have lights with him and dynamite. Nat was a sitting duck. Even if he hadn't hurt his foot, he was no match for the two of them. They were at least ten years younger and in far better physical shape. He eased the boot off his aching foot and felt his swollen ankle. He picked the boot up again up and ran his hand over it. The damn things were so stiff, especially the toes. *Stiff leather!* He struggled up once again and felt the stony surface of the wall. Making an estimate of where three feet would be from the floor of the ledge, he ran his hands over the face. "Got you," he muttered, as he found a good sized rock loosely embedded. Standing on his one good foot and leaning against the wall for support, he started to dig the rock out with the hardened toe of his boot.

He was sweating and swearing profusely by the time the rock became loose enough to ease it out of its hole. *I'm on the right track.* He continued to dig until the hole was big enough for his purpose. As he leaned against the wall to get the strength for the next part, Nordstrom called out to him.

"I can hear you, Southby," Nordstrom taunted. "I don't know what you think you're doing, but take it from me, there's no way out of there."

~

Maggie awoke to a tapping on her door. "You asked for a five o'clock call ma'am," the maid said.

She dressed quickly and packed her bag. The sun was just beginning to peep over the top of the distant mountains and the stunning natural beauty made her forget everything that had happened in the past few days, if only for a brief moment. Downstairs in the dining room she had the waitress refill her thermos. As she climbed into the jeep, she looked at her watch. *Five-thirty. Sit tight,*

Nat, I'll be there soon. She grabbed cheese and crackers from the picnic basket to eat while on the way, then slipped the jeep into gear.

The sun, drying up the wet road and causing swirls of mist to rise off the trees and bushes, was already bringing out the mosquitos. At first, Maggie tried to drive with the windows up, but as it got warmer, she had to stop to get out and strip off her jacket. The mosquitos took full advantage and within seconds had invaded the inside of the vehicle and she found herself steering with one hand and batting with the other. "Get out," she yelled, slapping wildly at the insects that buzzed round her head, neck and arms. Belatedly, she remembered the repellent she had packed and pulling off to the side of the road, she delved into the basket again, found the evil-smelling liquid and daubed it on.

If Maggie had thought the road to Horsefly was rough, it was a picnic compared to the one that followed the river to Shadow Lake. Her neck and shoulder muscles became tense with the continual strain of steering around and between potholes. The road was not only lonely, it also ran precariously close to the water, and the closer she got to the lake, the more she realized that she had no idea how to find Nat. *You didn't think this out, Maggie. You have only Jerry Harkness's word for it that Nordstrom's plane went to Shadow Lake. And Jerry could be part of the conspiracy!* But she knew that she had to take the chance that Nat was there.

At the head of the lake, she discovered the road branched to either side of it. She could see that the one along the west side veered sharply away from the water, but reasoning that Nordstrom's place would have to be near the lake in order to fly the plane in, she chose the one along the east side. Although this track rose high above the lake, between the trees she could still see an occasional white sail or the wake from a power boat.

She came to a stop when she saw a wooden notice board by the side of the road.

BILL'S FISHING RESORT AND MARINA
STRAIGHT AHEAD: 2 MILES.

So that's where the boats are coming from. Quickly she scanned the map, but the marina wasn't marked on it. *It says 2 miles.* She put the jeep into gear again and continued along the rutted road. *They'll know where Nordstrom's cottage is.*

"Al Nordstrom's place?" replied the man on the dock. "That's another six or seven miles along. Just keep going. He's right at the end of the road. You can't miss it. There's a road that branches off to the north, but that just leads to an old mine. Just stay on this one."

Shadow Lake Mine! Should she drive up to the mine and have a look around or try to find the cottage first? In the end she decided on the cottage. *Nat's more likely to be there.*

She continued on, passing the road leading up to the mine, hoping she would see a driveway that would lead down to a cottage or perhaps catch a glimpse of the float plane on the lake. But the road rose higher and her view of the lake was obscured behind banks of tall trees. She had just crossed over another small bridge when the clatter of a truck coming at full speed toward her caused Maggie to wrench the wheel of the jeep and try to pull over. And that's when the jeep's engine stalled. The driver of the red flat-bed jammed on his brakes and came to a screeching halt. "What the hell are you doing driving in the middle of the road?" he yelled at her. "This road's a dead-end anyway." He waited, fuming while she got the engine going again and pulled to the side. Then he slammed the truck into gear and roared off.

I've seen that man before. Where? She pulled into the middle of the road again. Nordstrom's cottage has to be here someplace. A short time later the tracks led into a clearing next to an old garage. Pulling up sharply, she jumped out of the jeep and ran down a path leading to a cottage on the edge of the lake. Pausing for a moment at the top of a flight of wooden steps leading from the house down to the beach, she saw a float plane tied to the pier. It was Nordstrom's all right. She was in the right place! The cottage seemed deserted, but she took a deep breath before quietly turning the handle and walking in. It was then she heard sobbing. "Kate," she called. The sobbing stopped. "Kate," she called again. "It's me, Maggie."

"Maggie!" Kate came running out of a back room and flung her arms around her. "How. . how did you get here . . . Oh, Maggie, I'm so glad to see you. . . .I don't know what to do!" Maggie disentangled Kate's arms.

"What's happened, Kate? Where's Nat?"

"It's all my fault." Kate started to cry again. "I'm so sorry, Maggie."

"Where is he?" she repeated.

"Nat's at the mine, but. . . ."

Maggie started for the door.

"Where are you going?"

"To get Nat."

"But what about Douglas?"

"I'm sorry, Kate, but Nat's safety comes first."

"But you don't understand! Douglas is up there too. I think he's going to . . . going to . . . kill Nat!"

Maggie stopped in the doorway. "Your husband is here?"

Kate nodded miserably. "He's not missing at all. Oh, Maggie. . . ."

The man in the truck! Kate's wedding photographs! "For God's sake, Kate, tell me what's happened." But precious minutes were lost before Maggie could make sense of what Kate was saying.

"Then Douglas came back a little while ago to get a flashlight," Kate finished, "and he said they had him cornered."

"What did he mean?"

"I don't know. I followed him up to the garage, but by the time I got there he was loading a box in the back of the truck and he told me to go back to the house and wait."

Without another word, Maggie turned, left the house and started back up the path to the road.

"Where do you think you're going?" The man took her completely by surprise as he suddenly loomed over her. "It's Margaret Spencer, isn't it? I thought it was you up there on the road. You should've kept out of my business, lady." He grabbed her arm, spun her around and frog-marched her back to the cottage.

Kate let out a wail as they re-entered.

"Isn't this touching?" he said, brushing past his wife. "Your little friend has come to join her boss." He pushed Maggie down onto a chair and held her firmly there with both hands on her shoulders. "I don't know if my Kate would do the same for me."

"Where's Nat?"

"Safe and sound," he answered. "Kate, you'll find some rope in the shed outside. Get it."

Kate hesitated by the door. "Douglas, I. . . ."

"Get the rope!"

Still Kate hovered.

"You want me to knock your friend on the head instead?"

Kate scuttled outside and was back within minutes with the rope. But the moment Guthrie took his hands off Maggie's shoulders she was on her feet and running for the door. She wasn't fast enough. As she fumbled with the door knob, he delivered a blow that sent her crashing to the floor. Kate screamed.

"Should have done that in the first place," he muttered as he tied Maggie's hands behind her back and then dragged her toward the back door.

"Where's Nat, you bastard?" Maggie demanded as he pulled her to her feet.

"Down the mine shaft. But don't worry. I'm going back up there to deal with that little problem. Open the door, Kate."

"But, Douglas, she's . . . ," Kate began fearfully.

"I said open the door!"

Kate scuttled to comply.

"Now open the shed door," he said, forcing Maggie in front of him. "When I get back, she's going to have a little boating accident." He waited impatiently while Kate swung the shed door open before giving Maggie a push which sent her sprawling onto the dirt floor. The door banged shut and Maggie heard it being fastened.

"Now, what the hell am I going to do with you?" Maggie heard him say to his wife.

"I'll wait here for you, Douglas. I promise I won't let her out."

"You must think I'm as stupid as you are. You're coming with me."

~

Taking a deep breath, Nat put his good foot into the hole that he'd dug in the wall and reached for the top. As his hands touched the crumbling edge he felt them slipping through the loose gravel and his body sliding back down the wall. To stop himself tumbling down into the main shaft, he twisted sideways as he fell and landed on the ledge in a crumpled heap. His outstretched hands touched nothing but air. He had been perilously close to following the stones clattering down the shaft. He lay still for a few moments, his body sweaty with fear.

On his feet again, he replaced his foot in the hole and reached again for the top. This time, gritting his teeth, knowing there would be excruciating pain, he launched his body upward and over the edge, desperately groping for a handhold. Digging his fingers into the piled rubble, he gradually pulled himself completely out.

"How's it going down there?" Nordstrom's mocking voice was distorted by the echo in the tunnel. Nat estimated that he could be no more than fifty feet away, but the sharp bend cut off all light so there was no way he could see him.

"Hope you haven't gone to sleep," the voice taunted him again. "Pity to be asleep and miss the big bang." *Keep talking, Nordstrom. You don't know it, but you're helping me out.* He crawled over the heaps of rubble as silently as possible until he reached the beginning of the bend, then inching his way cautiously on hands and knees, peered around the corner. Nordstrom had given up taunting him and was sitting on a slab of granite just outside of the mine entrance. His rifle was slung across his knees. Nat watched him raise one hand to shield his eyes against the sunlight as he looked down the hill. Waiting for his pal. *And I have to get to him before the other s.o.b. gets back!*

A large stone ready in his hand, Nat stood up and began moving step by step closer and closer. *Don't turn round. Please don't turn round.* Suddenly Nordstrom shifted his position on the slab, and Nat froze. On the path below the mine, an adventurous rabbit had run across the road and was nibbling at the grass. Idly Nordstrom raised his rifle and trained it on the animal. By this time Nat had reached the entrance, but Nordstrom was so intent on the rabbit that he didn't sense the danger behind him. With a sudden intake of breath, Nat raised the stone above his head. It was at that moment that the rabbit bolted into the brush, and Nordstrom, returning his attention to his prisoner turned his head. Seeing a movement behind him, he instinctively brought up his rifle at the exact moment that Nat threw himself at the man, and as the stone crashed down hard on Nordstrom's head, the gun went off. Nordstrom fell with a thud, but Nat was left looking down at the blood oozing from his own thigh where the bullet had entered. Fighting nausea as waves of pain swept over him, he dragged Nordstrom's unconscious body back as far as he could over the piles of rubble into the darkness of the mine.

Staggering out into the sunshine again, he realized he had to find a hiding place quickly before the other man returned. Slipping and skidding over the shards of stone, he stumbled part way down the hill and pushed his way through a clump of broom at the side of the track. Once through, he managed to keep going another few feet into a small clearing and flung himself behind a large boulder, where he finally collapsed.

Sawasky could see by the heavy equipment that the waitress had been right: the road was in the process of being paved, but luckily for him the crews had only just started the work of spreading and rolling the crushed stone. Covered in grey dust, his battered 1948 Ford rattled through Lac la Hache less than an hour after leaving Hundred Mile House. The lake, shrouded in mist, beckoned invitingly but, promising himself a return visit one day, he drove non-stop for another hour and a half until he came to the turn-off to Horsefly. Unfortunately, there was also a sign pointing straight on to Williams Lake, and Sawasky was reminded that protocol demanded he report first to the local constabulary. Reluctantly, he continued north. In his rear view mirror he saw the Chrysler that had been following at a safe distance behind him turn toward Horsefly.

Brossard was not pleased to see Sawasky. "I don't understand why you're here," he said scathingly. "I called into the ranch yesterday and spoke to Guthrie's son. An old friend of the family had brought him up."

"But I told you over the phone that Maggie Spencer got a message to me." Sawasky found himself raising his voice.

"Jamie Guthrie told me his father had been in contact and he was sorry that he'd caused so much trouble, but he'd just wanted to get away on his own for a bit."

"Did he say why?"

"I gather there had been some domestic problems."

"And the deaths of Sarazine and Chandler?"

"Sarazine was killed but Chandler's death, that could've been suicide."

Sawasky didn't know how to keep his temper. "Don't you understand that Guthrie and his friends were most probably mixed up in the Smith abduction?"

"We've no proof . . ."

"Maggie Spencer came to you with proof and for help. If anything happens to either of them. . . ." Disgusted, he turned and stormed to the door. "I'm going to Shadow Lake and I hope to God that I'm not too late." He slammed the door and ran to his car.

"Wait," he heard Brossard call. "I'll come with you."

Sawasky stopped dead in his tracks. "You will? Come on then."

Except for giving directions, Brossard said nothing until they were on the Horsefly Road. "You think a lot of those two, don't you?"

"Nat's not only a friend, he's a damn good detective," Sawasky answered. "And he's trained Maggie into one helluva good assistant. And if she says they're in trouble — then believe me, they are." He drove angrily on, trying to miss the potholes. "Why do you think I've come all this way?"

The road to Horsefly was murder on Sawasky's beloved Ford and he had to hold grimly onto the steering wheel as they bounced and swerved on the loose gravel. The whole area had an abandoned feel to it, but this was partly due to the many crumbling, empty shacks and barns along the way. It was close to mid-morning when they stopped at the gas station in Horsefly.

"Hi Ed," Brossard greeted the mechanic. "Did a woman driving a jeep come through this way lately?"

"Oh, it's you, Corporal," he replied. "This ain't your vehicle." He bent down to fit the nozzle into the tank. "Came through yesterday. Her jeep broke down. Fixed it and she drove on. What's she done?"

"Nothing. Did she say where she was heading?"

"Heard tell it was Shadow Lake. Old Perce, down at Annie's, told her it'd be rough going, but she sure was determined to go."

"I can see what old Perce meant," Sawasky said, as they bumped and slid on the washboard road surface. "I don't know how Maggie made it this far."

"Well," Brossard said, dryly, "any old jeep would hold the road better than this crate." With a jolt, Sawasky realized that Brossard was hiding a sense of humour beneath his dour official shell.

CHAPTER FIFTEEN

Maggie was struggling to her feet when she heard the faint sound of the truck starting up. *Got to get out of here!* There was little time to lose, and here she was locked in a shed with her hands tied behind her back. There was only one dusty hinged window about five feet off the floor with a stack of small logs piled underneath it. Standing on tiptoe, she could see that the window had been nailed shut in each bottom corner. Against intruders, she supposed. But her first priority was to get her hands free. There were plenty of hammers and screwdrivers hanging in wall racks above a makeshift work bench, but none seemed of any use to cut the cord binding her wrists. Then, stilling her panic, she looked more closely and spotted an axe hanging just out of reach. A yard broom leaned nearby and, turning her back, she twisted her fingers until she could grasp its handle and lift it. With her back to the wall, she looked over her shoulder until she located the axe with the broom handle. With each determined push it began to swing. *Come* on! *Fall, damn you!* Then, "Got you!" she shouted in triumph, jumping out of the way as it came crashing down.

Using her feet, she pushed the axe close to the generator and then concentrated on tipping the blade upward. Next she sat with her back to the axe, forced the blade between her wrists, and began sawing at the rope. It seemed that hours had passed instead of minutes before the strands began to give way. Although her shoulders were aching with the strain, and her fingers sticky with blood, she continued to saw until she felt the last strand part.

Now how the hell do I get out of here? She tried the door first, but it was unyielding to her frantic launches against it. *It has to be that window! I'll need a pry bar.* Unhooking one from the wall, she climbed up the log pile and forced the bar into the small gap between the sill and the window frame, close to one of the nails. Leaning heavily on the tool, she began levering, but nothing happened. "Well, there's more than one way to skin a cat!" And she swung the pry bar at the glass. A moment later she was bashing away at the glass fragments still imbedded in the lower sash. When enough had been cleared away that she figured she could climb out without cutting herself to ribbons, she returned to the floor, pulled the dinghy over to lean it against the pile, climbed back onto the pile, and — even though she felt the top logs shifting beneath her weight — perched on the square-ended bow of the dinghy. Then grasping the sill, she lifted one leg through the opening, then the other, and a moment later she was lowering herself to fall into the weeds below. Not waiting to see what damage the glass fragments had done to her hands and legs, she ran up the path. The jeep was where she had left it, and she pulled the ignition key from her pocket and jumped in. Guthrie and Kate were now a good half hour ahead of her. *Just let me get there in time!*

∾

"Nordstrom! Where the hell are you?"

He's back! Nat lay on his stomach to peer through the bushes. *And that's Kate he's got with him!* As usual, she was crying.

"Nordstrom!" the man yelled again. "I'll kill that sonofabitch if he's gone wandering off." He turned on Kate angrily. "Oh, for chrissake, shut up!" And he disappeared from Nat's view. *Just don't come looking for Nordstrom over this way.* Nat dragged himself further back into the undergrowth.

"He's not by the stream," he heard the man say when he returned.

"Please, Douglas, please tell me what's going on?" Kate bawled.

Douglas? My God! How stupid could I have been? Of course, that man is Guthrie! It all made sense now. *No wonder Kate was with him!*

"I'm going back to the truck. Stay here until Nordstrom shows up and tell him to stay put!"

"Please don't leave me here!" Kate was crying again.

"I'm going to get the dynamite."

"You're not really going to. . . ." There was no answer from Guthrie, but Nat heard his feet crunching past him down the hill.

Do I crawl back through the damn bushes and try to get Kate's attention? On second thought Nat decided he didn't need a bawling Kate on his hands. Guthrie is bound to go into the mine to look for Nordstrom and then the hunt will be on. *They'll find me in no time flat.* He began wriggling backwards into the bushes.

"Nordstrom's not back?"

Nat realized that Guthrie had returned.

"Maybe he went into the mine," Kate said.

"Not without a light. Probably got chicken," he continued, but Nat saw him walk part way into the mine entrance and play his flashlight over the rubble. "Nordstrom!" he bellowed, then stood for a moment waiting for a reply. When he came out, he told Kate, "If he doesn't turn up, you'll have to help me set the charges."

"Oh, no, please, Douglas!" and she picked her way past him and walked into the mine. "Albert!" she called. "Albert!" Guthrie followed her, their flashlights dancing little circles over the rubble in front of them.

Maggie drove up the mine road, stopping the jeep where the road began to peter out. A glint of red among the foliage fifty feet ahead told her the flat-bed was parked there, so the mine couldn't be much further up the hill. Keeping her fingers crossed that Guthrie had not heard the jeep's engine over the sound of the rushing stream, she climbed out, sidled past the red truck, and started up the hill. Avoiding walking out in the open, she used the scrub alder, broom and blackberry bushes as cover, pausing only once to hold her breath when she heard Guthrie's voice.

"Where the hell are you, Nordstrom?" he yelled, his voice receding as he and Kate went further into the mine.

"Maggie!" She whirled at the familiar voice. "Over here."

She glanced up the track, hoping Guthrie hadn't heard, then pushed her way through the shrubbery to where Nat was stretched out behind a slab of stone.

"How the hell did you get here?" he whispered.

"You're hurt," she whispered back, kneeling down beside him.

"Fell down the shaft." He pointed to his right foot. "Can't get my boot back on."

"But the blood?"

"Nordstrom got nasty."

As if on cue, they heard Guthrie calling from inside the mine. "Southby!"

"Go for help," Nat said. "He knows I'm out here someplace. And he must've discovered what I did to Nordstrom."

"But what about you . . . ?"

"Go," he insisted. "There's got to be someone with a radio-phone in this God-forsaken place."

"I passed a marina on my way in," she whispered.

Nat urged her toward the track. "Go."

213

She nodded miserably, pushed her way through the bushes, and started to run back down the trail.

Above her, the Guthries emerged from the mine, Kate in the lead, her flashlight under her arm so that she could lug the feet of the unconscious Nordstrom, while her husband followed, taking most of the man's weight by holding him under his armpits. They reached the entrance just in time to see Maggie fleeing down the track.

"Shit!" Guthrie exploded, dropping his end of their burden. "Hold it right there!" he bellowed.

But Maggie ran on down the track, past the red flat-bed, headed straight for the jeep, and Guthrie was powerless to stop her because he had put his rifle down in the tunnel in order to carry out his accomplice. Cursing, he snatched Kate's flashlight and ran into the mine again. Within minutes he was out, carrying his rifle at the ready and leaping down the path after Maggie.

Nat lay absolutely still as Guthrie passed. *Go, Maggie, go!* And he was rewarded moments later with the roar of the jeep's engine starting up far below him and the grinding of gears as Maggie turned it to race down the hill.

"I'll get you, you bitch!" Guthrie shouted but it was several more minutes before the truck's engine wheezed into life, and Nat began to breathe again.

∼

By this time Sawasky and Brossard had arrived at the head of the lake. "Which way?" Sawasky asked. "North or south?"

"North," Brossard answered, tapping the map he was holding. "According to Jerry Harkness, Nordstrom's cottage is the last one on the north road. "

"When did you find that out?" Sawasky asked in surprise.

"I called at the Harkness ranch after seeing Guthrie's son yesterday. I knew Guthrie and Harkness were friends." He paused and hung onto the door handle while Sawasky negotiated another pothole. "So I reasoned he would know of some place the bugger could've been hiding all these weeks."

"Is that what you think? That he's been in hiding?"

The other man was silent for a moment. "Yes," he said abruptly. "I figure Chandler had something on him." He gazed steadily ahead. "I just resented Southby and Spencer coming up here and trying to teach me my job."

Sawasky opened his mouth to reply, then thought better of it and concentrated on keeping the car on the road as it careened close to the unprotected edge of the lake. "There's a marina up ahead," he said, pointing to the sign post. "Do you want to stop?"

"No," Brossard replied. "According to this map we should see the road to the mine on our left soon."

"Wow!" Suddenly another vehicle was racing toward them, and he pulled to the side as it came to a skidding halt beside them, and the driver sprang out. "My God! It's Maggie."

"George! Oh, George, it's Nat. . . ." The words came tumbling out as she began to cry.

Climbing out of the car, he pulled her roughly to him. "Maggie, what's happened?"

"Nat's hurt and Guthrie's up there with a gun," she wailed.

"Guthrie!" Brossard said.

"Get back in your jeep," Sawasky barked. "We'll follow you."

Maggie drove as if possessed, but halfway back to the mine she turned a sharp bend in the road and saw the red truck hurtling towards her. She slammed on her brakes, and the jeep slewed at an angle across the road. She just had time to duck as Guthrie sprang from the truck and aimed his rifle at her. The first shot ripped through the windshield as Sawasky's car swerved around the bend and came to a grinding halt. Both policemen sprang out of the car, drawing their guns.

Guthrie swung to face them. "Put 'em down," he screamed, "or she gets it!" And he edged around to the front of the jeep in order to train his gun on them, too.

Furious that once again the man had the upper hand, Maggie sat up, rammed the jeep into gear and, hitting the gas, aimed the vehicle squarely at him. Guthrie, taken by surprise, was sent flying into the bushes at the side of the road. She slammed on the brakes but was too late to stop the jeep careening onward straight into the flat-bed, smashing the truck's radiator and sending a spume of hot water and steam shooting into the air. Then appalled at what she had done, she rested her head on the steering wheel.

George Sawasky leaned in the window. "Maggie! You okay?"

"I think so," she answered shakily. "I didn't kill him, did I?"

"He's a bit damaged," he answered her, smiling. "Brossard's taking care of him."

"We've got to help Nat!" And she began backing the jeep up so that she could detour around the truck.

"Wait!" Sawasky yelled. He pulled open the driver's door, motioned for her to move over, then leapt into the driver's seat. "Okay, let's go and find the boss."

Brossard was left to deal with Guthrie.

Nat, meanwhile, was succumbing to shock as he lay in the bushes, drifting slowly into unconsciousness, but he came suddenly wide awake at the sound of a familiar voice.

"Over-impetuous, I see," the voice drawled. "Couldn't wait for the cavalry to turn up."

"George! Is that you? How the blazes did you get here?" Nat said, trying to sit up. Then he saw Maggie and his face lit up. "What's happening?" he continued.

"First things first," George answered. "Let's look at the damage." Taking a pen knife out of his pocket, he slit Nat's blood caked trouser leg to reveal the wound. "Bullet?" he asked and Nat nodded. "It seems to have stopped bleeding, but we need to get you to a doctor."

"Where's Douglas?" Kate, running down from the mine entrance, burst into the bushes. "What's happened to him?"

216

Maggie stood up. "I'm sorry, Kate," she said as gently as she could, "but he's been hurt, too."

"He's hurt?" Kate repeated, her voice breaking.

"He was going to shoot me. There was nothing else I could do." When Kate still stared at her uncomprehendingly, Maggie realized she would have to come clean. "I ran him down . . . with the jeep."

Kate continued to stare, obviously not taking it in. "Is he badly hurt?" she asked again.

Maggie shook her head. "I don't know. He's with Brossard."

Sawasky had meanwhile climbed up to the mine and discovered Nordstrom. "You did a good job on him," he said to Nat when he returned. "He's still out cold." He looked down at Nat. "If Maggie and I can support you, do you think you could make it down to the jeep?"

Nat nodded wearily. "I'll try. But what about Nordstrom?"

"I'll stay and keep an eye on him." Maggie replied. "But hurry back," she said to George. "And you'd better bring some help to move him."

"I'm going with you," Kate said. "I want to see Douglas."

Nat's face was as white as a sheet by the time they managed to get him down the hill and into the jeep. As Maggie leaned over and shifted the picnic basket to make room for Kate, "What's in there," Nat asked.

"Food."

"Food!" He exclaimed. "There wouldn't be coffee in there too, by any chance?"

Maggie nodded and opened the basket and passed him a packet of sandwiches. "Dig into those while I pour you some coffee from the thermos."

"Maggie, my love," Nat said, grinning and taking a huge bite of a cheese sandwich, "you've come through again."

After they had gone, Maggie walked back up to the mine entrance and after having checked for Nordstrom's pulse, sat down beside him.

"It's getting stronger," she said. "I hope George returns soon, because I think you're coming around." The man's eyes began to flicker. She stood up and peered down the hill, but it seemed an eternity before Sawasky, accompanied by three other men, climbed the hill to the mine.

"They're from the marina," Sawasky said. "We've brought a chunk of plywood and the marina's pickup to cart Nordstrom back."

"How's Nat?"

"Brossard's patched him up as best he can," he replied. "It looks as if his ankle is broken. I left Brossard radioing for help. Now all we've got to do is get this bugger down the hill. I see he's beginning to come around."

As Sawasky prepared to follow the men carrying Nordstrom down the hill, Maggie took his arm. "Wait," she said. "I've got a hunch this is where they stashed the ransom money," she told him. She waved Guthrie's flashlight at the blackness of the tunnel then walked deliberately into the mouth of the shaft. Sawasky hesitated a moment, then called to the others to go on without him, and followed Maggie into the mine. She almost turned back when she rounded the bend and the entrance light was cut off, but keeping close to the wall and shining the beam on the rubble, she felt her way cautiously along. Sawasky caught up to her just as her light revealed the narrow ledge in the shaft. "That's how Nat broke his ankle," she told him, but she realized how lucky Nat had been to have survived his fall at all. Then raising the flashlight, she played it slowly over the walls, pausing when it shone on an opening to their left. Climbing over the small pile of rubble that partially blocked it, they found themselves standing upright in a secondary tunnel. Walking warily, they advanced down the passageway for close to twenty feet before the beam of her flashlight showed a blank wall in front of them. It was when Maggie was turning to retrace her steps that she stepped on something soft and yielding in the dark. She pointed the light downwards. She had trodden on a piece of clothing. Kneeling down to get a closer look, she stopped,

218

frozen, her face close to the skull that lay beside the clothes. "Oh, Jesus!" Stifling a scream, she sat back on her heels. Sawasky took the flashlight from her and, kneeling, shone the light over the rest of the skeleton. It was slumped onto its side. A decaying tweed jacket and some bits of tattered grey cloth which had once been trousers were all that remained of the clothes the man had once worn. Beside the skeleton was an initialled briefcase with the letters LS in gold. "We've found Leonard Smith," Maggie said in a shaky voice. "That's the brief case I saw in the other mine." Sawasky nodded.

"Poor old man. What a terrible ending for him, but at least his widow can give him a proper funeral now." Taking a handkerchief out of his pocket, he carefully picked up the briefcase. "I'll need this for evidence," he said. He swung his flashlight over the rest of the cavern. "No sign of the money."

"No," Maggie answered. "Perhaps they stashed it in the cottage."

"Worth a look, anyway," Sawasky agreed, leading the way out.

They arrived at the marina in time to see Brossard and the three injured men safely aboard the seaplane which had arrived in response to the RCMP man's message, and Maggie, George and Kate watched with mixed emotions as it taxied to the middle of the lake and took off. "They should be in the Williams Lake hospital within a couple of hours," George said as they retraced their steps to where they had left the jeep and his car.

"You might as well all come back with me," Sawasky said. "It's clear that jeep's not going to go anywhere for the time being."

Kate nodded. "Can I collect my things from the cottage first?" she asked.

"Nat asked me to pick up his tweed jacket, too," Maggie said. "He said he left it in the shed."

"Nordstrom found it," Kate stated miserably. "That's how he knew Nat was here."

"And I want to see if that ransom money has been stashed

there." But although the three of them searched the place from top to bottom, the only things they found were Nat's jacket and shirt. They set out soon after.

"Kate, do you want to call into the ranch before going on to Williams Lake?" Maggie asked after they had gassed up in Horsefly.

"I'd rather go straight to the hospital," she answered. "I managed to put a call through to Hendrix from the marina. He told me that Jamie had arrived and that he'd meet me there." She paused. "The line was so terrible that I had a job understanding him. He said somebody else had turned up but I couldn't catch the name."

~

It was late and they were thoroughly exhausted when they eventually parked George's car in front of the hospital. The three of them stumbled into the emergency entrance and confronted the nurse manning the desk.

"How's Mr. Southby?" Maggie asked.

"How is my husband?" Kate asked over Maggie's voice.

"Not more of you!" the stern-faced nurse said. "You'll have to wait with the others over there." She pointed to a line of chairs.

"Others?" Maggie looked to where she had pointed. She could see Jamie Guthrie, his head leaning against the wall, apparently asleep. Next to him was a blond man dressed impeccably in a pearl grey suit, pale lemon shirt and matching grey and lemon silk tie. He was talking to Jerry Harkness, who was seated beside him in his wheelchair.

"Maggie," Harkness said. "You haven't met Ray Teasdale, have you? He flew Jamie up here." As Maggie stretched out a hand to take Teasdale's, the door of the washroom burst open and Harry came rushing out.

"There you are at last!" he said.

"My God, Harry!" Maggie exclaimed. "What on earth are you doing here?"

220

"Do you realize that I've been traipsing all over the country looking for you?"

"Looking for me?" she answered in a daze. "What. . . . Oh, Harry, something hasn't happened to one of the girls, has it?"

"Will you please be quiet," the harried nurse said. "This is a hospital." Harry drew her further down the corridor away from the others.

"Just gather up your things," Harry hissed. "I'm taking you out of this madhouse."

"Just tell me what's happened," she whispered back.

"Nothing has happened. I already told you about Mother. But, Margaret, that's not why I'm here. I knew you'd want me to take you back to . . . to . . . civilization."

"Civilization? What are you talking about?"

"I've had enough of this nonsense, Margaret," Harry exploded. "Mother's coming out of hospital on Monday and you're. . . ."

"Oh, please keep your voice down, Harry," Maggie said, exhausted, "and do go away." And to her horror, she started to cry.

"There you are," Harry yelled. "You're all upset getting mixed up in that man's sordid business."

"Please leave, Harry," she sobbed.

George, noticing Maggie's distress, joined them and put his arm around her shoulders. "Come on, let's find you a cup of coffee. And," he said, turning to Harry, "I don't know who you are, but do as the lady says. Go."

"How dare you!" Harry spluttered, drawing himself upright. "I am her husband. And I'm taking her straight back to Vancouver and . . . and . . . sanity."

"I don't care if you're the King of England. She told you to scram, so scram!"

"I am a lawyer," Harry shrilled back at him.

"And I'm a cop," Sawasky growled, and taking Maggie firmly by the elbow, he led her away.

"You'll regret this, Margaret," Harry bellowed as they went down the hall toward the cafeteria.

It was quite late by the time the doctor allowed Maggie and George to see Nat. Pale-faced, he was lying back against a pillow with his plastered leg resting in an overhead sling. "It's so good to see you both," he said weakly. "What's happened to the others?"

George, who had managed a brief conversation with Brossard before accompanying Maggie to Nat's room, filled him in as best he could. "Guthrie and Nordstrom have been attended to and they're both in the next room, under guard." He moved toward the door. "Anyway, Brossard's coming back in the morning. He'll tell us everything. Meanwhile, I'm bushed!"

"You look all in," Nat said after George had left them alone. He took Maggie's hands in his. "What's this I heard about Harry turning up?"

"Who told you that?"

"Brossard came in to see me. He said Harry was making one hell of a fuss in the waiting room." He tried to shift his weight. "Are you going back to Vancouver with him?"

"Don't be foolish. I'm staying right here with you. We'll go back together when you're able to travel."

"But Maggie—"

"No 'but Maggies,' dear. George and I will get rooms over at the hotel for tonight and we'll be back in the morning." And she leaned over and kissed him on the mouth. "Oh, Nat. I was so worried about you." She let the tears run down her face unchecked.

Nat reached over and brushed them away. "You're one hell of a trouper, Maggie. Don't you ever dare leave me."

When she returned to the ground floor, she found that George was talking to Harkness, Brossard and Teasdale. "Where are the others?" she asked.

"Kate and Jamie have been allowed in to see Guthrie," George answered. "I've just been telling Corporal Brossard about us searching the cottage for the ransom money."

"We both searched," Maggie said. "It's funny, because we found the briefcase, and it had been with the ransom money when

222

I went into the old mine the first time."

"Ransom money?" Jerry Harkness mused, and they all turned to look at him. "I bet I know where it is."

"What do you mean?" Maggie asked.

"Vivienne. She's gone."

"Gone!"

"Yep. Left a note saying she's fed up being tied to me, and that she's off to greener pastures." He shook his head sadly. "Been expecting it for some time, truth be told," he added ruefully. "But you can bet your boots that she wouldn't have left unless there was money involved."

"Is that why you're here?" Sawasky asked. "Were you hoping she'd turn up?"

"No. I came to give Kate some moral support," he answered. "I think she'll need a lot of it in the next few days."

Brossard stood and replaced his cap on his head. "Well I guess that's everything for now. . . ."

"Just a minute," Maggie interrupted. "Jerry, Vivienne had been married before she married you, hadn't she?"

"Oh yes. To a fellow named Sean O'Connor."

"The sixth partner," Brossard said.

"Not him," Maggie contradicted. "Her. The sixth partner was a V.M. O'Connor. Vivienne M. O'Connor. So she lost all her money in the Shadow Lake Mine too."

"And that's why she married me," Jerry said. "How could I have been so dumb?"

The RCMP office was on the same street as the Williams Lake Memorial Hospital, so the following morning, Brossard walked along to visit Nat who was propped up in bed, his leg still elevated. Maggie was seated at his bedside.

"I hear that Mr. Teasdale has agreed to fly you back to Vancouver," Brossard said, handing Nat a bag of grapes then settling into a chair.

"Yes," he answered, "I'm being transferred to the Vancouver

223

General. By the way, where's George?"

"Outside. He'll be in to say goodbye before heading home."

"Sawasky tell you about the skeleton in the mine?" Nat asked.

Brossard nodded. "Oh yes." He turned to Maggie. "It looks as if you were right about the kidnapping, about everything, actually. We're sure that skeleton will turn out to be Leonard Smith."

"What about Vivienne Harkness?" Maggie asked.

"Early to tell. But it looks as if she was in everything up to her eyeballs," he answered. "When I told Guthrie that she'd split with the money, he started to spill his guts out. I think he gave it to her to look after, and when she realized we were onto him and Nordstrom, she took it and ran."

"Do you think you'll find her?"

"Eventually. Sooner or later, we Mounties always get our woman. Anyway, we've put out an APB on her."

"But how did she know we were on to Guthrie?" Maggie asked.

"Kate Guthrie told me that Nordstrom had called someone on the radio-phone. We think it must've been her." He turned back to Maggie. "I have to hand it to you, Mrs. Spencer, that was very courageous to go and look for Southby on your own."

"We're partners, Corporal," she answered him with a smile.

"When are you going back to Vancouver, then?"

"Today. I'm flying back with Nat."

"Look, I'm sorry we got off on the wrong foot." Brossard stood up and put his hand out to her. "I guess I was out of line."

Maggie shook it and gave him an impish grin. "No harm done. It takes a big man to say that. Well, we'll soon be out of your hair."

CHAPTER SIXTEEN

A week after their return from Shadow Lake, George Sawasky
called the Southby Agency to say that he would be collect-
ing Nat from the hospital and stopping by the office with
him so they could all hear his update on the Cariboo affair at the
same time.

"The boss, he be his old self?" Henny asked for the umpteenth
time.

"I doubt it," Maggie answered. "The cast itches, the bullet
wound hurts, he's bored to death, and he's sure I'm not running
the office properly. In fact," she finished with a chuckle, "he's ready
to come back." Southby had been driving Maggie and Henny to
distraction with his constant phone calls — to see how things were
going.

"He be using the clutches?"

"You mean crutches," Maggie answered.

"*Ja*, clutches," Henny answered, reaching for the phone. "Ah! It is that nice Sergeant," she said, handing it to Maggie.

"Have some coffee ready, Maggie," Sawasky said. "We're on our way."

"Is exciting, *ja?*" Henny said, as she lugged Nat's chair to the outer office. "Make easy for boss to sit when Sergeant Sawasky tell us all."

Maggie smiled. *And easy for you to hear everything too.*

"They here!" Henny, who had been anxiously watching from the window for her boss, ran to the door. But it took several minutes before the ancient elevator creaked to their floor and a pale-faced Nat hobbled in and collapsed into his chair. Henny immediately rushed over, lifted the plaster encased leg and rested it on an upturned waste paper basket. He looked imploringly at Maggie who was doing her best to hide a smile.

"You've got some answers for us, George?" Maggie asked, as soon as everyone was settled.

"Where to start?" George said, and paused teasingly.

"The skeleton, *ja*," Henny chimed in. "I want to hear about the bones."

Maggie laughed. "Yes, George. Let's hear about the skeleton." Maggie would never forget the shock of stumbling onto it.

"Right! The skeleton. It was definitely Leonard Smith. Not only did the dental records prove it was him, but his widow identified his watch and the scraps of clothes found on him."

"How terrible for her," Maggie said sadly.

"Yes," George answered. "Well, she's remarried, of course, and doesn't seem to have all that much good to say about the man, but at least she now knows what happened to him."

"*Ja*," Henny said, passing cups of coffee around. "She is going to have big funeral bill now."

"How about the briefcase?" Maggie asked. "I'm sure it was the same one that I found earlier."

"It was," George answered. "Guthrie's prints were all over it."

"I guess he wanted to make sure it would never be found again."

"Who did the actual abduction?" Nat asked.

"What is duction?" Henny asked, as she settled down to listen.

"Ab-duction, Henny. It means kidnapping," Maggie explained.

"Oh, I see." But Maggie could see that Henny was wrestling with that word too.

Sawasky continued, "We think it must've been Guthrie, Nordstrom and Sarazine, though Guthrie and Nordstrom are denying everything. But Guthrie was no newcomer to kidnappings. I eventually got the report from the Seattle police, and it says that they were on the verge of arresting him way back whenn on an abduction charge themselves when he skipped out of the U.S.. Then he just turned up here, supposedly to take over his father's ranch."

"Yes. Just a few years before the war."

"That's right."

"Was Vivienne Harkness part of the Smith scheme?" Maggie asked.

"I'm sure she was."

"But the abduction went wrong?" Nat said.

"Yes. They knew Smith from having approached him as an investor. But they couldn't know that he had a bad heart. They got the $750,000 ransom but then they had a corpse on their hands and couldn't figure out how to explain away the money."

There was a sudden gasp from Henny. "Poor man," she said sadly. "Like my aunt Wilhelmina. She has bad heart."

"Hence the explosion!" Maggie said, ignoring Henny's aunt's bad heart.

Sawasky nodded. "Right. They couldn't risk using the ransom money to openly develop the mine, and it was such a huge sum anyway, so they decided to blow up the entrance and bury Smith inside it. What they didn't know was that Fenwick was in the mine at the time. Luckily for them the police found Fenwick first and didn't check any further down the shaft."

"Chandler and Fenwick weren't in on the kidnapping then?" Nat asked.

"It doesn't look like it. Guthrie just told them they'd have to close down operations because Nordstrom had been unable to raise more capital, and the two of them went back to pick up their gear."

"Fenwick was still inside when the charge was set off."

"And Chandler got blamed for it," Nat said.

"Yep. At his trial the Crown produced witnesses who had seen the two men having a drunken brawl the night before."

"But how did they find out that Fenwick was in the mine?" Maggie asked.

"Chandler," Sawasky answered. "According to him, he had been in the mine when Fenwick showed up, and they picked up their fight where they'd left off the night before. He admitted slugging Fenwick and knocking him out, but he insisted that he was still alive when he left him in the mine."

"And no one would believe him," Nat said.

"They found dynamite and caps when they searched his cabin. Also he was known for his foul temper. He was the perfect fall guy."

"What about Sarazine?" Maggie asked quickly, before Henny could ask what a fall guy was. "What was he doing on the old mine road?"

"Putting two and two together, I think he got greedy. Guthrie and Nordstrom had been dipping into the ransom money a little at a time over the years to avoid suspicion and giving Sarazine enough to keep him quiet, and then they found out that he had been helping himself as well. When Chandler appeared back on the scene, it was the perfect opportunity to get rid of Sarazine and blame his death on Chandler."

"Do you think Guthrie shot Sarazine?" Nat asked.

"I'm putting my bet on Vivienne."

"Then it was Vivienne who shot at me?" Maggie mused.

Sawasky nodded. "Looks like it. But to ease your mind, I think she was just trying to scare you off." He smiled at her. "With her eagle eye, I think she'd have got you if she'd really wanted to."

"But why did Guthrie do his disappearing act?" Maggie asked.

"Same reason. To avert suspicion. If he was out of the picture, then it had to be Chandler who killed Sarazine. I guess he and Nordstrom thought no one would suspect Vivienne." Then he added, "But I think it was Guthrie who killed Chandler."

"And he must've seen you that day at the old mine, Maggie," Nat chimed in.

"And he started that rock slide."

"I would think so. Probably saw you speaking to Chandler too."

"So Chandler had to be killed."

"Guthrie must've been worried that you were getting too close to the truth for comfort."

"What about the others mentioned on the contract?" Nat asked.

"I was coming to that," Sawasky said grinning. "Jock Macleod was included, like the other two, just to do the hard work at the mine. The real work."

"If they were hired just to get the mine going, their share must have been very nominal."

"And Jerry Harkness?" Maggie said. "How does he fit in?"

"He insists he knew nothing about any of it. I believe him. He had no part in the mine, and in fact, he told me that he and Vivienne were on the verge of splitting up when he had that terrible riding accident that paralysed him."

"Was it an accident?" Maggie asked. "He insists that he heard a gun shot just before the thunder."

"Brossard had a long talk with Hendrix," George answered. "He knew nothing about the kidnapping, but he was always very suspicious about Jerry Harkness's accident. He had no proof as Vivienne immediately had the animal put down and buried. If there was a shot, I'm putting my money on Vivienne as the shooter."

"To collect his insurance money," Nat suggested.

George nodded and stood up. "Most likely. Well, I have to go. Do you want me to run you home?" he asked Nat.

Nat shook his head. "No. I'm going to go over a few things with Maggie."

"I'll take him home, George," Maggie said.

"Won't it be fun to settle down to normal, unexciting investigations for a while," Maggie said after George had left and she and Henny had helped Nat into his own office.

"It sure will," he answered, painfully shifting his leg. "And I'll be damn glad to get this cast off too."

Maggie could see it was going to be a very long five weeks before his wish came true.

"You sit quiet, Mr. Nat," Henny said, patting his shoulder. "I make you tea." She beamed at him. "I got your favourite — camomile."

Southby cringed. "Don't bother, Henny."

"No bother. Do you good."

After she had left, he turned and whispered to Maggie. "I hate camomile!"

Maggie laughed. "She's worried about you."

"Have you heard from Kate?"

"No. But I feel so sorry for her," Maggie said as she spread out the new files on his desk.

"Any idea what she's going to do?" Nat asked.

"She apparently wants to come back to Vancouver, according to her sister." Maggie answered slowly. "Jodie's asked me to give up my suite so she can move in there for a while."

"Are you going to?" Nat asked.

"I don't think I have a choice."

"You could always move in with me," Nat said, but his tone said he didn't expect her to say yes.

Smiling, she shook her head.

"Think about it."

"I'm still married to Harry, Nat," she said gently.

"I haven't forgotten," he answered.

"And you know, I think I really enjoy living on my own."

There was a long silence between them.

"Have you got your cat back yet?" he asked at last.

"I'm going to collect her from Harry tonight."

"Can't you get one of your daughters to do that for you?" he asked, fearfully remembering Harry's performance in Williams Lake.

"No. It's something that I have to do for myself," she answered.

Harry was waiting for her when she arrived to collect Emily. "Come in, Margaret," he said calmly as though nothing had happened. He led the way into the living room.

"How's your mother?" Maggie asked. "Is she here?"

Harry shook his head. "No. I took everyone's advice and got a nurse for her. She's in pain but doing quite well at home."

Maggie relaxed a little. At least she would not have to face the old battle axe as well. "I'm sorry I couldn't help you, Harry," she said, "but you know, even if I'd been here, I wouldn't have looked after her."

"I know that, Margaret," he answered. "You and Mother have never been that close. Why don't you sit down? I've made coffee."

As Maggie sat, Emily appeared in the kitchen doorway. The cat walked sedately over to her, and sprang onto Maggie's lap. Gathering the cat up into her arms, she snuggled her face into the soft fur as she looked around the familiar room. It hadn't really been such a bad life here.

"She's very fond of you," Harry said, putting a china mug of coffee in front of her. "I think she's missed you." Then pulling a chair up to the table he said, "There's something I'd like to ask, Margaret."

Maggie took a sip of her coffee. "What is it, Harry?" she asked, steeling herself for a fresh round of unpleasantness.

"Look here. Mr. Crumbie is having his annual tea party next week and . . . " he hesitated for a moment before continuing, "would you consider going with me? You see, I've never told him or Mrs. Crumbie that we are . . . we are living apart."

Margaret looked intently at her husband of twenty-eight years. Not haughty any more, he just looked worn out, defeated really. They had been through a lot together during their marriage, they had two beautiful daughters and now a grandson. Harry was stuffy and she knew he would never change. And she knew too, there was no way she could ever go back to the old relationship. But all those years together had to count for something. And the gallant sod had driven all that way up to the Cariboo to rescue her! She owed him at least this minor act of generosity. "Yes, Harry," she said, "of course. I'll be pleased to go with you."